THE HUB

THE HUB

A CITY AMONGST THE WASTE

AARON C. LEMKE

BEAVER'S
POND
PRESS

Book design and typesetting by jamesmonroedesign.com

ISBN 13: 978-1-64343-555-8
Library of Congress Catalog Number: 2024904004
Printed in the United States of America
First Edition: 2024
28 27 26 25 24 5 4 3 2 1

Beaver's Pond Press
939 West Seventh Street
Saint Paul, MN 55102
(952) 829-8818
www.BeaversPondPress.com

To the author, our son, Aaron. Celebrating you.
It is life, not death, that defines you.
Within the pages bound in this book, your spirit lives on.

Until we meet again,
Love, Mom & Dad

CHAPTER 1

It had been exactly 301 years since the Lexington Company sent the wealthiest people in the world to Mars. Earth had become unstable due to the massive strains that the human population had placed on her. Pollution was mostly to blame, and in its wake the polar caps continuously kept melting. The water levels rose and rose.

However, that is neither here nor there. This story begins as Jack Erdman finds himself awoken by his cryo-pod at daybreak, April 2, 2392.

...

Psssssshhhh. The hibernation cryo-tube sounded as the air pressure inside the tube equalized to the pressure of the room, as the tube's plexiglass door opened. A needle attached to a small robotic arm injected a chemical concoction into Jack's neck, jolting him out of hibernation and sending him flying back into consciousness. Jack took a large gulp of air and exhaled it dramatically. He then slowly opened his eyes and let them adjust to the almost overly bright glow of the fluorescent LED lights that cast a slight hue of light blue over everything. He slowly sat up; as he did, every vertebra in his back cracked in linear succession. Now sitting and rubbing some feeling back into his leg, he surveyed the room.

The life-support room was a small ten-foot-by-ten-foot square. The cryo-tube Jack sat in was placed along one wall; the life-support computer ran the length of another. The tube itself was constructed of steel framing and a plexiglass lid. The inside of the tube was a foam-padded enclosure stitched with a white cotton covering. The smell that hung rank in the air of the room was that of a stagnant, closed-up old house. The fresh air that had once circulated through the vents was now old and pungent. The steel door that led out of the life-support room was located in the farthest corner of the room; the tube sat diagonally from the door.

Jack, once certain he could walk, clambered out of the tube. As he stood on the cold steel flooring, his head throbbed, and his body felt like gelatin shaking in a soup bowl. *Worst hangover ever,* Jack thought to himself as he slowly proceeded toward the door. He pushed through into a hallway that ran the entire length of the pod. There were three doors in the hallway on the right side. There were also three doors on the left side. Jack crossed the hallway and entered the first door on the left.

He emerged into a very small bedroom that housed a small night table with a lamp in its nearest corner. To the immediate right of the night table was a queen-sized mattress, a box spring, and a solid brass bed frame. To the right of the bed was a dresser constructed of some sort of alloy, with three four-foot by two-foot by one-foot drawers. At the foot of the bed was a two-foot by four-foot by two-foot black carbonate trunk with bronze inlays running along its sides and corners. Jack walked over to the dresser, and upon opening the first drawer found two pairs of boxers and two pairs of socks. Naked as the day he was born, he proceeded to dress himself in the boxers and socks. In the second drawer, he found two white T-shirts and two gray boiler suits, with the number *7* on the back of the boiler suits in yellow lettering. Jack pulled on one of the T-shirts and finally the boiler suit. In the third and bottom-most drawer, he found a pair of black sneakers and a pair of black steel-toed work boots. He decided to go with the work boots.

Once fully clothed, Jack crossed the hallway and entered the door that sat kitty-corner to the bedroom. The utility room within contained a furnace, a water heater, an air conditioner, a power bay, a breaker box, laundry machines, and a small metal locker. None of these items resided in the room in any particular order except for the locker, which was situated in the deepest corner of the room. Jack crossed the utility-room floor to the two-foot-square, six-foot-tall locker, then pulled up on the latch and opened its door. The locker was filled to the brim with every hand tool one could ever think of needing to repair and maintain every system in the pod. Jack closed the locker door, exited the utility room, and continued to walk across the hallway to the next door.

The next room Jack found was a bathroom. It was the smallest room in the entire pod, four feet wide by ten feet long. It housed a standing stall shower, a small toilet, and a very small sink with an accompanying mirror hanging over it. Jack moved on to the next room along the same wall. This was the dry storage room, containing nonperishable goods such as freeze-dried food with no expiration dates. There were also toiletries and an entire pallet of liter water bottles stacked to the top of the ceiling. *Won't have to worry about starving anytime soon,* he thought to himself as he closed the door.

Jack proceeded to enter the last door on the right side. This room was obviously the office. One wall in the office included the entrance door and was lined with filing cabinets. Directly across from the filing cabinets was a small steel desk. Instinctively, Jack walked up to the desk, took a seat in the chair, and turned on the terminal.

The green-hued screen turned on. After a long "Loading, this may take a moment" screen, it flashed the only page that Jack could view; the terminal had no mouse, no keypad, and no interactive touch screen. The page read as follows:

Temperature: 80.7° F
Precipitation Today: 0%
Solar Panel Efficiency: 11%
Minimum Efficiency Requirement: 3%
Stored Power: 72 hours
Radiation Outside: Safe
Toxicity Outside: Safe
Date: 04/02/2392
Time: 05:47

Jack opened the drawer under the desk and found nothing there but three books. The first was titled *Operating on Yourself: Surgery for Dummies*; the second, *You're Lost: What S.O.L. Stands For*; the third, *Becoming a Caveman: Which Berries Not to Eat*. A troubled, very puzzled expression crossed Jack's face as he thought, *This is an attempt at humor.*

When he opened the books, he found the titles were dead serious—no attempt at humor was to be found. The first book was a real wartime surgery book. The second book was a real survival guide, and the third was a how-to for procuring food and water safely. Jack was not only perplexed by their presence but also confused as to who had written the books so despairingly—describing just how truly shit out of luck you really are as soon as you have to leave the safety of your pod.

He returned the books to the only drawer in the desk. Leaving the terminal on, he turned his attention to the filing cabinets. Each was empty except for one. Its bottom drawer was crammed full of pencils, pens, highlighters, permanent markers, composition notebooks, and large sheets of graph paper. Jack grabbed one of the composition notebooks, a pen, and a single sheet of the poster-sized graph paper. He then closed the cabinet, exited the office, and entered the open kitchen and dining area of the pod. The airlock doors were at the farthest corner of the pod, dead center of the window that Jack was drawn to.

As he approached, the first golden hues of the morning started cascading through. Outside, he saw nothing but a vast expanse of shore, a white sandy beach, and a calm sea resting in a channel.

"I'm still on Earth," Jack said aloud to himself in a panic. "I'm still on Earth!" he said again—this time it reverberated off the walls of the kitchen and echoed softly through the hall.

"It can't be," he said with the grimness of denial. His mind furiously tried to search for any reason, no matter how small, that the "Martian planet" he was on could bear such a close resemblance to Earth. *Maybe people have found a way to colonize it?*

He pushed this thought right out the proverbial door—even he knew that if he'd just woken up, so had everyone else. Which still left him on Earth—but why?

• • •

Jack had been sitting at the two-chaired dining-room table, which rose abruptly in the middle of the kitchen. He had been going through the scientific processes of creating theory after theory, then running through the steps of testing each one, all of them dissolving like strawman arguments. He had rummaged through every drawer, nook, and cranny of the pod in hopes of finding something, anything really, to explain why he was still on Earth. He had been twenty-two years old when they put him in hibernation, with a fresh college degree in geography—he knew the Earth when he saw it.

Jack kept turning the situation, analyzing every possible angle. Each presented the same simple answer: *Does it really matter which planet I am on? No, not for the moment. I need to figure out a plan of action. The inevitable truth is, I will at some point, sooner rather than later, have to adapt to my surroundings and make wherever this is my homeland. This is the reality, the truth.*

As soon as the thought had come, it was gone, replaced by the weight of how to go about getting acclimated to his new surroundings—also, the dubious thought, *What if I'm the last man on Earth?* This thought continued creeping into his mind, starting to plant dreadful, thorny seeds in its landscape.

April 2, 2392 (Journal Entry)

I have been in hibernation for 301 years, which makes me 323 years old. I am not on Mars but have for some reason woken up on Earth. The computer is not helpful as it only gives me today's data, and a very limited amount of it. I have not eaten today, as the stress of waking up on the very planet I wanted to leave has left me without an appetite.

Tomorrow, I will embark on phase one of my plan. I will need not only to become familiar with my surroundings through navigation, but through doing this task to find a clean source of potable water. A man can live for weeks without food but can very well die in a day without water—especially seeing how the midday temperature today was 100.5 degrees.

Also, I am becoming very tired of the blue hue reflected everywhere in this pod by the steel surfaces. It's almost as if I am in a proverbial fishbowl, in which to be examined.

...

The next morning Jack was cooking powdered eggs, gravy, and biscuits over the stove. The coffee gurgled as it percolated on the far left burner. It was nearing eight in the morning, and his thoughts were tidying up the loose ends of his plan.

The first part involved special orientation for points of navigation; in short, he was going to make a compass in the sand with the cardinal directions for the headings. Then he would simply walk 150 paces, after which he would place another marker of some kind, then continue to place markers every 150 paces until he reached 1,050 paces in all the cardinal directions. Once north, south, east, and west had been adequately identified, he would venture forward in each direction until he no longer could—until some features of the terrain blocked him from doing so or he reached areas where the geography made a drastic change, such as beach biome to forest biome, or beach biome to water. Once he had ascertained what was directly around him, each day he would venture farther and farther out until he'd found a source of potable water.

The coffee was done before the eggs, biscuits, and gravy, which tasted marvelous for being some three-hundred-odd years old. The coffee was black, just the way he liked it. While he was chowing down the tasty breakfast, his thoughts were on safety. Earth may have once been under the oppressive thumb of man, but now Mother Nature had reclaimed what was hers. Jack had no doubts regarding the fact that hostile wild animals and the wild in general had reclaimed the Earth. Also, he was not naive enough to think that just because he had known the habitats of animals before the human race had either died out or left Earth, they had remained unchanged and were still the same today. *Hell, there might even be completely new creatures roaming around.*

After cleaning up his cookware and stowing it away, he found himself in the utility room, rummaging through the hand tools. The best-suited weapon he could find was a twenty-four inch red pipe wrench. He grabbed the heavy wrench, shut the locker, and proceeded to the airlock entrance door. In truth, he was nervous, for he did not know what stood on the other side.

He worked the yellow-painted lever and switched it to the down position, which unlocked the inch-thick, solid-steel hatch door. He strenuously pushed against the door, opening it, then entered the four-foot-by-ten-foot airlock chamber. He then forcefully pushed the door closed and switched the lever for the airlock door up, sealing it. Jack proceeded to the far end of the airlock's exit and pressed the red button over the door lever.

Pssssshhhh! "Pressure stable," an automated voice called out from the intercom. For a moment, Jack paused; then, sweat now forming on his brow, he pulled the yellow lever with his right hand and the door opened. Again he strenuously pushed the door open, and was met with an ever-increasing amount of blinding white light.

His eyes took several moments to adjust while he still stood within the safety of the airlock. Slowly, the white sandy shoreline came into view, along with the rolling, gentle waves of the sea that filled the channel between the landmass he was on and the one directly across from him. Jack scanned for predators and found only scuttle crabs, herring gulls, and great cormorants. Closer to the water, he saw massive green turtles and some rather unpleasant-looking toads. *Looks clear,* he thought to himself as he proceeded to take his first steps onto the hot, sandy surface. He then turned around and sealed the airlock door behind him.

As he deeply inhaled through his nose, the fresh sea breeze, carrying a hint of salt with it, stung his nostrils sweetly. The air was pure, and if the airlock had allowed it, he would have opened both steel doors wide open, flushed the stagnant air out of the pod, and filled it with this amazingly salty, sweet freshness. For a long moment, he just took it all in. The sky was bright blue and clear, with only a few wispy clouds. Off in the distance was another landmass—Jack noted what appeared to be an island. The sea was a brilliant blue with turquoise reflections, its calm waves breaking upon the shore. Jack gauged the distance between where he stood and the island to be no more than three miles. He realized the seagulls now appeared to fly in larger flocks and were quite large in size—they had obviously grown since Jack's days in college, over three hundred years ago.

Jack kept his eyes constantly moving as he foraged around the life-support pod. He gathered five grapefruit-sized rocks of all denominations, stowing them in the front pockets of his boiler suit. Sweat had begun to form droplets and drip down in small streams from his buzz-cut brown hair. He wiped his brow with his right sleeve and made his way back to the pod's airlock door, his shadow dwarfed by his six-foot, one-hundred-eighty-pound stature as it followed.

Once at the airlock door, his brown eyes looked into the face of the sun. Ever so briefly, he walked toward it, counting the paces aloud: "One, two, three, four . . ." and so on, until he reached 150 paces, roughly one hundred yards. He dug the first rock out of his pocket and placed it directly in front of his right foot's last footfall. This rock served as the center marker. He then turned on his heels and began counting his paces again: "One forty-eight, one forty-nine, one-fifty," he said aloud. This time he placed the rock in front of his left foot's last footfall. This marked due north, as the sun rises in the east. Jack then double-checked his paces on the way back to the center rock and found them to be correct. He then turned on his heels toward the sun and began a fresh set of paces; as he marched, he found two more rocks to replace the two he had just used to mark the center and the north bearings. Once he reached the end of the paces he had made previously, Jack placed the rock directly in front of his last footfall, marking east.

He continued this process until he had the south and west marked as well. The western heading landed smack dab in the middle of the airlock door. Jack verified the spacing and his paces one last time.

His boiler suit now had sweat stains under the armpits and around the collar. As the temperature kept climbing and the sun's rays continuously beat down on him, his exposed face, scalp, and hands started to burn. He had retracted the earlier idea of continuing the pacing until he reached a count of 1,050. He now felt that marking his steps out to three hundred was adequate enough to get the general idea.

Just before high noon, Jack had completely marked out his rough compass. However, he had incurred enough sun that his face was beet red and his exposed hands and wrists mimicked that of a lobster. Thus, upon reentering the airlock, its blue hues were a welcome relief to his sun-scorched hands and face. After the pressure had equalized, Jack emerged into the kitchen and dining area, closing and sealing the airlock behind him; once he placed the pipe wrench down on the table, he was off to the bathroom.

Jack took a quick pee, and then, while washing his hands, took a look at his almost crispy complexion. "Lesson one: don't go out after ten in the morning, stay indoors until six in the evening," he said aloud, the cool water refreshing his burned hands.

After his bathroom break, he went into the office and checked the stats on the computer terminal.

Temperature: 102.3° F
Precipitation Today: 0%
Solar Panel Efficiency: 17%
Minimum Efficiency Requirement: 3%

Stored Power: 72 hours
Radiation Outside: Safe
Toxicity Outside: Safe
Date: 04/03/2392
Time: 11:46

Jack proceeded to write down this information in his journal. He found this helpful in deciphering the area around him. After he had jotted down the pertinent facts, he returned to the kitchen and put his journal back on the table next to the pipe wrench. Jack then made the quick trip into the dry storage. He took two more liter bottles of water and a nonperishable bag of mashed potatoes and turkey, then rummaged around to see if there were any first-aid supplies. To his dismay he found none. *Huh?* he thought to himself as he put the newly acquired items on the countertop next to the stove. He then got a stir spoon and the stew pot from the cookware cabinet. He then dumped a liter of water into the pot and set the electric stovetop on high in order to bring the water to a boil.

Once the water was on, he turned his attention to his journal. Jack jotted down the fact that he hadn't seen a first-aid kit. His only theory as to why he hadn't seen one was that maybe whoever made this place couldn't have made nonperishable bandages, medications, and the like. However, Jack couldn't quite figure out why he hadn't seen a doctor's bag, which would have the necessary tools to operate on himself. Why would they have given him a book about how to operate on himself if they hadn't provided the tools?

A good question, one Jack would ponder during what he now considered his indoor hours. When the sun's rays were the fiercest outside, he couldn't afford to burn his skin again—he already looked like a lobster.

While he cooked his meal, Jack drank up half the water

bottle he had set aside for himself. Once lunch was ready, he chowed down. Jack discovered that he would be saving the turkey and mashed potatoes for a time of desperation—the meal tasted wretched, and the smell was the worst part. Its nasty aroma had replaced the stagnant smell of the pod with what Jack could only assume was the smell of *turkey farts held in a jar for three hundred years to be smelled later.* Later, he would chuckle aloud whenever he remembered this thought.

After his meal and the cleanup that ensued from the utensils used, Jack was on a scavenger hunt to find anything that resembled some kind of medical instrument or first-aid collection. He started with the dry storage, as it was filled to the brim with nonperishable food, drink mix, water, soap, hygiene products, and even a do-it-yourself wine and mead beer kit. However, after a good hour spent looking high and low, there was not a single thing pertaining to first aid other than the general antibacterial soap. He then began searching the bedroom, the utility room, the tool locker, the office, the kitchen, and even the hibernation room. To his trepidation, Jack found not a single thing pertaining to a first-aid kit. He even looked at every dial and the now-black screen of the hibernation tube's life support module, and found nothing other than a busted button reading "power." However, through his scavenger hunt he had found the basic locations of everything and anything *other* than a first-aid kit; thus, if he hadn't found it now, he never would.

This was quite unnerving to Jack. How could one survive alone without anything resembling aid? An even darker thought occurred to him: *How does one survive without another watching their back?* This was a truly depressing question to him, another one of these isolating and desolating thoughts that crept up like squirming maggots in one's own brain.

April 3, 2392

I made my compass today; however, in doing so, I also gained a bad sunburn. Upon searching for a relief cream such as aloe, I found out that whoever made this pod must have forgotten to put a first-aid kit in here. Today the temperature reached 103.9 degrees by 15:00, which discouraged any thought of going back outside today.

The turkey and mashed potatoes meal has stunk up the pod something fierce, which has now, unfortunately, wafted into the bedroom (super disgusting).

Tomorrow, I plan on making a trek north, as long as the sun isn't too terrible to endure. I'm roughly thinking of walking about five or so miles out, which would make for a ten-mile hike. I am thinking of walking that far, since all I can see around the pod's position is white sandy beach. I have no idea how far this stretch of beach goes, or if the entire landmass that I am residing in is just a vast expanse of sand and rock. In either case, the sun is setting, and I have to get up very early tomorrow.

CHAPTER

Jack awoke to a bloated feeling in his lower abdomen, which was the direct result of the one and a half liters of water he'd drunk before he went to bed. He pushed the covers to the vacant side of the bed and, like a flash, disembarked from the mattress. He then clapped his hands twice, and all the lights came on. He ran out into the small hallway and flung the bathroom door open. He had his organ in his hands before he reached the toilet, and still almost missed it by a hair. "Ahhhh," Jack exclaimed as the pressure relieved and the near miss was avoided.

Once he was finished, he washed his hands in the sink and then proceeded to splash the brisk water on his face. When he looked up into the mirror, he found that his once smoothly shaven face had sprung up a thick four o'clock shadow. The water dripping off his chin was soothing at first, but as he woke from the stupor of his slumber, he found that his face and hands felt like someone had violently rubbed eighty-grit sandpaper over every inch of his now-pink complexion. *Damn,* he thought to himself—the fact that someone had forgotten something so vital to survival baffled him. Jack knew he was going to have to proceed with an overcautious attitude from now on.

The thought of being truly alone also bothered him mentally as much as the burns on his hands and face did physically. There was safety in numbers, and the number on the back of his boiler suit read *7*—shouldn't there at least be six others? If they had, in fact, left people behind for a reason—though, until he found any sign of other human life, it was a moot point.

Jack proceeded to grab his journal from the dining table, then jotted down the information that the computer had to offer.

Temperature: 75.1° F
Precipitation Today: 0%
Solar Panel Efficiency: 4%
Minimum Efficiency Requirement: 3%
Stored Power: 72 Hours
Radiation Outside: Safe
Toxicity Outside: Safe
Date: 04/04/2392
Time: 05:52

Jack made his way over to the window and found that the sun was starting to cast the first dim rays of the morning, announcing that its presence would be coming soon. Jack placed his journal back on the table and proceeded to grab a liter bottle of water and a lab-developed never-expiring synthetic protein bar. He ate it quickly and found that his pile of plastic packets and wrappers had grown to a small mound on the far-right side of the counter. "I'll have to take it out today and dispose of it far away from the pod," he said aloud to himself. He then got dressed in the same clothes he had worn yesterday. On his return to the airlock door, he grabbed his pipe wrench, then shoved the trash in his left pocket and the half-drunk water bottle into his right pocket.

When he finally emerged into the fresh air and onto the surface of the beach, the morning's first golden-orange rays were illuminating the sand. In the distance, he saw the reflection of the sun on the still waters of the sea. He took in the beauty of the scenery for a moment, and then, with a walk of purpose, began his trek north. Jack consulted his roughly accurate compass on the beach before truly making headway.

As the sun began to reveal more of itself, it began to change from a welcome, radiant beacon to a hatefully oppressive force of never-ending fire. Jack's eyes were constantly scanning in every direction; for every hundred or so paces he walked, he would take a glance over his shoulder to make sure nothing was stalking him like prey. His ears were really listening, trying to hear everything, slowly becoming able to decipher the natural flow of things; he breathed through his nostrils, allowing the scent of the fresh sea air to fill them. Jack did all these things almost out of instinct, without a lot of forethought put into it. He relied on the concept of scanning the area around himself with his eyes to catch the stimulus, and hopefully he would see what was hunting before it was upon him. One listened for the unnatural twig snapping underfoot, or for the brush that rustled when there was no breeze. One smelled the air to ascertain if something dank, primitive, and hungry was lurking just past eyeshot. These things came to Jack easily, but he still had to, at times, train his brain to become almost entirely primitive. He realized that even letting his mind wander was a mistake, as even a moment's distraction from what was truly going on around him was just enough time to be eaten.

By seven in the morning, the sun was standing at full attention above the horizon. Jack had made it about two and a half miles since he left the pod at roughly six in the morning. The beach was coming to life, as birds of all denominations began to sing and call out. The crustaceans scuttled and burrowed. The small lizards and turtles began to come out to warm their cold bones from the chill of the night. The beach was coming alive. Jack's once desolate and isolated march now filled him with the knowledge that he was never truly alone. However, the sudden call to attention amongst all ranks in the biome meant that the predators were also in accompaniment—the only difference was that they were silent.

Jack was nearing his full-mile mark when, about a hundred yards in the distance, the landscape took a dramatic change. To his left, northwest, a long field of tall, dark-green grass stretched for about half a mile. Past the field were giant oak, pine, poplar, mahogany, and spruce trees that denoted the start of the forest. He could now see from his position that the forest encompassed the entire northwestern side of the landmass. In the distance were the peaks of a long mountain range, which looked to span as far as the eye could see, running north to south.

As his gaze returned to the field in front of him, he saw three flashes of fur and scales coming toward him. He readied his pipe wrench, as he knew trying to run would be the worst idea—they were coming on way faster than he could in fact run.

As they drew closer, he saw the nasty creatures full on. They were three to four feet tall at the shoulder, ran on two back legs that resembled those of an ostrich, and had the body of a massive rat. The pink tail trailing behind each one made their overall length between ten to eleven feet long. However, their front arms resembled those of an alligator, as did their massive heads, which were clad in green scales, followed by gray fur starting at the neck. "What in the fuck is that?!" Jack said aloud in true disbelief and horror of the creatures, now twenty feet away.

As the first one came upon him, Jack swung the pipe wrench but missed. The creature ducked the wrench, and as it did, it swiped its nasty clawed hand with talons as sharp as razors into Jack's left hand. Jack cried out in a rage of pain. The second one was now approaching, and fast; as the third one followed suit, the first one circled around again.

This time when Jack swung, it flew true and smashed the second creature down to the ground, stunning it and crushing the bones in its neck. Out of the corner of his eye, he saw the third jump headfirst at his neck, its jaw wide, brandishing its sharp teeth. Jack saw it in the nick of time—as the creature flew at him, he raised the pipe wrench and the creature bit down into it, breaking its teeth against the steel. The force of the impact sent Jack flying, the creature's jaws now locked around the pipe wrench.

Jack and the creature hit the ground hard. When he came to a stop, he tried to pull the wrench free, but the creature's locked grip was too strong. The other two creatures were now circling, coming down upon where Jack and his foe lay.

Jack threw a wild left jab at the creature's now violently shaking head, but missed. The creature tried desperately to dig its front claws into Jack, while he tried to shake its grip on the pipe wrench. The other two creatures were within striking distance now. "Come on, come on!" Jack shouted wildly, as he knew if he lost the pipe wrench, he would most certainly die.

In one very swift action, Jack drove his left thumb into the creature's right eye that lay atop its head, then kicked both his feet into the creature's stomach, causing it to lose the grip of the wrench. Then, still on his back, he swung the pipe wrench like an axe to wood, crashing down hard on the top of the creature's skull, sending it reeling backward. The other two creatures collided with it at full speed ahead, sending all three of them falling over each other in one lumped mass of fur and scales.

Jack jumped to his feet, sprinted up to the second creature, leapt into the air, and sent the pipe wrench down upon its exposed abdomen with fury. The audible fracturing of ribs sent the creature spilling over onto its back in a protest of defeat, the other two still struggling to regain their upright position. The wrench came down again upon the second creature, which pushed fragments of its ribs into its heart, killing it. The other two were now up but still semi-dazed. Jack rushed up to the third one and sent the wrench flying upward, like a bowler does with his arm on the follow-through. The wrench made perfect contact with the creature's chest, smashing through its ribs and pulverizing the organs behind the now-shattered protective rib cage. The creature called out in a high-pitched hiss and staggered off in defeat.

However, the leader of the pack wanted to finish what it started—it pounced upon Jack's left side, driving its left claws into his left hand and its right claws into his left shoulder blade, the full weight of the creature pushing him down flat to the ground on his right side. Jack tried to break free but only succeeded in unhooking the talons that were dug into his left hand. However, the creature then sunk its now-free left talons into Jack's abdomen, sending grievously agonizing pain through his body.

In response, Jack put everything he had left into a right kick that he sent into the creature's left kneecap, popping it instantly from its socket and sending it tumbling down off of Jack's body. As it fell, its talons ripped out of Jack's abdomen, causing three massive lacerations to open, which immediately began bleeding like sieves. Jack, still fueled by adrenaline, got up to his feet while the creature was still reeling, and sent a right-handed swing of the pipe wrench into the creature's exposed shoulder. It was a loose swing that did not connect with its intended target—the creature's head.

The creature let out a high-pitched hiss and was on its feet again. Jack immediately brought the pipe wrench back around and caved in the creature's skull with one final blow. It instantly dropped into death throes, expelled its last breath through its reptilian nostrils, and died.

The last creature that had bowed out of the fight had disappeared amongst the tall grass. Jack looked down at his boiler suit and saw that three talon marks had ripped not only the fabric but also his stomach, in lacerations of no less than six inches apiece. These were accompanied by an ever-growing crimson stain that ran all the way to the tops of his thighs. "Oh fuck! That ain't good . . . I just have to make it to the pod," he said aloud, refraining from looking at the wounds in his stomach. They had been only a hair shy of gutting him like a fish, and that thin lining was hanging in an ever-present balance as he walked as slowly as he could to avoid tearing the thin lining. However, he knew he couldn't walk too slowly either, as that would cause him to bleed out.

He no longer listened to his surroundings, or really even considered them. He was grievously wounded, and his life hung by a very thin strand. All Jack kept thinking about was the next step, and the next.

The journey back to the pod was the most painful and agonizing thing Jack had ever had to go through (so far, though he did not know it yet). When he returned to the pod, he barely had the strength to open each door just wide enough for himself to squeeze through. Once in the kitchen, he proceeded very slowly to the dry storage room, then carefully pulled out three things from the hygiene effects shelf. The first was a roll of toilet paper, which was tightly wrapped in plastic packaging to preserve it for all time. Jack ripped it open with his teeth and then pulled out the roll, discarding the empty packaging to the floor. The second item was a squeeze bottle of antibacterial soap, and the third was a roll of dental floss.

He staggered backward, almost passing out when he reopened the dry storage door. He slowly walked to the bathroom and deposited the items in the sink basin. Then, with baby steps, he emerged into the utility room and opened the tool locker. He rummaged until he found a box cutter, in which the blade was a very thin triangle about an inch long. With the box cutter in hand, he made his daunting return to the bathroom. Jack then painfully undid the top of his boiler suit, exposing his mostly crimson-stained white T-shirt. He then delicately cut the white T-shirt down the middle with the box cutter and agonizingly removed it from his body. The lacerations, now fully exposed, looked very red and angry, with a small stream still flowing from each one.

Jack proceeded to cut three two-yard strips of dental floss, tying a large knot at the end of each. He then placed the items on the ledge around the basin and filled it with water. Jack dumped the entire bottle of soap into it and flopped his left hand around in the stinging solution, making his teeth bear down against each other. Once a copious number of bubbles had formed, he took his right hand, made it into a cup, and began pouring the solution into each one of his abdominal lacerations. "Eh . . . eh . . . eh . . . eh . . . *fuck* . . . eh . . . eh," Jack howled through gritted teeth—any more pressure and his jaw lock was bound to start breaking them.

Once each cut was now thoroughly inflamed, he began the true torture. He hooked the first unknotted end of the floss to the tip of the box cutter, then cut himself until he could delicately grab the floss on the other side of the skin. "Ah . . . God damn it," Jack exclaimed with every cut, followed by bitter red-eyed tears and multiple deep breaths. He kept going like this until he had ten stitches in each wound pulled as tight as he could get them to go, almost completely closing each, but not enough to stop the bleeding. He then wrapped the entire roll of toilet paper firmly around his abdomen.

At this point his vision was very far off, as if looking at the light through a very distant tunnel. His hands were now shaking with tremors, and as the last wrap came around, he cut into a layer of the toilet paper bandaging and tucked the loose end into it. To finalize the procedure, Jack cut his T-shirt into two strips and tied them around his abdomen as firmly as he could, to hold pressure around the absorbent makeshift gauze.

Then, as he took one step out of the bathroom to go lie down on his bed, the light at the end of the tunnel was gone, and he hit the ground hard as he passed out.

• • •

Jack awoke face down on the cool and very hard surface of the steel floor. His tongue felt like sandpaper, and his mouth was drier than a desert. He began to rise, but a wave of excruciating pain put an end to any movement at all. His abdomen throbbed with very sharp and intense pain, whereas his left hand was dull and void by comparison. However, he knew he was going to have to dress his hand and at least look at his left shoulder, which felt no pain in comparison to the rest of his injuries. Over the course of an hour, he eventually rose to his own two feet. The first movement was the worst of all—as he got up on his hands and knees, he felt that delicate balance of the thin lining holding his guts in place as it tore a little more. Once standing, he slowly shuffled into the dry storage room to gather a water bottle, another roll of toilet paper, and another bottle of soap.

Once situated in the bathroom again, he drained the sink basin, then refilled it with water and another entire bottle of soap. He then sloshed his left hand in it once more, and this time the soap really bit into his skin. "Ow . . . shit," Jack begrudgingly bayed. Upon inspection of his left hand, there wasn't much to work with—it looked like a mangled mess of appendages, tendons, and bone. The majority of his left hand starting at the wrist was practically cut into three separate pieces. He tried to move his fingers, but nothing happened; he doubted if it would ever work again, even if he could put Humpty Dumpty back together again. However, at this point, trying was better than dying.

He proceeded to cut three more pieces of dental floss and began stitching up the separation of his thumb to his hand, in which he felt nothing. It took twenty stitches to get his thumb back to some kind of resemblance to where it once was. He then started stitching the split between his pointer and middle finger, which traveled all the way down to the wrist. Tears filled his eyes as he continued to make sixty incisions that consisted of thirty stitches. At the very tail end, Jack felt like he was going to pass out again. He took a minute to collect himself; once he had, the copious amount of red that cascaded down on almost every surface surrounding the sink and floor made him dry heave as he thought of all the blood that had come from his body.

He shifted his gaze to the ceiling, and once he calmed down again got back to "playing surgeon." The last split was by far the worst—he decided that he would have to cut off his pinky finger, which was hanging on by a limp thread of muscle and tendon.

The pinky fell in the sink basin, and he felt a sudden urge yet again to pass out and vomit at the same time. "Oh . . . oh . . . oh . . . GOD," Jack muttered to himself as he set seven stitches into place where his pinky used to be attached—

He vomited in his mouth and held it until he made it to the toilet, the violent spasms sending ripples of agonizing pain throughout his abdomen. Once the sickness was over, he dabbed his hand in the water again, then wrapped the entire roll of toilet paper over it. Once the hand was concealed, he no longer had the urge to be sick, but seeing the pinky finger at the bottom of the sink was another thing entirely.

He looked at his back in the mirror and found the talons of whatever the fuck that thing was had only bored skin deep. Cupping a couple of handfuls of the soapy water, he dumped them over his affected left shoulder, which stung in such a tiny amount compared to everything else that he didn't even notice. After that, he shuffled his bitter and scornful body into the office, as he knew if he lay down, he would never get back up again. He carried the unopened bottle of water with him, then ever so slowly sat in the metal chair behind the desk.

As he gazed at the computer terminal, what the computer relayed baffled him deeply.

Temperature: 96.1° F
Precipitation Today: 0%
Solar Panel Efficiency: 11%
Minimum Efficiency Requirement: 3%
Stored Power: 71 Hours
Radiation Outside: Safe
Toxicity Outside: Safe
Date: 04/06/2392
Time: 17:04

He had been unconscious for over two days. This thought made him start pounding down water—it explained why he'd had such a bad case of cotton chops when he woke up. Jack stared at that screen over the course of the half an hour that it took for him to finish off the bottle of water. Once he had done so, he had fallen fast asleep, his head hanging down over his chest, a pool of drool running down his stubbled chin and forming droplets, which fell to the floor and created a small pool of their own accord.

...

The humming of the computer terminal's green screen read 05:14. Jack saw through the fog of pain that surrounded his mind and body, like a thick wool blanket filled with red ants, constantly biting and nipping at his skin. He was also semi-delirious—a fever had started in the early morning hours, and to his dismay had continued. However, he knew he needed soup, or some kind of meal with a thick broth. He also knew he needed to drink; with his unconscious spells ranging from a couple of hours here to a couple of days there, it was almost impossible for him to implement any proper method of keeping hydrated.

As he stiffly, slowly, and agonizingly got out of the metal chair behind the metal desk, beads of sweat formed and trickled down his cheeks in streams. He walked hunched over in an unnatural fashion as he tried to keep his abdomen as flaccid and unused as he could. He reached the dry storage room, where, to his surprise, he found a boil-ready bag of chicken noodle soup. He then grabbed three liters of water, which felt extremely heavy now, as his entire body was more or less adapting to the functions it had lost in the fight with those bastards.

The fact remained that he had no use of his left hand and was now debating if he should just cut the damn thing off. However, he had already lost enough blood, and the pinky that still sat in the bottom of the sink in his mind's eye would always bother him. He was a hurting unit for sure, and the absolutely absurd fact that some idiot had forgotten the one thing he would surely need, a first-aid kit, began to kindle a fire of hatred within him for a man or woman he didn't even know. The other task he wanted to keep out of his thoughts for as long as he could was undressing his wounds, taking an antibacterial soap shower, and then redressing his wounds. That was a task that had to be done, as his dressing had become saturated in weeping blood and sweat.

Once the water was at a full boil, he dumped in the powdered chicken noodle soup and began to stir it for the ten minutes that it recommended on the package. *Beep! Beep! Beep!* The computer terminal sounded its weak, ebbing alarm chirps. Jack turned the stove down to a simmer, then turned his attention to the task of painfully walking back to the computer terminal. Once he was upon the screen, everything looked normal—until he read, "Radiation Outside: Advanced/Not Safe."

Such a quick change in the radiation level did concern him gravely, almost as if the world were adding insult to injury. He slowly shuffled back to the kitchen and approached the small window that looked out along the southern shoreline.

The sky, even in the early morning hours of dawn, had turned a bright green, and multiple orange arcs of blazing lightning flashed through the sky with blinding intensity. A moment later, the once-calm sea was in a tremulous white-capped stir. From the distance, Jack could only assume that waves were cresting at five to six feet tall. Then, with a streak of lightning dawning upon the distant mass of water, the rain began pouring down in sheets, accompanied by baseball-sized hail that rattled and smashed into millions of tiny pieces against the thick steel walls of the pod. The sky, now a brilliant green, was alive with massive fireballs striking the nearby beach surface, creating a massive crater. Massive clumps of smoldering sand hurtled out a hundred yards in every direction.

I hope the pod can take whatever's next, Jack thought to himself, as he begrudgingly returned his attention to the soup.

He turned off the heat on the left rear burner of the stove, then placed the stew pot on the cool right front burner. He then began taking sips from the pot with the large stir spoon. The soup wasn't half bad; however, he did miss the chunky chicken pieces that had been replaced with a chicken flavoring. *Not at all close to how Mother used to make it,* he thought as he continued to slurp the tiny noodles and broth.

Crack! Thump! The lights temporarily flickered as lightning struck the top of the pod. Out of reflex, Jack jumped to attention—this sent rippling waves of sharp pain throughout his entire abdomen, making him double over with trembling cramps. Once he recovered himself, he slowly and carefully moved the stew pot, which was now half empty, and placed it in the small refrigerator. Jack then grabbed a bottle of water from the counter and returned his attention to the small viewing window.

The storm was blindingly bright, the tremulous sea reflecting the burning lightning in the sky. Off in the distance, he saw a very dark cluster of wall clouds forming into a cyclone. The tornado of the air met with the water in a stunning explosion of force—the cyclone twister was massive, looking as if it were going to suck the entire sea dry. As it grew nearer, the pod began to violently tremble. The cyclone, now filled with its own orange and blue streaks of lightning, was coming upon the pod now, no more than a mile down the southern shore. The increasingly powerful winds were whipping rain and hail so hard against the little observation window that visibility was at a complete zero, other than the ever-increasing darkness that was besieging the pod. Jack, like a deer caught in the headlights, didn't move but just held a silly *O* on his lips. His face was now covered in a sheen of sweat, and his expression was one of true terror—if the twister did not change course, and soon, the pod would be sucked into it.

When the twister disembarked from the water's surface and hit the white sands of the shore, the cyclone left it behind. It held its rotation on the water's surface for a brief moment before the hundred-foot wave crashed down and sent a massive tidal wave in every direction, as if a giant troll's hand had performed a cannonball. The wave was upon the pod before the twister was—it submerged the enclosure under twenty feet of raging water, pushing it ever so slowly up the beach and away from the shore. Then, almost as if the heavy steel box had decided to float, the pod was being sucked up through the wave and into the twister.

Before Jack knew it, he was thrown into the air and crashed into the corner where the airlock door rested. *Thump!* His body hit the steel wall hard, and a very acute need to vomit filled him. Farther and farther up the twister sucked the pod, whipping it horridly in long circles. *Crash! Smash! Dong!* The steel casing that surrounded Jack reverberated as if the pod had made contact with an object equally as heavy, but not as strong. Then Jack's body lifted off the steel floor. A sudden loss of gravity had just hit.

"Oh fuck!" Jack screamed out—the pod's violent twisting had suddenly stopped, and the fear of falling filled the air. He screamed horridly as the pod came hurdling back down toward the earth. *Boom! Crash! Boom crash!* Jack was being thrown around like a ragdoll as the pod made contact with the earth, then flipped end over end for a quarter mile until it crashed down again into its final resting place.

He lay there in an unconscious slumber, his life hanging on a very finite thread, deciding whether to accept the luminous white or keep fighting to get back to the gray.

CHAPTER 3

The pod rested upside down, nine and a half miles from where it had originally sat upright. Jack, lying spread-eagle, awoke to the almost rambling *Beep! Beep! Beep!* of the computer terminal. His body felt limp and lifeless, every inch of him now filled with either numbness or a constant flow of pain.

Inching himself upright, he found his stature very decrepit. After a quick examination of his body, Jack didn't think he had broken anything, but almost every inch of him was covered in some fashionable yellow, blue, or purplish bruise. He slowly limped to the now upside-down and ajar office door, climbing over the top of the door frame—that sent a rippling and now-familiar sharp pain through his abdomen, shooting up his spine. Once underneath the upside-down terminal, he found that the screen had cracked and the small letters that it flashed were unreadable from his position. In either case, Jack knew what they were saying: *If you thought you were fucked before . . . guess again.*

He felt hot tears of desperation rising up from behind red eyes. "Why did you people leave me here?!" he bayed out, sending even more hot waves of pain through his abdomen.

He slowly clambered out of the office and reemerged into the kitchen. The supplies from the dry storage room were now scattered about the entire length of the hallway—he realized that in his stupidity, he'd forgotten to close the door. When he entered the bedroom, he found that all the drawers in the dresser were wide open, their contents dumped on the ground. Jack slowly and painfully donned a fresh boiler suit and T-shirt, as his old pair were beyond tattered and soiled. He then grabbed a bottle of water that rested amongst a large pile of nonperishable goods resting on the ceiling, now the floor.

Jack then proceeded to the airlock door and pulled the handle backward, as it was now upside down. When he climbed through the first door, he found the airlock hallway had taken the brunt of the impact—it looked like a concave lens. The side exposed to the impact had compacted into the hallway airlock. At this sight, Jack wondered if the outer airlock door would even work. He hit the switch to depressurize the airlock; it returned a metal voice of "Compromised, pressure stable."

An airlock on the fritz meant that a hole, possibly a microscopic one, had been punched in either the door or the now caved-in outer wall. As Jack operated the handle, the outer door reluctantly unlocked with a great amount of effort on his part; he was then able to open the door. What he saw struck him dumb.

The path in which the pod had traveled was marked by the immense clearing it had made through the trees. Jack had a clear line of sight to where the tall grass met the white, sandy beach. There were two craters of about twenty yards in diameter where the pod had undoubtedly made contact with the earth; as it had, it had left its large footprint behind. It had uprooted all the trees in its path, leaving what looked like a giant skid mark in the now-cleared ground.

He disembarked from the pod into the late evening hues of the afternoon. The air was cooler in the forest, and it was heavy with humidity, making the biome very muggy indeed. At the end of the skid mark, there was dark-brown mud. Jack turned around and saw all the trees that the pod had taken with it. A massive logjam rested against the side of the pod farthest from where he stood. It looked as if a square acre of trees and brush had been compacted into the space of just thirty yards. The foliage that rested at the front of the pod was so thick that Jack doubted if even a mouse could find a clear way through it. The tops of the trees that had snapped free of their trunks rested on the top of the pod, making it seem as if nature had provided him a massive lean-to shelter to reside in.

However, he doubted the point of staying in the pod longer than tonight—if the life-support systems had in fact crashed, the only purpose the pod now served would be as a cold and very large tomb. The fact that he now had not even a sliver of a rough idea which direction was north made it seem to Jack that his compass on the beach had been an exercise in futility—everything, including the pod, had been thrown miles in every direction from its original position.

As Jack took a sip of water and took in the scenery, the direness of his situation now seemed to sneak up on him. What he needed was rest, but the fact that he now had to find another suitable home disallowed that entirely—he could only guess how cold it might get at night in this biome. Who knew anything about this biome? He hadn't even come close to scratching the surface of understanding the pod's surroundings on the beach. The present facts amounted to "shitola"—he knew nothing of where he was, what day it was, how long he'd been unconscious, or even where to get water. All his tasks had been futile, and that thought alone made him weep bitter tears of frustration.

I haven't cried this much in my life . . . well, ever! Why is it that it took me being marooned on an alien concept of a planet to make me cry? Why is it that they left me here to die? That's the real question. If there were at least six others, how long ago did they die as well? How long will it take for me to die? Jack's thoughts became more and more despairing as he dove further into self-pity.

Once he had finished of his bottle of water and thrown it on the ground for the wind to take, he returned to the catacomb of the pod. Jack grabbed the blanket that had fallen off his bed and curled up in the fetal position in the far corner of the bedroom ceiling. He was on the brink of giving up hope entirely, as the lights of the pod had gone completely out within an hour of his return to his bedroom.

...

Morning came. Jack had slept restlessly as his thoughts proceeded to torment him. These were no longer the happy, good old days of college. These were no longer the days in which your house was built by a team of contracted construction workers. And they definitely were not the days in which you sat on the couch with a beer in one hand and a hot dog in the other, watching mindless television. These were the days you wept and gnashed your teeth. These were the days of primal living. These were the days of only *surviving*, not living.

He spent the first hours of the morning pacing around the pod and scanning his surroundings. Jack did this very slowly, as the pain that encumbered his body only allowed for a slower process of movement. His plan would now have to include all of the following: food, water, shelter, first aid, fire, navigation, and signaling. All these things would also have to be done in a manner that could withstand the volatile environment. The area that he was working with was a hundred yards long and sixty feet wide, which the pod had made easy work of clearing. He would build his shelter and accompanying structures in this area. He was living in a primal time, which meant he would have to adapt to becoming a primal being himself if, in fact, he truly wanted to survive.

However, first things were first—what he needed to do first was to gather up all the tools inside of the pod. With an accurate list of what he was working with, he could then hopefully make the primal form of whatever tools he was missing in order to serve his purposes. Summing all this up into a nice little package was easier said than done. Thus began the long process of inventorying and piling all the tools outside of the pod's airlock door.

The pod's tool locker offered the following multipurpose tools: a claw hammer, needle-nose pliers, channel locks, a utility knife, a hacksaw, standard and Phillips-tipped screwdrivers, a twenty-five-foot measuring tape, a twenty-four-inch pipe wrench, a crescent wrench, a propane torch and spark lighter, a putty knife, a handsaw, a hatchet, a speed square, a pry bar, a cat's paw, a plumb bob, a round-point shovel, and a bricklayer's hammer, which would now be assigned as his melee weapon. After inventorying the tools, he knew the basic fundamentals of how to use each; his father had taught him throughout his teenage years, in the hours they'd spent together working on various household projects.

It was going on what Jack assumed was late morning by the time he had the tools out of the pod and had gathered three bottles of water, as he was about to work up quite a sweat. He had the general rough draft sketched out on a sheet of graph paper: the most basic floor plans of how he was going to build his new home. The plans were for a ten-foot wide, ten-foot long, four-foot deep dugout trench shelter, using the hard-packed soil and timber to construct retaining walls. In essence, he was going to build a timber-constructed bunker that would be able to withstand any storm of the likes that he had just been through. The first phase of the plan was to outline the ten-foot-by-ten-foot square he was going to cut out of the ground.

He grabbed the tape measure, standard-head screwdriver, and putty knife, then proceeded to count out twenty-five paces from the airlock door as he walked into the clearing. Once roughly fifty feet from the pod, he stabbed the putty knife into the soft, dark soil. He then clipped the tape measure's edge to the far side of the putty knife and walked backward from it until he reached ten feet, then stuck the screwdriver into the ground to mark the spot. Retracting the tape measure, as evenly as he could, he began dragging the putty knife through the soil until he reached the screwdriver. He repeated this step four times until he had the outline of his square cut out.

The next part of the plan was what his body begrudgingly pleaded against him doing: breaking first soil with the round-point shovel. He started at the closest corner toward the pod and planted the shovel into the ground with his boot, driving the bit. He then laboriously pulled up the first shovelful of dirt and tossed it as far from the corner as he could, which was a little less than a yard away. He continued shovelful after shovelful, following the outline until he'd made a complete round trip—it had become more pronounced now, as four inches of dirt had been removed from the outline's surface.

He took a quick water break and let his abdomen rest, as it was completely engulfed in flaming pain. He then returned to the corner that he'd started at and began again, occasionally looking up from his work to scan his surroundings. He had dug a complete foot down into the outline of his trench by midafternoon; he had made more progress than he thought he would. Ultimately, it was not he who made himself retire for the day, but the dull, throbbing pain in his wounded abdomen and limp left hand, as he had to crane his left wrist around the shovel to get any use out of it at all.

The second phase of today's plan was to get a fire started, which would hopefully ward off any predators that decided to come by his new residence. Jack had decided that he would burn the midnight oil for as long as he could, giving his body rest only when it truly needed it, switching from heavy, labor-intensive work to light work as needed to allow his body enough breaks while continuing to work as long as possible. Thus, he switched gears and began foraging the forest floor and dense flora that surrounded the clearing with hatchet in hand, hoping to find some dried wood that wasn't too damp or rotten.

First came the handfuls of dried twigs and sticks, necessary tinder to get the fire going. He made four piles of the tinder at each one of the four corners by his newly formed trench outline. The piles were in decent enough proportion that Jack was confident he could start a fire in each corner. He returned to his foraging, gathering sticks and logs that were no smaller than his thumb and no longer than his wrist, which would provide the starting fuel for the fires. This process, however, took an excruciating amount of time—he could only truly carry six to eight logs at a time back to each fire, as he had no use of his left hand other than using his left arm to pin the bundle of logs to his chest in order to transport them to the designated fire locations.

It was late evening by the time he had gathered enough fuel to hopefully last through the greater portion of the night. Returning with the propane torch and spark lighter, a notebook held against his chest by his left arm, he spent a moment feeling for the wind. When he found its direction in the dim and fading rays of light, he began to make lean-to fires, in which the largest log was set against the face of the wind as a wind block. He filled the lowermost portion of the lean-to with scraps of dry paper, small twigs, and sticks. Then he laid the smaller logs over the tinder; once they were in position, resembling a proper fire structure, he sparked the lighter, ignited the propane torch with a hissing sound, and then lit each fire successfully. He killed the propane torch and watched as each corner fire cast its warm glow over the "construction site." He found that the four corner fires were just enough to make out the ten-by-ten cut-out, in which the extra hues and rays from the fire were cast about three yards past the site.

As the sun set and Jack began digging again, the horseflies and mosquitos were ravenously hungry. Digging side by side with the fires wasn't too bad; it was when Jack got to the middle of the trench and the smoke no longer provided its bug protection that things got bad. For every shovelful of dirt came his right hand swatting at a quarter-sized horsefly that bit into his exposed skin, which was mostly his neck and face. However, eventually the work fell into a natural and very numbing routine of more pain and swelling from each bug bite; it made him forget momentarily about the pain in his hand or abdomen, although both these areas were screaming and throbbing with pain.

By what would appear to have been midnight—the fingernail moon was highest in the sky—Jack had dug an additional foot into his trench, which was now little more than knee deep. He took a quick break as he refueled the fires and drank the last liter of water he had brought out of the pod earlier in the day. He stood as close to the corner fire as he could as he drank his water, to avoid the ever-increasing swarm of mosquitos that had replaced the majority of horseflies that had already gotten their fill for the night.

He scanned the ominous edge of where the fires' glow met the black blanket of night, where a few pairs of small, beady eyes lay just beyond the glow. If they were predators that could kill him, they already would have, he concluded. More than likely they were some small nocturnal creatures that were staring at him bitterly, due to the fact that he had taken out quite a large area of habitat when he and his pod came crashing through the air, thrown violently into the dense forest flora by a tremulous twister. "Yeah, we're all upset around here—we're all bitter, aren't we?" Jack howled into the cool night air—he had only now noticed how cold it had become, his perspiration beginning to cool from inactivity. Nevertheless, he pushed on.

■ ■ ■

Jack awoke to the first true-yellow hues from the sun's broadened face, which had just risen above the horizon. He had dug an additional foot—he now lay in a three-foot-deep, one-foot-wide, ten-foot-long trench. He had succumbed to his body's eager yearning for sleep at some point late last night; it was now very stiff and tender from the forced, overtaxing labor, making it ever so difficult to clamber out of the trench. When Jack stood up on the dirt floor of the clearing, his abdomen jerked and twitched with furious muscle cramps that sent him to his knees. He began drawing deep breaths until the cramps passed, then resumed trying to achieve his upright stature. That done, he proceeded to walk to the pod.

After entering the pod, Jack grabbed four bottles of water and an instant biscuit and gravy boil-ready meal pouch, along with the last clean stew pot. He then rekindled and refueled the closest fire, filling the pot with a liter of water. Jack scanned the forest floor for a couple of nearby rocks; once found, he threw them amongst the coals of the now-flaming fire. While Jack waited for the rocks to heat up, he restoked each fire, then went rummaging in the nearby woods for more fuel. This, Jack knew, would become another one of those constant battles, keeping at least one fire burning at all times. That propane torch was a nifty tool, but God only knew how long it would be till he could leave this forsaken planet, and how many fires he would have to light in the interim.

Once the wood piles were restocked and the rocks had heated,

Jack placed the four stones into the pot, and the water immediately hissed and gurgled in response. As the water boiled, Jack took a moment to sit next to the fire and warm his cold bones. His mind was miles away from attending to the boiling pot as he thought on the last two weeks. They had been a very long and hard two weeks—he felt that he had grown a year older. More than a year, actually—he felt old, he felt beat up and rejected.

He knew that around noon he would have to change his bandages and rinse them with more of that ever-so-nasty anti-bacterial soap. If the feeling kept receding from his left hand, he feared he would eventually have to cut it off at the wrist, due to its higher chance of turning gangrenous. That, however, was another battle for another time; right now all he wanted to do, in truth, was quit. Death didn't seem so bad at this point; the main selling point was, you guessed it, *no more pain, just receding into darkness.* That thought alone felt welcome for longer than Jack would like to admit.

And then there was the even bigger trouble he was facing. If he truly were the last man alive—which, with every day gone by, seemed entirely more possible—*what's the point in prolonging the extermination of the human race on this planet where the wild has restored its dominance?* The questions he was asking himself bordered on self-pity, bitter frustration, and self-doubt. All those things, as he knew, were not good thought processes in a survival situation. The last question that slipped its way out of the dark box in his mind that he was trying to close was *Who is there to survive for? Everyone I know is either long dead or on a planet millions of miles away.*

Jack chowed down rather fiendishly, as he hadn't eaten in . . . well, truthfully, he couldn't remember. All he did know was, with the hunger now filled and the thirst quenched, it was time to start digging again.

■ ■ ■

The hours rolled past, the sun made its traverse across the sky, and a little after high noon, Jack had the outline of his trench dug out. Now came the more daunting task of digging out the massive pile of dirt which remained separated from the new walls of the trench. He was nevertheless determined to dig the rest of the dirt out; however, he knew the status of his wounds would prove whether or not he had the ability to keep digging and to keep running that ever-uphill race of survival.

Standing half naked, with his boiler suit opened down to his upper thighs and his brown, bloodstained T-shirt removed, Jack slowly unwrapped his abdomen; as layer after layer came off, more and more brown and crimson color came through. With the last wrap of toilet paper gauze off, he saw his profound abdominal wounds in their full glory. To his surprise, they were not infected—they had actually begun the process of healing, and thus far, it was going along nicely. A few stitches had loosened, but that wasn't the end of the world; it just meant he would have to restrain from quick and far-reaching movements. He retrieved the antibacterial soap from the crook of his left elbow; once a nice lather was created, he rinsed it off, which felt good in the noonday sun. He then dropped the antibacterial soap and the empty water bottle on the ground and began blotting the water off of his stomach with handfuls of toilet paper. Once thoroughly dry, he rewrapped his abdomen for compression, then donned his ripped T-shirt and zipped up his boiler suit.

Looking at the last wrap of toilet paper that had come off his left hand, he winced. "Jesus, that stinks." The tissue surrounding his hand and just below his wrist was black and purple; pus had started to leak from where his pinky used to be. At the least, he would have to cut off his ring finger and middle finger all the way back to his wrist, begging the even bigger question: *Cut the entire hand off, or cut half of it off and hope to save my pointer finger and thumb? Who the fuck can make that decision?* He knew he had to cut off the whole hand, knew it had to be done—but how?

A bead of nervous sweat that had started at his right temple began to run down his face. The limp, mangled member no longer looked like part of his body but more like an alien squid that had decided to hitch along, holding him by the wrist. His mind was made up, but the follow-through of the action was the hardest part.

...

He spent the next hour boiling the hatchet head in a pot of water and jerry-rigging the putty knife to the end of the propane torch, lashing it to the nozzle with some wild vine cordage. He set a stump high enough to act as a chopping block, which was tall enough for him to get a full swing out of the hatchet before it would fall on his left wrist—specifically the soft part between the bones in the hand and the bones in the wrist, "the tendon part." Procuring a shoelace from one of his boots, he twisted and twisted and twisted it around his arm and a large stick, cutting off all circulation to his hand.

Now, ten minutes later, came the moment of torturous truth. The plan was simple, but the time frame was incredibly short—about ten seconds. He would have to swing the hatchet down on his numb hand, whose few parts that still had a bit of feeling to them would send him into almost immediate shock—his eyes would comprehend that he had just lost a very large member. Then, in the ten seconds before he passed out, he would have to press the putty knife's steel, now brightly glowing orange with the propane torch's heat, into his stump, cauterizing it before he lost consciousness. Then he would simply fade into the darkness of unconsciousness—but before he did, he would have to loosen the tourniquet just enough to allow minimal blood flow to circulate through his stump.

This knowledge was purely based on a very long reading of the emergency surgery book. The book said nothing about cauterizing the wound; he had heard that from a different survival book. However, the cauterizing was for fingers and toes, not for stumpy wrists.

Sweat now profusely flowed down every nook and cranny of his stern, set face. He would not count to three—he would not flinch. He would visualize the stump, and only the stump on which his hand rested, and would swing.

"Oh Christ. Oh boy!" he said through a small parting of his lips.

Sching! The hatchet rang true. Jack didn't look right away; when he did, his vision was that of a faraway trance. He grabbed the makeshift cauterizer and pressed it hard against his stump, the flesh burning and filling his nose with its dank and grotesque smell. As the vision of his stump grew ever so far away now, almost like the tip of a nail in size, he unwrapped the stick—one, two . . . *thump!*

He fell backward, hitting the ground hard. The propane tank rolled onto the dirt, burning unwaveringly.

CHAPTER

4

Jack awoke to the last fading rays of light that cascaded through the trees and their full leaves like whispering coins, constantly shifting their position, ever falling upon the forest floor dimmer than they'd started. His body was in dismay as a confusing and tangled cluster of unmoored nerve endings shot rambling messages back to his brain.

He slowly sat upright and found that his hand had truly been cut clean off. The only thing that remained was a very charred and black stub, which had wept not a single drop of blood—to his relief, this meant that the wound had been truly cauterized. With that thought, he looked over to where the now silent and dead propane torch lay. He picked it up and found that because of the bindings, the putty knife had kept the trigger depressed long after he had passed out; the entire propane tank had now completely drained out. He threw it far off into the nearby foliage and cried bitter tears of disappointment in himself.

Rising slowly to his feet, he felt an acute wave of dizziness that prompted the sickness that followed. Once the sickness was over, he looked to where the closest fire had dwindled down to only small coals. He then, as hurriedly as he could, restoked the fire with kindling, and small flames licked at the twigs. Then, as the fire progressively accepted the larger fuel, he began the task of hazily restoking all of the fires. To his surprise, all were on that thin thread between going out and staying alive.

Once the fires were stoked and going again, he grabbed one of the bottles of water and pounded it down. He was somehow still in shock—he just couldn't place why. Then he remembered the tourniquet; however, after feeling its pressure was loose enough to allow some blood flow through it, he deemed that it wasn't that either. It took him up until the point when he saw his severed, mangled, blackish-green and blackish-purple hand to remember that he had just hacked it off.

It wasn't that he was surprised in some way, as he had known why he passed out in the first place. It was simply the act of visualizing the thing that made him feel as if part of him was no longer whole. The other thought that kept jumbling and tumbling around was that he hadn't really planned on waking up at all. He had kind of grimly expected to die from bleeding out, or shock, or something along those lines. He was definitely "shook up," the modest term for waking up and going, *Sir, did you know your hand is off?* Then responding, *Why, yes. It's only a flesh wound, I think I'll go for a brisk walk in the park.* The reply: *Well, that sounds like a marvelous idea, sir, if I don't say so myself.* That is the way his distant and convoluted thoughts were now jamming up his mind—sitcom humor and unrealistic thoughts. He was out of his mind, but he hadn't considered that a possibility.

With his old member thrown far off into the forest underbrush, he began to laboriously collect as much fuel for the fire as he could. He now no longer felt any of the pain that was still screaming in fiery shots around his body. He only felt distantly numb, like he wasn't even in his body at all. He was somewhere else, somewhere warm, some fond memory comforting him, as he paid little to no attention to the world around him. He was still dealing with the disconnect wrought by the actions that had led up to his now-severed nerves—they were still trying to tell him that his hand was there, but they couldn't really send the message of where that hand was or what it was doing. It was a very odd thing that he was dealing with, a queer thing.

Once the wood had been collected and the dark blanket had descended upon the forest, only then did it hit home for him. He, himself, had just cut off his fucking hand and lived to tell the tale, no matter how much his dead-end nerves wanted to tell him his hand was still there. "What a day," he whispered to himself as more tears came rolling down his cheeks, followed by bitter resentment. No! This feeling was different. It was no longer bitterness, it was hatred. He had hatred for the people who had deemed it a good idea for him to stay behind on this far-gone planet. Then he collected himself and began taking his anger out on the massive mound of dirt that still lay in wait to be removed from the trench.

The night continued on, and as it did, so did the swarms of horseflies, the mosquitoes, and the beady little eyes that lay in wait, just beyond the light of the fire's reach. As he continued, he paid no mind as the stinging things bit into him, draining him little by little. The action was repetitive, mundane, yet somehow soothing: burying the shovel in the mound with his one good hand and right boot, scooping it up with his left forearm craned around the shovel shaft and his right hand doing most of the work, sending it forcefully into the air. The dirt then landed upon the ever-increasing piles that lay around the far edges of the trench and just beyond the fires.

The night passed on in its peculiar, yet now usual way; the only sound that disturbed the mundanity was the very distant howl of a lonesome wolf. However, as the morning approached, the throbbing pain in his abdomen made him yield in his non-stop effort of digging. The fires remained lit; as daybreak fell upon the forest, Jack traded the shovel for the hatchet and searched the ever-farther distance from the clearing to find dry fuel for them, as the fuel he was burning was not being naturally replenished fast enough.

He ate the same thing as he had the other morning. He no longer ate it for the sake of how it tasted; he ate it for its nutritional value. He no longer cared about why people had thought it a good idea to leave him here. He no longer cared about the aches and pains in his body. He simply cared about survival and the continuous construction of his trench shelter. He continued his labor-intensive job of digging, foraging for dry wood, cutting the larger pieces of wood he found with his hatchet, then quenching his thirst with yet another bottle of water that would eventually end up on the outskirts of the forest, where the wind would be left to deal with the trash as it wished. This was followed by stoking the fire with a large amount of fuel before taking a catnap during the day just before high noon; he'd wake up an hour or two later and return to feeding the fires and digging the trench. Once night befell his "construction site," so did the never-ending swarms that he no longer slapped at, or even waved his hand at to shoo away. He didn't care if they eventually did suck him dry, for he had nothing to lose. *What did you say? Oh, you want the other hand too? Well, go ahead and bugger off!* he thought hatefully to himself.

The hatred fueled him, drove him. He no longer had anything to lose, and the burning desire for payback in any way, any shape, or any form, drove him further along. He wanted them to see the consequences of just leaving him behind, essentially abandoning him; he wanted to be able to overcome the odds so that one day, just maybe, if in fact they returned, he would be the first one waiting for them. What he would say would be simple: "Go fuck yourself and die!"

He did, however, have to admit to himself in a very small dose: the chances of ever actually meeting the bastards who'd left him here were slim to nil, but so were his chances of survival. "I guess it balances itself out," he said to himself in a whisper.

▪ ▪ ▪

It took four days of almost nonstop, around-the-clock digging, but by late afternoon on the final day, the trench was dug. However, it was far from done, for now came the even harder part: phase two of the trench-shelter build. He needed to procure sixteen pieces of timber that were roughly six inches wide by eight feet long. After that, he needed to procure an additional sixteen pieces of timber that were six inches wide by ten feet long. He would stack them log-cabin style, in alternating square lengths, to keep the walls even but also structurally sound. This would be the first retaining wall that would keep back the mud and dirt in even the heaviest of storm showers.

Dragging the procured length of timber through the forest would be the bitch of it. The fact that his body was still tender, not to mention missing a member, didn't help the math of how he would get the loads of timber back here. However, for now, he would relish in his progress while he pondered how to proceed with the next phase.

He sat with his legs crossed in the afternoon glow of the temperate forest, stirring a steak-tip and potato-chunk stew in the stew pot and sipping lukewarm powdered fruit punch from a liter bottle. His thoughts wandered as he stirred his earned victory meal, turning to his dog days of college. He would save money from his summer job as a Mississippi barge deckhand, but it always seemed to run dry by the beginning of February. Paul, his old college roommate, would come up with goulash-style dinners and one night had suggested, "Why don't we sign up to become high school tutors and set up our operation at one of those rich-prick private schools?"

Jack could see where Paul was going with this idea right away. "What if we got caught, huh? What if we get the boot from the dean because we decided to do high school pukes' homework for a fee?"

Paul's smile had widened just enough to show a little white. "We won't get caught, because we'll set it up through my friend Dan's computer. He said he could disguise the IP address of his computer through the entire high school's mainframe and all the computers connected to it. If questions were asked, it would look like someone from within the school was doing it. We can charge different fees for papers, tests, and homework assignments. We make it look legit by doing standard tutoring as well as the other stuff."

Jack had sighed, dumbfounded—even if he had a friend that could do that, how were they supposed to hide the money trail? "What about the online banking accounts? How are we supposed to hide that?"

Paul looked down at the single gummy worm that lay on the three-day-old plastic plate, and with the same bitterness all his great ideas came to, said, "Not so great . . . right."

That look of scorn that came from being poor for no reason other than to get a future career . . . it was the same look that Jack had never been able to decipher until now. It was the same look he subconsciously embraced when he thought, *What's the point? Who cares about my trials and tribulations? Who's waiting with that gold statue for first place at the end of my finish line? Why do I have to suffer for so long just to get that brief passing glance at victory?* Jack understood completely now how his roommate had felt, and that revelation saddened him.

After the large and very filling meal, by far the tastiest thing amongst all the other boil-and-serve meal pouches that lined the hallway floor of the pod, Jack stoked the fires and lay down for his first true night of rest. His new "first-place prize" was a large meal, clean water, and a muddy trench to sleep in. He lay with his face to the barely visible stars as large, ominous black clouds rolled past him in the night.

...

To Jack's surprise, when he awakened, the clouds had dissipated and the ground was dry. "It didn't rain on my proverbial parade," he said to himself. He slowly got up; as he did, his knees gave off a loud crack as each popped from stiffness. He then began the morning routine of gathering more fuel for the fires, restoking and resupplying the fuel piles, cooking biscuits and gravy, and pounding a bottle of water as the breakfast cooked. The morning air was cool, just below seventy degrees. The air hung damply around the forest floor; the birds just beyond the distance of the clearing, who had relocated in their dispersed habitat, fell into their morning routines as well, singing the forest to life. Thus far, Jack had thought himself lucky—no mammals, other than the ones behind those beady eyes in the distance of the night, had even come within eyesight of the clearing in the past week.

With breakfast over, Jack walked back to the pile of tools that sat just in front of the pod's airlock door. He pocketed the tape measure, slung the hatchet through the right belt loop of his boiler suit and the bricklayer's hammer through the left belt loop, and carried the handsaw in his right hand. Since the mangled mess of trees and foliage was too thick and entangled to attempt to make a use of, he decided that a new side phase would be added to his plan.

He thought it would be a great idea to continue down the farthest side of the clearing. Then, once upon the undisturbed foliage in the direction the pod had descended from, he would begin to clear a ten-foot-wide path, which would eventually lead back to the tall grass that rested between the beach and the edge of the forest.

His ultimate goal in making that path was to connect his home with the beach; however, he had a darker initiative behind the plan as well. He wanted to start the long, mostly dry grass ablaze, in hopes of clearing it of all those fuck-ugly creatures he'd had the pleasure of gaining his battle scars from. At the same time, if there were any other survivors within his general area, they would see the blaze from tens of miles away. The plan would thus also accomplish the goal of signaling. But mostly he was set on giving those . . . *What should I call them? They looked like a cross between an ostrich, a rat, and an alligator . . . maybe osators? No, that's stupid . . . allegatos? Yeah, that sounds right . . . I like it.* Those ugly bastards would now and forever be called *allegatos.*

In any case, Jack had crossed the length of the clearing and now sat on the far east end of it, where the cleared floor returned to dense forest. Surveying the area, he found smaller poplar trees that only reached a height of around twenty feet tall. The poplar trees were scattered everywhere among the large oaks, pines, redwoods, and mahoganies. However, this posed no problem—it would create a nice snakelike trail that wouldn't make his home a directly obvious thing. After all, who knew what "smarter" predators lay in wait for their chance at him?

He proceeded to walk up to the closest poplar tree, which was about three paces from the eastern edge of the clearing. He set his handsaw on the ground and retrieved his tape measure from his right pocket, then worked it out to a foot with his right hand; he then placed the tape across the tree's trunk and found it to be six and a half inches wide at the base. "Close enough," he said to himself as he replaced the tape with the hatchet, then began the long and laborious work of cutting down a tree with an implement made to cut small logs and branches.

Swoosh, swing, thud. Swoosh, swing, thud. The rhythm of it chimed out in the still forest air. He had progressed halfway through the tree's trunk around late morning. The rhythm was much more rewarding than the overtaxing rhythm of the digging. Plus, he only needed one hand to swing the hatchet; he thought grimly to himself that he was lucky they hadn't supplied an axe, as he would have been forced to consider other options. The rhythm went on, with Jack changing positions around the trunk from time to time as he tried to cut the trunk so that when it fell, it would fall toward the clearing, making less work of the hauling process.

Crrrrraaaaacccck. THUD! The poplar tree fell close enough to where he wanted it. The sun was nearing its noon position, and he found himself drenched in sweat; now that it had been at least four days since he had taken his last bird bath, Jack found that he reeked with dank body odor. With the tree down, he began to make quick work of the smaller branches at the top of the tree that would serve no purpose other than to be used as burning material. Once all the nonworkable twigs, sticks, and branches had been cut off, he found after some rough measurements that the tree would offer two ten-foot-long timbers and four eight-foot-long timbers. "That's a good start," he said aloud as he placed the hatchet back in his belt loop and began making piles of the scrap branches. From there, he could bundle the ends of the piles into his right hand and begin dragging them back to his trench.

Once the last bundle was brought to its final resting place, ten paces to the east of the trench, he grabbed another bottle of water, pounded it, and then began his walk back to the felled poplar tree. Once upon it, he grabbed the handsaw and began cutting the tree into the desired sections. First came the four eight-foot branches that stemmed from the trunk. Then came the longest part, during which he had to take multiple breaks—this new physical activity made Jack a doughy lump of huffing and puffing in quick succession.

Snap! The final timber sounded as he strenuously jumped, then came crashing down with all of his weight behind his feet, making the wood finally give way. He regained his stance, then took a step back from the now fully processed tree. It was nearing early evening; at this rate, he could estimate a tree a day, which would result in this phase being completed nine days from today. *Not too bad a time frame. The shelter will probably be done before the snow falls . . . if the snow does still fall,* he thought to himself in an obscure way, as if he had to question every "fact" that he had known about his home planet.

The dragging of the timber proved a more difficult task then he had expected. It was true that he had gained quite a bit of strength from his previous endeavor, and his right arm had picked up quite a few new "ropes" of muscle as well. However, the tension that he had to keep in the crook of his left elbow was fundamentally painful. He had never had to use his bicep and stubby forearm in this fashion before, which was proven by the way he had to stop and regrip the timber he was hauling almost every ten paces as he dragged it. The work of dragging the six total timbers was the most physically exhausting part of all. The sun was only a sliver above the western horizon; by the time the last timber was dropped, half in and half out of the trench, he could not even see it.

Pounding two more bottles of water, he stoked the fires that surrounded his trench. Large mounds of ashes now accompanied each fire. Jack began by placing the first two eight-foot-long sections at the east and west sides of the trench's floor. He then grappled and struggled to place the two ten-foot sections at the north and south sides of the trench's floor. With the first frame in position, he began kicking the timbers firmly into place, securing them into the dirt walls. He then placed the last two eight-foot pieces of timbers atop the ten-foot timbers of the north and south side of the trench. He then grabbed the shovel that still lay in the middle of the trench, clambered out, and began shoveling the loose, muddy dirt that lined the outskirts of the trench into a decent-sized pile in the middle. Clambering back into the trench, he began packing the dirt into the crevices between the overlying eight-foot timbers and the underlying ten-foot timbers, which, once firmly packed, held their place in the wall firmly.

This task alone had taken its over-encumbering toll on Jack's body; by the end of the night, it was screaming at him to take a rest. With the timbers in place and the fires stoked again, against the black carpet of night, he lay down in the middle of his trench and fell into an exhausted slumber.

▪ ▪ ▪

The days passed in much the same fashion, with each night ending a little later than the last and each day beginning a little earlier. However, today the high noon marked multiple endings and beginnings.

The first ending came only eight days, not nine, after he'd set out to build the first interior timber wall of his trench. The interior wall was finished, but so began the next phase: placing twenty six-foot-long by one-foot-thick timbers in an upright position and setting them two feet into the ground, thus acting as retaining barriers, giving the interior wall a much-needed strengthening.

The next ending was the thought, *Why haven't I observed the mammals yet?* This thought came to him on his last trip to haul the timber back to the trench. Out of the corner of his eye, he noticed fresh and very large hoofprints. The prints were from a very massive bovine creature. If it were a deer, it would, in Jack's mind's eye, have been at least ten feet tall at the shoulder. It reminded him of a moose documentary he had seen as a very young boy. The man in the film had put his hand over the print of the moose they had been tracking; it had been a little smaller than his hand, and the depth of the impression had been that of an index finger. The print that Jack saw reminded him of the exact same thing; however, the print was larger than the width of his own hand.

This startling print was all it took for Jack's perception to change all the more drastically. Not only that, but the last few nights he had been accompanied by more sets of eyes around him than he could count. This also marked the beginning of a rebirth of the habitation—nature, as it has always done, began to overcome his new home.

The clearing had begun to sprout small grass and moss about two days prior, and all these new observations marked the end of his dim theory that he "controlled" his surroundings. Strikingly, a lot more patterns of growth had arisen in the areas around him; it was especially noticeable in the morning. Everything had grown distinctively differently than the previously dispersed life, and had grown back to the outskirts of the clearing. What Jack was most concerned about was what would happen when some alpha mammal or predator decided to try its luck in reclaiming the clearing itself. This thought alone made the now almost-healed talon scars on Jack's abdomen tremble, burning with remembrance of what hostile things truly lay in wait for a prime opportunity to attack and possibly kill him all over again.

In a way, he had become more vigilant; the thoughts of what was observing him began to make him look very hard through the foliage, listening very closely for that unmistakable twig snap. As he enjoyed his midday steak-and-potato victory meal, his eyes constantly scanned the underbrush and forest floor for any movement. This was a consistent problem Jack had also noticed: all the eyes seemed to come out at dark, and the possibility of the biome becoming a nocturnal one suddenly dawned in his mind. This could very well be a reality; however, he was still an unadapted human, his eyes made for daylight. Nonetheless, Jack felt keeping the fires going was another primal but very valid reason for keeping the scary creatures of the night away. However, how long would it work? That he didn't know for sure. What he did know was that keeping even those four fires burning was a chore enough in and of itself.

Once he had finished his meal, his eyes were back on the prize. In the previous days of cutting down the small poplar trees, he had also cut out a large notch in the growing mahogany trees that would serve his six-foot-by-one-foot material purpose. However, the shortest mahogany tree he had come by looked no taller than sixty feet, and the trunk was roughly fourteen inches wide. With what he assumed to be forty feet of workable timber length, he would have to cut down a total of three trees, which was no small job—and the hatchet would make it all the longer a process. Nevertheless, he approached the first notched tree twenty paces east of the clearing, on the north side of a somewhat pronounced path on whose vegetation he had trampled over at least a hundred times in the acquisition of his poplar timber.

He made it back just as the blackness of the night encompassed the forest. He heftily rolled the mahogany timber into the trench before he stoked up the fires. This night proved queer, however—not even one pair of beady little eyes emerged in the darkness just beyond the light of the fire. The hairs on the nape of his neck were standing at attention, but he just couldn't put his finger on what was disturbing the subconscious part of his brain the most. Jack thought aloud, "It is a rather starkly quiet night, but red sky at night, sailor's delight . . . right? Maybe the animals have grown bored of my company."

With no real present danger to be announced, he began the task of digging the first two-foot-deep hole, which was seated a foot from the true-center line of the southern wall. He did this on purpose—he would leave a two-foot gap between the pylons to allow for the staircase that would eventually set into the timber. He dug the hole exactly two feet deep, then proceeded to roll the mahogany timber to the hole, the far end pointed toward the south wall. He then put all of his strength into lifting the end of the log; once it was up to his chest, he pushed it forward. It fell into the hole and stood at attention, firmly pressed against the interior wall. He then compacted the dirt he'd removed from the now-occupied hole around the bottom of the log, which kept it firmly in place.

Once this was done, he subconsciously decided to scan his surroundings. *Something is out there, but I just can't see it,* he thought to himself. He strained his eyes to see any reflection of light coming back to him through the eyes of another, and still saw nothing. His ears were alert, and the hairs on the back of his neck still stood at attention, but he couldn't understand why. He stood scanning every direction for what seemed like an hour; when not even a leaf rustled, he bedded down for the night.

■ ■ ■

The days that followed that precarious night were increasingly strange. No birds chirped or sang in the morning, and not even the nocturnal animals came to watch him at night. Nothing seemed to come within miles of where he resided in the clearing. It was as if there had been a mass evacuation of life, which was very unsettling. For the eleven days it took Jack to cut, haul, and set every pylon into the trench, nothing moved, nothing talked—not even a mouse fart could be heard in the stark silence. However, the morning after he had finished his pylons, he saw something he would never forget.

Six of them stood within ten yards of the trench's south side. It was as if they were the ones that decided if life continued in the forest. Jack stood as still as his trembling body would allow. They appeared to have been watching him trench through the night.

Four of them stood a hand taller than a man at their shoulders. Two others had shoulders that would come up to a man's navel. The creatures stood on hooves that held up very long legs connected to their bodies. Their faces closely resembled those of white-tailed deer, but their massive, gnarly, backwards-twisting horns were theirs alone. The bodies resembled those of moose but were more agile in build, like those of massive deer. Their eyes were wide and very large, their long, horse-like ears twitching like little radar arrays.

One clopped a hesitant hoof in Jack's direction, as if to say, "We see you." The two smaller members of the group were obviously fawns that remained at the back of the four adults. All twelve eyes were on him, waiting for him to move, to do something that would cause an equal or greater reaction. *Demoose,* he thought to himself, the best name could place on them—the massive deer *were* like moose.

However, their giant horns spanned at least six feet wide and cascaded about four feet behind their heads. This was what really concerned Jack, along with how massive they were in build. All that lean muscle behind those horns would kill Jack in one blow—he knew this just by the size of these giant creatures.

They stood staring at each other for the better part of the early morning, the herd's eyes on Jack and his on the herd. It was like some sensitive, hair-trigger standoff, one in which he was outgunned and outmanned. All he could do was stare and stand where he was, nothing else. The courtesy he gave by standing his ground was much repaid in the same fashion by the herd.

A call from the largest of the group, which Jack denoted as the alpha male, broke the stark silence and reverberated through the trees. It clopped its right hoof as if to draw the proverbial line in the sand; then, as abruptly as the call had ended the silence in the trees, it turned its massive head away from Jack and began walking back into the dense growth of the forest. After a moment, the herd followed suit; within five minutes, never looking back to where he stood, the herd had vanished amongst the dense foliage.

With a great exhale of breath, Jack thought, *What the fuck was that?* As soon as that alpha male had spoken, the birds and the rustling small creatures had returned to their songs and movements.

It was as if they had been lying in wait for the demoose to decide that it was okay to proceed. For eleven days he had heard nothing, seen nothing—for the forest to return to how it was before was something he could not comprehend. He stood for an entire hour, baffled by the experience—he couldn't understand it no matter how hard he tried to figure it out.

It was approaching noon—for hours he had been standing with his jaw dropped, just breathing through his mouth in nothing shy of amazement. Jack could have comprehended the situation if it were a pack of massive wolves standing there—if, after they'd eaten him, the forest had returned to its normal song and dance as the predators left with their stomachs full. However, a herbivore ruling the wilds, in a hierarchy the other, smaller beings respected, was beyond him. It was as if even the wolves and allegatos were afraid to show their snarling teeth around what seemed to be a divine moose herd in the new natural order. It was just plain strange.

The whole experience was above his understanding. By noon he had decided to give his brain a rest, as it obviously was not going to make a connection for a very long time.

■ ■ ■

The natural order had been restored, if it could be called natural at all. The last eight days had been filled with the last phase of construction. He had cut down the remaining poplar trees he needed for the six-foot-by-six-inch timbers, as well as the eight-foot-by-six-inch timbers. He had his exterior wall firmly established against the pylons; when it was all put together, it formed a very sturdy type of soil bin wall. The last part of the building process was shoveling and packing the dirt into the openings between the exterior and interior wall. However, Jack assumed that process would take only three days.

Once that was accomplished, the easiest part of the entire plan would come together in the construction of the roof. The first part of this work would consist of cutting down another ten poplar trees, of which he would then use the ten-foot-by-six-inch timbers to place over his trench walls. Next would come the piling of about a foot of dirt over the beams that made up the structural support of the roof. Lastly would be the piling of a foot's worth of brush, sticks, and twigs that were readily at his disposal, as his unworkable wood pile had grown to a pile about twenty feet around and five feet high that lay next to his trench shelter, just ten yards beyond his east trench wall.

Along with crafting a makeshift grass bedding area, which would rest in the farthest corner from the south door, this work would take about fourteen days. When all was said and done, when the roof was in place, the door would be just wide enough for him to crawl through. Yes!

CHAPTER 5

This morning marked sixty days of survival since Jack had awakened in his newly placed pod, thanks to that cyclone twister. The forest had seen around-the-clock rain for the past twelve days in a row. He'd had most of his roof completed by the time the showers had started—if the roof had not been almost completely finished, his trench would now be as good as a duck pond. The crater in which the pod sat was completely filled with water; about four inches of that water had filled the interior of the pod itself due to Jack's inability to close the outer door.

Small rodents had occupied most of the corners of the pod, and to his frustration, they had gotten into quite a bit of the food reserves. The last eight days since he had finished the construction of his trench shelter had been spent inventorying and storing what food and water reserves remained and moving them into his trench shelter. Jack figured that if he ate two meals a day, he had ninety days left—he had 180 bags of boil-and-serve pouches of nonperishable food. If it weren't for the rain, his shortage of water would have concerned him—at a minimum of three liters consumed per day, he only had ten days left, or thirty liters of water.

This, however, had led to his two new projects, which he sketched out in the only notebook he had been able to salvage from the soggy remnants of the office supplies that were now completely submerged in the water that occupied the pod. The first project: he needed to establish a way in which to collect the rainwater. Storing the water would have been easy—until recently, clear plastic bottles had lain throughout the clearing in every direction. However, due to the rain, most of them had been washed into the foliage of the forest. The second project: building another structure where he could simultaneously hold a fire above ground level and block it from the rain. This was the priority at the moment—Jack had not been able to eat for the past two days, as his last remaining fire had succumbed to the heavy rains. He was also very wary of having a fire in his trench shelter, because even the smallest risk of burning it down was too much—it had taken a lot of hard work to build the damn thing in the first place, and he was not going to have it perish in a blaze if he could help it. All in all, things were looking up for Jack—even his wounds had healed up, and it no longer bothered him to look at his nub.

He was still in the process of sketching his fire shelter by the time noon came around. However, as it was constantly raining now, it was hard to distinguish the sun's true position and the time it held. It was also a chore to even go outside, as he then had to dry out his clothes and skin to avoid getting a bad case of trench foot. He had also found that survival really boiled down to what injuries and losses were worth incurring for gaining even the most basic things.

The first step of building the shelter was to acquire eighteen four-foot-by-six-inch timbers that would act as the base and the roofing material to get the fire off the ground and shield it. The second step was to cut four eight-foot-by-six-inch posts that would hold the roof over the base. The third was to cut two six-foot-by-six-inch pieces that would bind the roof to the posts with lashing of cordage. Once completed, the four-foot base would stand three feet off the ground, with a four-foot space between the base and the roof. The roof would be one and a half feet thick. On the base would be a six-inch layer of dirt to keep a heat barrier between the wood base and the fire. An additional six inches of dirt would be thrown on the roof to absorb the water that the logs and brush didn't displace back to the surrounding ground. The timber length amounted to cutting roughly four poplar trees down, which would result in a little timber being left over. Thus, Jack could accurately assume the structure would take roughly the next seven days to complete—he could manage a tree a day, and then the construction would take about three days after. Today would mark the first day.

Jack took a look outside through the opening in the trench-door roof, uttering a small curse to the rain, then turned to the tools he'd jockeyed into the corner that sat kitty-corner from his bedding. He dug out his bricklayer's hammer for a melee weapon, the hatchet, the tape measure, and the handsaw. Once he had all his tools ready, he began to clamber out into the rain in his still-damp clothes and accompanying boiler suit.

As he stood on the soggy ground, the constant pitter-patter of rain was more pronounced, as the rain fell through the clearing unobstructed and crashed into the small pools that had formed. He began his march. For the first time since he had taken up residence in the forest, the air hung with a chill, unpleasantly accompanied by the heat-absorbing rain. Jack was thoroughly soaked again; he felt not just a chill, but cold.

He walked along his beaten path, which now spanned the greater part of one hundred yards. At the end of it stood just what he needed: yet another small poplar tree. He grabbed his hatchet, and in the somewhat annoying rain, he began his rhythm, an unimpeded *swing, swoosh, thud. Swing, swoosh, thud.* As the hatchet came down in its usual fashion, Jack again found some strange normality; in fact, he had become a little stir-crazy in the small confines of his trench shelter, his new home.

The hours passed quickly now, as they seemed to do whenever Jack was having fun or engaged in laborious chores. Once the tree was down, he began his methodical measurements, scored the notches that marked those measurements, and began trimming the nonworkable branches and limbs off. After piling the branches, he started dragging the first bundle back to the brush-and-burn pile that was now a true walk back and forth from felled tree to clearing pile.

Crack! A streak of orange lightning came down a hundred yards past the clearing, followed by a resounding *snap!* A large oak tree had been cut in half, and the half that still stood burned with intensity. Jack had jumped a bit as the immense bolt of lightning shook the ground and the accompanying thunder rumbled close overhead. *Never have I ever before in my life seen such intense lightning, except in this new age,* Jack thought to himself as he returned to his felled tree. The rain came down in sheets now as the wind picked up and slammed through the treetops. On the forest floor, all he could feel was the sheeting rain and a light breeze on the right side of his face. *If I have to go through another fucking tornado, I'm going to seriously shit a brick,* Jack thought to himself as he grabbed the last bundle of branches and began the journey back to the clearing.

Crack! Crack! Crack! Three bolts hit the pond encompassing the pod at the same time, which resulted in a fire starting in the thick brush that lay around the far end of the pod. For a split instant, it seemed as if the water had become engulfed in electric fire—upon the last bolt strike, most the bottoms of the trees entangled in the mass of foliage were set alight.

"Holy Christ!" Jack shouted at the lightning strikes' close

proximity to his trench shelter. *Guess you can't have any structure of steel around here,* he thought to himself as he watched the unimpeded flames lick around the mass of damp foliage. The lightning was so intense now that he thought of calling it a day, but at the same time, his chances of being crushed under his roof and burned alive if the lightning hit his shelter were greater than coming to harm if he continued his work. "If it's not a twister, it's lightning," he said to himself after he threw the last bundle on top of his brush pile.

By late evening, he had the felled tree cut into its sections accordingly and was carrying the first four. Each was four feet in length. He cradled the timbers with both arms, crooked at the elbows. The lightning had halted for the past hour or so, but the wind, even on the forest floor, was a fresh breeze to his back. As he'd predicted, the fire had spread very quickly to the surrounding foliage. An afterthought occurred to him: *What wildlife will it displace, and how soon will I meet a bigger creature that will silence the forest floor for weeks on end?* That was the question, as the fire looked as if it were going to continue on its war path for miles. The thick smoke rose a thousand feet into the sky, casting an even grayer, almost black hue over the overcast sky. The wind took the ever-increasing wall of smoke high into the sky in massive plumes.

Jack stacked the timbers next to the brush pile and began his walk back to the felled tree. The sky had turned that ominous, terrifying ghastly green hue in the direction past his path. He could tell the wall of clouds was forming over the beach again, as in that general direction the green turned into a looming and impending wall of black. "If I had to bet on the chances of shitting a brick," he said sarcastically to himself, trying to hide his boiling fear. These were the times he wished for someone, anyone, to be here with him, to share the weight of the bad times. However, no one was. He had to bear the massive and frightening load on his very small shoulders, which even after months of nothing but strenuous labor were still not large enough. Jack doubted they ever would be large compared to the massive and frightening creatures that roamed these new lands.

His pace quickened, as the edge of the green sky was directly above him. He knew he had enough time to continue with the load he was carrying, but there was something else about the green sky—as if it wasn't the worst that the storm could offer. It was almost like some indescribable frequency was carried in the air underlying it . . .

Jack shouted, "My God, radiation! It's a fucking fallout storm!"

His ears were ringing, every hair on his body stood at attention, and the skin on his uncovered right hand had begun to take on a pink hue that stood in great contrast to the green sky. Once he reached the brush pile, he dropped the load of timber next to the previously placed ones and made a dash to his shelter. As he ran, the light green now became a placid green, which, in truth, scared the living daylights out of him. Once at the small entrance to the trench, he jumped through and crawled in the darkness until he reached the fluffy dried grass.

Crack! Crack! Crack! Crack! Crack! Thud! Smash! Whack! The lightning that had receded had now come back in a deafening array. Jack could not tell exactly how close the firebolts were, but with every flash the interior of the trench reached a light level comparable to that of an overly bright day. The opening to his shelter now howled from the wind passing over it. "Fuck me!" Jack bayed, furious tears of frustration and anger streaming down his face. He had a feeling that a twister was coming, but whether he was going to truly shit a brick was still questionable . . . as long as he didn't hurtle through it this time, which would surely kill him without the protection of the pod.

"By God, the pod!" Jack cried out, but then a stone face came over him—he knew going to it was certain death. For now, the pod was in a pond of water—with the water that had reached the interior of the pod, one strike of furious orange would send him into an uncontrollable convulsion before certain death took him.

The wind kept up its constant howl but did not increase. The deafening bolts did not waver as their strikes continued. "As long as it doesn't hit the roof, I'm fine," Jack said aloud to himself, half believing it. As of right now, he didn't really believe anything—he certainly did not trust his surroundings, as time and time again they left him beaten and battered. His mind could never come to a full conclusion as to why the world was the way it was now.

The storm did not reach its climax until late into the night. Jack curled up into a ball, rocking back and forth with his right hand and nub cupped over his ears, though his nub did nothing to keep out the sound. His ears rang constantly as the concussive blasts continued, and at one point he was sure he was suffering permanent damage to his hearing. He was beyond scared—he was withdrawn, a living conduit into which terror continuously curdled his blood, his face drawn and pale. He rocked endlessly until the first glow of early morning followed the break-up of the storm. His head pounded like a massive gong; even hours after the concussive bolts had ceased, his ears still falsely heard them through the ringing.

When he finally had a grip on himself again, which was primarily due to the cessation of the ringing in his ears, he slowly crawled to the opening in the trench and peeked his head through it. What he saw could only be described as little more than the aftermath of a heavy explosion, such as artillery ordnance being dropped from the sky. Fires raged in every direction of the forest, and most of the once-standing mass of entangled trees on the far side of the pod had burnt down to a large smoldering pile. The fire still raged half a mile from where it had started, spanning what looked like a wall of flames a mile long. The four- to six-foot-deep craters created by each and every deafening bolt had hit the ground in no particular order around the floor of the clearing; they were still smoldering and charred with black dirt.

His brush pile and his small trench seemed to be the only things not struck by the furious firestorm. However, the winds had picked up and blown a large portion of his pile into the surrounding forest, which no doubt had added to the small fires that raged within its depths. The smoke was thick even on the ground, and the persistent rains that continued now only added to it in a musky stream.

▪ ▪ ▪

The fires would rage for the next six consecutive days; by the time Jack had built and erected his fire stand, he was malnourished and had lost about five pounds of the muscle he had gained. The smoke to the north would proceed long after the small fires around him smoldered out; the forest fire that had been started would not quit or falter but only grow in size and length, leaving nothing but mile after mile of barren, scorched earth behind it.

The sixty-ninth day found Jack eating a large breakfast which consisted of the two allotted bags of food rations for the day. He was sitting on a charred log that he'd acquired on one of his passes through his path that led a hundred yards east of the clearing. The log sat four feet from the fire stand, which now held a healthy fire burning in it. He had not eaten since yesterday, and his spirits were low as the rain continued. It was not only the rain, but the stale smoke that stood dank in the air from the still-raging fires to the northwest of his clearing. As the fire progressed, it had left miles and miles of burnt and charred earth behind it.

The sight he had seen this morning was a grizzly bear with its fur still smoking and a few patches still alight. The bear had run nonstop for what Jack could only guess to be miles, maybe even tens of miles total. It was running at his clearing in a full run when it suddenly stopped three hundred yards from the edge. It began to laboriously walk, its ragged breathing audible in Jack's right ear from a hundred yards out. It had then dropped and sprawled out fifty yards from the edge of the clearing, and with one final baying plea, it had died. This disheartened Jack a lot. He knew all too well that the bear he'd seen was only one of the probably thousands of animals that had suffered the same fate—other than the birds, which now flocked to his surrounding forest in droves. It was so overpopulated that for every branch, two birds followed suit.

He himself had suffered his own wound—he had lost most of the hearing in his left ear, as it was the one he couldn't protect without a hand.

Hatred for his situation rose up in his chest. He no longer found himself crying, for the tears he had wept seemed to have drained him of all his reserves. He just felt that rising hate in his chest, burning and churning in his stomach, flaming behind his eyes.

One thing, however, was different. His left ear had gained the ability to hear the lowest of decibels, things he wasn't able to hear before. More like vibrations that carried from miles and miles away through the earth. That's the way he liked to think about it—in reality, he probably was suffering from the same dysfunction as when he'd cut off his hand. He just wasn't ready to accept it was no longer there.

The other core problem he had, now more than ever, was that he could count the days since he'd last said something—and of course, it was always to himself. He didn't even bother to dredge up the thought that everyone he knew and cared about was either long dead or millions of miles away. God bless them for it—only those who needed to suffer were left here. This was the grim root of all his problems, all life seemingly miserable. For now, his plan was just to spend the day on his stump, drink the rest of his last water bottle, and wallow in his problems—after all, what was the point?

This was also another fundamentally disturbing question in his mind. It seemed now that all he did these days was categorize the things he couldn't think about, placing them in the dark recesses of his mind, never to ponder them again. The birds, with their songs of demise, at least had other birds to respond and sympathize—Jack was alone.

...

The next morning found him in a better state of mind. The question *Why think about anything, then?* had a validity to it—it was true that if he couldn't think about anything in the past, he couldn't think at all. Thus he retreated to his primal thought processes on the next two things he needed to do, at the same time. His water had run out, and that alone posed a serious problem. However, all that was needed was to collect it.

After Jack woke up to another rainy day, he made his way to the pod, which was rank with smoke. The smoke had entered the pod's airlock door and proceeded to stain every inch of the interior with the smell. With no real lighting, he had to feel his way around the floor—all the dishware in the kitchen had dumped out of the drawers, making his job a lot easier. Once he gathered all the cookware he had stumbled around in the dark for, he piled his treasure in front of his fire stand. He had three bowls that would collect a quarter liter of water each, three mugs that would collect half a liter of water each, and an uncleaned stew pot that he had left the chicken noodle soup to ferment in—this he was cleaning through fire. The stew pot would collect two liters easily once it was cleaned, and three additional coffee mugs would also collect a quarter liter of water apiece. All totaled, if the rain remained constant, he could gather up to five liters of rainwater a day, and he assumed at the very least nothing shy of a liter.

So he placed all the dishware and the stew pot, once it was cleaned, around the edge of the roof of his trench shelter, which would hopefully gather the runoff from the roof as well as the droplets of falling rainwater. As of now, he was fairly confident that he had his water problem solved. *Who knew?* he thought, unable to stop the negativity. Maybe it would rain for every day of his life.

The second need he had was to acquire meat or other food, as his ration supply would run out soon. This was what was truly on his mind, which had been toiling around the problem since last night and had offered many ways to solve the problems. The first problem was getting yet again acclimated to the wildlife, which had almost cost him his life the first time. Now Jack seemed to not care as much—what could his death from a wild animal really take from him at this point, anyway? The second problem was figuring out a way to capture, trap, or kill each one of these animals. Jack decided on crafting many weapons such as spears, bows, arrows, etc. He would also start the crafting of traps, such as pitfall traps, snare traps for small game, and maybe even massive deadfall traps, if he felt up to it. The third and final problem, which involved multiple factors, was the cooking and preserving of the game and/or fruits and vegetables that he procured. To be honest, he didn't really want to risk eating bad berries or fruit; those usually proved a very painful end indeed. However, without salt or refrigeration, he was looking at smoking meat, which would take a smoker of some kind. He could probably just cover the fire stand and use this as a smoker as well—problem solved.

After warming up by the fire and restoking it so it wouldn't go out when he was gone, he grabbed the bricklayer's hammer, the utility knife, and the hatchet before taking off down toward the trail. He was going to mark his way with notches in trees on his way down to the beach. He was headed in that direction as it had some of the most obvious features that he would find, making it harder to get lost—he just had to look for the craters that the pod had made as it bounded and crashed its way through the forest. He didn't know how long it would take him, but he surmised that just past noon would be the turning-back point.

Once he was off his beaten path, he began to embrace a slower pace. For every ten paces he would walk, he would stop and scan his surroundings and count out ten seconds before taking another ten light-footed paces. Upon reaching a hundred paces, he would notch the closest and preferably largest tree within his vicinity. Once the tree had a giant *X* cut into it with the hatchet, Jack would begin the process all over again. As he scanned and absorbed as much as he could from his surroundings, he found that most of the life that resided within the forest did so amongst the tops of trees. In rare instances, a flash of fur could be spotted as a mouse or shrew would run amongst the underbrush and fallen leaves. He continued his surveying and scanning, as he was desperately trying to learn the habits of the world around him. He saw a very few large spiders that made massive webs, and knew instinctively that these webs were for snaring birds, not insects. The spiders were comfortable twenty to thirty feet up in the air. They looked to be the size of a throwing disc; their thick bodies bewildered him as to how they were not ground hunters, making funnel webs.

A mile into his walk, he came upon the first massive crater that the pod had made. It was an astounding twenty feet wide by ten feet deep at the surface of the water that now filled it. Jack could only guess how deep the crater truly was, and if the rain didn't cease sometime soon, it would become a very large pond. He skirted along its edge; once on the other side, he marked an *X* in the closest tree, pointing in the direction straight across from the crater to get his bearings correct once he skirted back to the other side.

He continued through the dense flora and rich foliage until he reached the edge of the forest, where the tall grass lay before him, and just beyond it the beach. The memory of those nasty little bastards in all their glory came back to him, and that hate rose in his chest again. "Oh, yes. Your time will come too. However, I have traveled and seen enough for today—but mind you, I will be back tomorrow. Now that I know for certain where you live," he whispered to the grass that was waving as if to say goodbye, as the winds whirled through it and played with it.

Jack made it back to his trench in the early evening. He had collected a nice amount of rainwater and drank from the first mug that was half full. The water tasted crisp, yet had a small hint of pine and grit from the runoff of the trench roof. He polished off the other two mugs, then foraged for a couple water bottles that lay in the dirt nearby. He filled three bottles near-completely full from the water collected in the bowls and stew pot. He took the bottles with him into his trench shelter, stripped stark naked, wrung out his clothes and set them to the side to dry, and lay down for the night.

CHAPTER 6

The trio found themselves staring at the distant smoke of some raging forest fire off in the distance, on the other side of the vast mountain range that seemed to divide one side of the island from the other. Their individual pods were within fifteen miles of each other, so they had come together. They were residing in what seemed to be the plains region of their area. Upon their initial encounter, which had only been four days after the trio awoke from hibernation in their individual pods, they had agreed that they would move into one pod and share it, while the other two served as the group's fallback if the one they were sharing decided to crap out. Since that decision, the group had made quite a few journeys around the realm they now occupied.

They had in fact made four very long expeditions to survey what lay around them. The first expedition had brought them west, where they landed upon yet another mountain range, this one not quite as long as the one to their east—however, the height of these mountains dwarfed the ones in the east. Upon getting closer and closer to the massive mountains, the trio had each begun breaking out in a pink rash, which was followed by an even more intense morning sickness for the following two days. Matt had deciphered that they were all suffering from radiation sickness—his vision on the second morning had become grainy, and his rash had intensified, similar to his fellow travelers'. Thus they'd decided to make the long trek back to Olivia's pod—especially Nicole, as her rash was the worst and in the most uncomfortable areas.

The second expedition was to the south—after fifty miles of walking, they had found a great vantage point on an overlying hill of the southern islands. To the southwest, the lands consisted of a red-sand desert. Due south were more plains, grass followed by a beach that formed an ocean shoreline, though they were unsure of which ocean it was. The southeastern region consisted of a forest that sprung starkly out of the plains, which was accompanied by multiple rivers and streams just beyond it, flowing and forming into a delta. After the two days it had taken them to explore, Matt, the only cartographer amongst the group, had sketched a rough map of their southern surroundings, and they had agreed to head back.

The third expedition had consisted of walking due east. They had arrived at the shorter but longer eastern mountains; however, they had also found a break in the mountain range, the length of which was about ten miles, forming steep hills and deep valleys. In Matt's mind, this was a key find—if they ever needed to cross from one side of the realm to the other, they could pass through this passage they had discovered. The sketching for this new area only took Matt the course of one day. Once completed, the trio had again made another long journey back to Olivia's pod.

The last and most important expedition was when they traveled due north. They had traveled twenty-five miles, which plopped them down on the border of a massive forest that stretched as far as the eye could see; it only took Matt a few minutes to sketch and fill what was to the north. To the west of the forest's edge and off in the distance was a massive city—not one that was occupied and operational, but a decayed remnant of the previous world. They had agreed to walk the extra twenty miles east in order to see the city firsthand.

Once they'd arrived, it was just as they had expected it to be, yet different. The roads and concrete structures were now encompassed by vegetation and vines. Trees grew out of manhole covers, and each office tower looked as if it were an attempt to recreate the Gardens of Babylon. More than that, the entirety of the city was filled with life, just not the kind they'd expected. They saw a deer walking down the long and very wide street that led into the city, grazing on grass that encompassed almost the entire street, leaving only sparse patches of concrete to reveal that it once had been a road. Cars sat rusted and abandoned, acting as flower beds, and most of them looked just like small mounds of dirt—the glint of a steel frame would hit the eye just right, revealing that it once had been an automobile.

Matt, Olivia, and Nicole had proceeded to walk down the street that led through the top north corridor of the city. However, after three hundred yards, they all agreed that they felt like they were being watched, giving them a peculiar urge to run. It was as if something just past the openings and crevices where doors and windows used to stand was stalking them. In abrupt agreement, they had decided to leave the city and return to it later, as they had all the time in the world to explore. Obviously, their expeditions and travels had not been that of Jack's.

Once they'd returned to Olivia's pod, Matt had finished his rough outline and map of the realm in which they resided. They were going to set out again yesterday morning—however, the raging forest fire just to their northeast on the other side of the mountain range appeared as if it would never stop, placing a halt to their plans. They had remained inside Olivia's pod all of yesterday; only this morning, when the plumes of thick smoke had begun to wane, had they decided they would cross over to the other side and investigate, as the storms that were ravaging the other side of the mountain range seemed to dissipate before ever crossing over.

They'd suffered the rains of the past month, but nothing compared to what Jack had gone through. The rains on the plains where they resided resembled the showers they were used to seeing on Earth. They were calm, but constant, which did puzzle them a bit—how had the entire realm seemingly just decided to rain for the past twenty-three straight days?

■ ■ ■

"What do you think? I mean, do you think it's safe?" Nicole asked in an unsure tone of voice, her aggressively dominant stature evident even as she sat in one of the chairs which accompanied the small kitchen table. Her dark-brown eyes scanned Matt for any indication of a falsehood in the words that would come out of his mouth. Her straight black hair ran neatly to the small of her back and collectively hung in a long ponytail. Her golden brown face was that of a black widow—beautiful to look at, before the fangs came out and wept their poison into you.

"Well," said Matt, "I think the fire is what poses the greatest threat—in the past two months, we haven't even seen or heard a lone wolf cry at the moon. We have seen one deer; other than getting a small dose of radiation from whatever lies beyond the western mountains, we have only felt something's presence. That lack of life, then a sudden reemergence of it, is why we felt stalked. I would bet that we will come back in exactly the same shape as we leave, only stronger from the strenuous work it will take to cross the eastern mountain range twice."

All this reply was genuine, as he could see behind those dark, beautiful eyes that she was waiting for any inconsistency in his mannerisms to jump upon and twist into a garbled heap of lies. He was not blind to the ways of Nicole—nor was he blind to the ways of Olivia; the two women in his present company were completely opposite forces.

Matt scratched an itch on the upper corner of his brow after Nicole's probe was completed. He was a simple kind of man; this was the first time anyone of the opposite sex had ever spent this much attention on him for this long a time. He used to be called names, a recluse shoved in the back office of a large map-making company. He was the dog that got beaten and kicked and shrugged off as a loser in his past life. However, in this new realm, as the only man around, he was actually valued for something more than a train track needing to be redrawn, or a new road being drawn in. For the first time, he mattered. His light-blue eyes reflected that new concept every time he looked in the mirror. He was well built and tall, jet-black hair done in a fifties-style greaser haircut that accentuated his height. He had thin shoulders, but they were filled with generous amounts of lean muscle. His once-thin mustache had now grown into a full, masculine upper-lip curtain.

"When are we leaving, and how long do you think it will take us to get over there?" Olivia chimed in to the conversation as she stirred two stew pots filled with a biscuit and gravy meal. Her dark-blue eyes scanned her peers for a moment, then returned to the spoon she was using to stir the breakfast concoction. Her shoulder-length and very straight blonde hair swung nicely as she stirred the meal. Her short stature made it swing more than expected—she had to almost stand on her tippy-toes to see how the breakfast was coming along in the pots. Her curves, in Matt's mind, were nicely proportioned and very firm, whereas Nicole's seemed to be a little overproportioned for his liking. However, life was no longer some strange popularity beauty contest, which was a nice relief for Matt.

"Well, it's hard to say. I would think a day to get to the mountain pass, three days to get across the pass, and maybe three more days to get to that fire, if all goes as planned," Matt replied while he scanned the rough map he had completed earlier. He knew the map would grow larger and more defined as they crossed over to the other side.

"Let's say three weeks total at the most," Matt finally concluded.

▪ ▪ ▪

The trio ate breakfast at a leisurely pace, enjoying banter about their previous travels and reminiscing on days past. Once they had finished breakfast, they began to pack the gear they would need. Three weeks was a long time, and thus came the decision to improvise a bag for each one of them out of their extra boiler suits. Olivia's sack read *4*, Matt's sack read *8*, and Nicole's sack read *1*. Each one had their specific items to carry in their sacks. Nicole was going to carry the food they would share—twenty-one meal bags, a one-third portion a day, as to keep the load as light as possible. Nicole tied off the legs and hands of her spare boiler suit, then stuffed the meal bags and stew pot into its midsection, tying the tops of the arms together to close off the neck hole in the suit. She then tied the legs into the knots at the top of the arms, creating a makeshift and very snugly fitting backpack.

The other two undid their knots in an attempt to make towable sacks, following suit in Nicole's nifty idea. Olivia stuffed hers with half the load of water they would need, which was thirty liters or almost seventy pounds. Then, while she was tying her heavy load to her back, Matt followed suit and stuffed thirty liters into his pack, which was also tied to his back. "How much does your sack weigh?" Matt asked Nicole, as he and Olivia were almost hunched over with the weight.

"A lot less than your does—how about I take five bottles from each of you?" she replied, almost giggling at their impossible postures under the weight before they threw their hefty sacks back on the floor of the pod. Once the weight was redistributed amongst the group, each was carrying just a smidge over fifty pounds of gear. Each had their own hatchet from their individual pods in their accompanying right belt loop.

"Everybody ready?" Matt asked; at the two women's nods, they departed from the safety of the pod.

▪ ▪ ▪

The looming, overcast gray sky prevented the sun from shining its bright face upon the group. They had set off about an hour ago and had kept a steady three-mile-an-hour pace. Each of them was now soaked, as the drizzling rain had continued to embrace them with its presence. It was cool on the plains, and the wind whispered past them in a gentle breeze. The thigh-high yellow grass they walked through left a clear trail behind them as they stomped it down under their boots as they walked. It swirled in various dances as the wind gently blew into it; grass that had looked gold in the sunlight now almost looked as if the color had been sucked out of it by the overcast gray sky.

"You know what I find funny?" Olivia said as she took a quick glance at the other two in their present company.

"No, what? That you're a three-hundred-year-old hag?" Nicole said jokingly. But it was this same kind of joke that asserted her as the alpha female of the pack. It was the same kind of way classmates had joked with Matt in high school, jokes with underlying tones of dominance and placement.

"Right back atcha'! Because you're the same age as this old hag too. But anyway, what I find funny is the fact that I can only remember the first interview I had with the Lexington Company. I can't seem to remember anything that happened after it. What about you guys?" Olivia replied with the same mannerisms a person has when they're teased by another who has no right to do so. As far as Olivia cared, Nicole was a black-hearted and very angry person, and would probably only grow worse every year she got older. Olivia could read into Nicole, just as Nicole could read into Olivia. The bottom line was they would have become fast enemies in any circumstance outside the one they were presently in.

"Personally, I can't even remember the interview," Matt replied. "I just remember the last day at work, where for the first time in my life I stood up to my boss. It was the day I told him to suck shit through a straw and die, and then I quit. I had been denied a raise or promotion for the ten years that I worked for the company, whereas all the people who started five years after I did had positions over me. It's the kind of situation where it's a lose-lose. I know I quit my job for some other position . . . and now that I think about it, it was the day after my interview with the Lexington Company. That's right, duh," Matt said, huffing very deeply by the end of his reply. The weight on his back and the exertion it took his body to plod through the grass left him so breathless that by the end of his explanation, he was truly hoping someone else would take a turn.

"Sounds like you had one shitty job. I bet they stuffed you in the corner cubicle where the last guy had died long before he ever saw a promotion either," Nicole joked. However, Matt just gave her a quick, stern glance that firmly expressed, "*Fuck off!*"

"Well, I personally think you made a wise decision," Olivia said to Matt, hoping to make Nicole drop the topic. She knew all too well what it was like to be forgotten in a far-off corner, in one respect or another.

"Geez. If I'd known it was such a sensitive topic, I would have left it alone, crabby cakes. Anyway, all I remember is being sold some mumbo jumbo about how great life on Earth would be with so few people on it—once all the people died, of course," Nicole said, trying to keep her zingers rolling. However, her expression changed dramatically when she thought of that last part, as if it were too grim a topic even for her to think about. Nicole hoped the others hadn't noticed it, but they had. "All right, that last part was a bit too much, but isn't that how they put it?" She quickly tried to clear herself with the last comment, but it only received cold and obviously distant glances, as if Matt and Olivia were trying to pretend she hadn't said what she had just said.

The party continued on in stark silence, now that Nicole had once again, as she had multiple times before, unsettled the others in the group. It was starting to dawn on both Matt and Olivia that Nicole was an unsettling person to travel with—to her, it was always about herself and herself alone.

The group had traveled another six miles, their total distance up to this point just over nine miles. It was also starting to get darker out—not because of the time of day, but because the clouds seemed to grow an increasingly darker and more ominous gray as they approached the mountain range. It was almost as if the mountains were put there for a reason: nature's way of blocking the easy side from the hard side, or the tame side from the wild side. In either case, it was unsettling to all three of them, although even to her death, Nicole would never admit anything had unsettled her in her life. Nicole was the strong type, the hard case—she was the type of person who would never know what she truly felt. Nicole locked that shit down deep somewhere inside her and forgot about it as soon as it had come.

After another hour of walking, the silence was broken by

Matt, who suggested the group take a water break. He let Olivia lighten her load first as she pulled three water bottles out of her pack. Each took one and drank the thirst-quenching liquid. A thought seemed to crawl out of the recesses of Matt's mind before he could filter it—he blurted out almost subconsciously, "I could really go for a smoke right about now. I use to smoke a pack a day before the whole hibernation thing, and yet even after three hundred years of not smoking, I suddenly feel the urges to bend my elbow. You know what I mean?"

The two women only looked at him for a moment. Nicole truly did not have any thought on the matter, snarky or otherwise. "I think I know what you mean," Olivia said, "because for the past three days all I have been wanting to do is go to church. I used to go every Sunday and never missed a single sermon, even if I had a nasty flu. I made time for it. I always did it, and now that I can't, it seems to bug the living piss out of me," she finished, as if that distant urge had come back to her full on now.

"Well, maybe you guys are ex-addicts or something and don't even remember it yet. I bet you were especially closely acquainted to the powder!" Nicole replied, laughing to herself. The zingers had come back now, and she thought the two of them were perfect for each other, as she didn't understand what the hell they were talking about.

"Again, very funny. What I was trying to get at was deeper-rooted than just the fact that, for whatever reason, I am really craving a cigarette right now. What I truly think is happening is that every day we are starting to embrace our old mannerisms more and more, as if somehow we had lost them in time, and now time has returned them to us," Matt said with a deepness of expression. He was trying to convey that slowly but surely, their true selves were coming back to them. At first, he had believed himself to be a blank page, a very vanilla type of person, but now it was as if his own thoughts were surfacing again.

"Very trippy, Matt," Nicole chimed in again. Truthfully, Matt and Olivia were both getting very tired of Nicole—their stress-relieving activities were beginning to grow foremost in their thoughts, to decompress from Nicole's never-ending negativity and aggressive nature.

...

By nightfall they had reached the basin of the mountain range, its steep hills and deep valleys sprawling out before them. Matt was unsure of how to traverse this obstacle. If they took the low ground valley, they could very easily become lost; however, if they took the high ground, who knew how many of the steep hills ended in drop-offs to the underlying valley below them? It would also add a lot of time to their limited timetable, which would make for a very short window to explore the other side. Matt decided he would sleep on it; when he woke up, he would have his decision.

The camp they had made contained no fires, since there were no logs or twigs around for them to burn. This meant they would go to bed hungry in the little clearing they had stomped down with their feet. Each lay on their back with their eyes to the dark sky, constantly annoyed by raindrops. Each one of them would awake the next morning from a restless night.

...

Morning's first light dawned on the now completely soaked and frustrated group. Each was more restless than the last, as the rain had continued to disturb their attempts to sleep. Matt was the first one to get up off the soft and very wet ground. He performed his morning routine out of earshot of the women, who still lay on the ground but were wide awake and very tired, just as he was. He returned to the camp and pulled three bottles of water out of his pack. The morning air had a chill to it, and it took the group quite a while to loosen up for the day's following journey. Matt had decided that the high ground would be best, as the valleys were probably vast rivers at their bottoms now. He led the way once everyone had polished off their water and shaken some warmth into their bones.

The hills were indeed steep, and their progress was a snail's pace. Still, up to this point the group had been lucky—with each steep incline, they were met by a plateau and a steep decline on the other side, which gave them options as to the next hill they were going to climb. The valleys were laid out like jagged veins in the hills, just as Matt had presumed they would be, wet and very muddy rivers at their bottoms. The trio continued to snake and traverse around the middle ground of the mountain range, as a very wide and jagged valley lay in front of them; it looked as if they would have no other option than to traverse to the only gap that was short enough to jump.

The gap was about ten feet wide and would take a fully unencumbered sprint to make it across. From where they stood, it was about a half-mile hike back around to the lower hill they had crossed. They would have to traverse a steeper hill that lay a horizontal three hundred feet to their right. The group hiked the full mile around the smaller valley that blocked their direct route to the gap of the larger jagged valley they had to cross. Once they reached the top of the steep hill, which had a plateau of only twenty feet before the hill collapsed into the valley, they stopped.

"What do you propose? That we jump that gap? From the distance we were standing from, it looked a lot smaller. Now that we stand right in front of it, I can tell you there is no way we can make it!" Olivia said sternly to convey the serious repercussions if one them missed the other side by even an inch.

What she said had a lot of truth to it. Plus, the other side rose to a steep incline right away—they would be landing on a hill, and gravity would make it almost impossible to stop if one of them began to backslide from the rebound of the jump. However, Nicole had her pack off her back and had already tossed it across. The pack landed on a small flat outcropping about five feet from the hill they would be jumping to.

"Wait, why did you do that? How do you expect to get your pack back now, dumbass?" Olivia yelled at Nicole, who only gave her a fiery glance as she walked backward the exact length she would need to get to a full sprint.

"I agree with Olivia. We haven't even looked for another route that is safer to cross yet!" Matt shouted at Nicole.

As soon as he did, it was like his last word was the shot fired at the sprinting block. Nicole was off and running, then sprinting, and then, with one powerful last thrust from her right leg, she was flying, her ponytail gliding behind her. Then she crashed into the other side of the jagged gorge and dug her fingers into the hard soil with all her strength, sliding down two feet, her feet stopping only six inches from the edge. If Nicole fell, she would fall for a very long time before hitting the bottom.

Nicole crept over to the outcropping that her bag sat on, grabbed it very slowly with one hand, and began to grapple up the twenty-foot slope to the top of the plateau on the other side. Once she was at the top, she turned to look at the duo across from her—they stood flabbergasted, *O*'s planted on their faces. "Pansies!" she shouted. "Look, I made it and so can you! If not, you can walk back to the pod hungry, since I have the food!"

Matt and Olivia stared at each other for a long time. The question they were both asking each other, without verbalizing it: "Is it that important that we cross at all? I mean, if we left her alone, the chances are great that she would bugger off and become someone else's problem." However, both of them knew all too well that they were not the kind of people who left a man behind.

"Well, are you just going to stare at each other, or are you joining me?!" Nicole shouted again, a nasty gleam of superiority in her eyes.

"Here's the plan," said Matt, turning to Olivia. "I'll help you toss your bag over on that ledge, just the same as she did. I will tell her to grab your bag—then we'll throw my bag and I'll jump. I will carry my bag up to that plateau and come back down to make sure you make it. Okay?"

He finished with such a firmness that Olivia could read it was no use to argue. "Okay. Fine," she replied, still in utter dismay at the fact that they were going through with this stupid plan. Olivia was deathly afraid of heights.

"All right, we're going to throw the first bag over—we need you to grab it and drag it up there. Then we'll throw the next bag, and I will jump over and grab it. Then Olivia will jump. You got that?" Matt shouted to make sure the communication was received by Nicole.

"Yeah, throw the bag!" Nicole shouted, in disbelief that the two chickens she was rolling with were actually going to attempt it . . . in her heart of hearts, it worried her. It was one thing for her to be reckless—that was who she was. It was another thing for a plain-Jane, follow-the-rules type to try to be reckless, and it usually never panned out.

"One . . . two . . . three," Matt and Olivia counted aloud as they swung the bag in unison, then finally let it sail through the air. It flew, then dropped precariously close to the edge of the outcropping. Nicole climbed down once again and grabbed the bag. This bag was heavier by about ten pounds. She dug deep and climbed back to the top of the plateau successfully. The duo on the other side then threw the next bag, which they put a little too much power behind. It hit the side of the steep hill, slid, then fell down into the gorge for a very long time before its audible thump echoed back up the sides of the valley and out through the mouth of the gorge.

"Fuck!" Matt cursed at himself, as he was the primary reason for the excess of power behind the throw.

"Sucks to suck!" Nicole shouted at the duo with the nasty little glint of victory showing through again, as if to say, "*No one can do it better than I can.*"

With the rage of past mental wounds opening, Matt took a few calculated paces back and then shot like a bolt. The one sport Matt was ever any good at was track. He leapt, flying gracefully through the air like a gazelle in a meadow. Matt hit the slope hard, almost too hard. He began sliding, sliding, and then stopped just a hair above the gorge's mouth.

"Holy shit," Matt whispered as he began climbing up just a hand higher than a man's height. He found a firm handhold in the slope's steep side and called out once he'd gotten a white-knuckled death grip on it. "Come on . . . jump! I got you!"

Olivia was ghostly pale, her body fighting her the entire sprint—as she predicted, she fell short. *Slap!* Somehow, she found herself suspended—she should rightly have been falling to her death.

She looked up, green at the gills, and saw that Matt had her outstretched arm in his. His grip was firm, almost like a vise, and if he squeezed any harder she felt that her forearm would crush under the pressure. Hoisting her up, he shouted, "Dig your feet in!" She responded in turn and firmly planted her feet into the side of the slope, just a couple of inches above the gorge's mouth. "You got it?" he asked, every vein in his neck popping out with strenuous effort to hold not only his weight but hers as well.

She gripped her right hand and dug deep, holding her own,

then replied just shy of a whisper, "Yes." The two of them climbed to the top of the plateau—and what happened next shocked Olivia more than her own near encounter with death.

Once Matt's feet were firmly planted on the ground and his lanky standing stature regained, his eyes were wild with fire. Nicole began saying, "I'm supr—"

Slap! This time it was not the lifesaving throw of a firm grasp to an outreaching arm for help. It was the firm-knuckled smack of a backhand, one that knocked Nicole sometime into next week for a moment. Nicole's head remained strained to the right for a moment, before her face became bright red with furious anger, her left cheek showing the most color. She stared at Matt for a moment with eyes of pure fiery hatred. Then she delivered a swift knee to Matt's groin.

Matt gave an unexpected yelp, both hands cupping his groin as his knees went out from under him. "You done fucked up, right and proper like!" Nicole screamed a hellish war cry as she brandished the hatchet in an upward stroke.

"*No!*" Olivia shouted as she bounded forward, then threw all her weight into a forceful shove into Nicole's chest. Nicole fell backward, landed on her behind, and then simply stood back up with the hatchet in hand and a murderous way about her eyes. Her intentions had shown clearly: she desperately wanted to kill the two of them. Her dark eyes alight with anger, she had now shown the two of them her true colors.

She stood her ground, staring at the two of them for a long time; then she simply hooked the hatchet back into her belt, grabbed her pack, and turned her back on them. It was that simple a decision for her. How could she remain among the only other two people left in the world, who now knew her monstrous secret? The fact was that her character traits had also come back to her. Unlike smoking, or attending church, she had been a murderer, and it showed clearly through her.

Matt and Olivia watched as her silhouette disappeared down the adjacent slope. "What the fuck just happened?!" Matt asked, bewildered that his simple loss of temper had resulted in such a furiously passionate attempt at murder. If it had not been for Olivia's quick reaction, he would have been as dead as a doornail. The life debt had been repaid that quickly.

"I don't know," Olivia responded in a whisper, but she did now—they both knew. Nicole had killed people—that was no secret now. However, how were they to take all of this in? What were they supposed to do now?

"I think we should cross back and never return to this side again!" Matt said with a finality so strong that Olivia knew she had a choice to make: either stay on this side with a psychotic killer, or return to the side she knew with Matt.

"Okay," Olivia replied. None of what had just happened made any sense at all.

Matt grabbed the bag of water that was left and, with a furious toss, cast it onto the other side of the gorge. He then took a few paces back, sprinted without saying a word, and bounded back across. When his legs made impact with the ten-foot drop, they went out like noodles, and he began to tumble and roll to a rough and abrupt stop. It was easier coming back, but it was also more painful. He looked to where Olivia stood, not sure if she was truly going to make the jump again, but after a moment she did. She tumbled and rolled a little more harshly upon her landing, but all the same, she was intact.

They looked at each other for a brief moment; then Matt picked up the bag and hoisted it around his shoulders, and they began the long walk back to Olivia's pod in complete silence.

▪ ▪ ▪

The end of the day found Nicole at the basin of the mountain range she had just navigated across. She was alone now, more so than ever before. The horrible thoughts she kept locked up in a box within her mind were now seeping out through the thick walls that normally kept them in. She ignored their pleas to be heard and made camp for the night, throwing her bag onto the sandy red ground and resting her head upon it. She knew she wouldn't get very much, if any, sleep tonight, as her true personality had slipped out.

It was true that she had killed people, but under the circumstances she had grown up in, she knew there had been no other way out of her horrible situation. She felt bad, or as bad as one could, for killing people who truly had it coming to them, if not from her hands then someone else's farther down the road. The box had finally burst open, and she regressed into a catatonic state. Her thoughts tormented her more than the knowledge of being truly alone in whatever desert she had just entered.

Nicole lay awake when daybreak came around. However, she now had a grip on herself, the box locked back up and neatly stowed away. As she picked up the bag and slung it over her shoulders, the thought of going without food for two days was pressing on her mind more than the agonizing thought of being alone. The sandy orange desert unfolded around her, and the sands soaked up what rain was still falling as quickly as it made contact with the ground. She stayed close to the mountain range that she was following north toward the thick plumes of smoke rising in the distance. Her travels were faster than they had been crossing the steep hills, but the sand proved a slow and tedious surface to walk on. The air was becoming very hot, and to her surprise, it was still a dry kind of heat, only a hint of humidity in the air.

She had progressed ten miles by noon, and the heat had reached a sweltering degree. If she had to guess, it was over a hundred degrees, and that was even through the now-ominous gray clouds that blocked the sun from the sky. She had drunk two liters of water already and had only peed once, and that had been from pure impulse. It felt as if the water entered her as quickly as it exited her through her pores.

As she continued on in the desert heat, she saw only snakes move under the sands in the distance. The wind was a lot fiercer on this side of the mountain range, whipping the sand constantly into her body. She was far off now, somehow avoiding her grim reality. She had only a hatchet, a stew pot, and maybe a month's worth of food rations, if she could find water, and soon. She only had seven liters of water left, and if the desert spanned the entire length of this side of the island, she would be dead of dehydration by week's end.

Late evening found her in higher spirits as she exchanged the desert for a span of white, sandy beach with a forest spanning to her north as far as the eye could see. She foraged through the edge of the forest floor with her hatchet and gathered up a large enough amount of wood to get a healthy fire going.

However, it dawned on her . . . that most vital fact . . . she was so stupid. She had gathered the wood for nothing. She had no way of starting the fire in first fucking place. "God damn it!" she bayed—Matt had been the one with the torch sparker in his pocket. "Fuck you, Matt . . . back atcha', you fuckin' whore, Olivia!" She begrudgingly laid her bag against a nearby oak tree and lay down herself, in contempt of her dire situation.

That night she slept, but very lightly, as something was watching her through the tall grass that lined the edge of the forest.

When she awoke to the sound of shuffling grass, she jumped to her feet in the almost pitch blackness of the minutes just before dawn. Something was out there. She could feel whatever it was watching her. She brandished the hatchet in her right hand and screamed, "Come on, you fucker!"

It did, except this thing was big and mean. It had sharp talons, the face of an alligator, and the body of a rat. This was one of Jack's "allegatos"—in fact, it was the one he hadn't killed, its scars healed, and it was hungry for Jack.

It hissed and then charged at Nicole, jumping and swinging its nasty claws at her throat, but in the broadening daylight, she saw it, dodged its attack, and countered with her own. She drove the hatchet into its chest with all her body weight behind the blade—it hit home and made a mess of whatever was pumping the creature's blood inside of it. However, it didn't go down—it had minutes before it would die, and it came back at her. This time its attack did not miss—it dug its left arm and very nasty talons into her right shoulder blade, and as it readied to dig its other talons into her and drag her down into the ground, she countered again. As the talons dug into her shoulder, she swiped the hatchet back toward its face, but the creature's neck lay before it.

She had severed some major artery, more vital than what pumped its cold blood. A fountain of crimson rained over the front of her body. For a moment, as she was being dragged down by the creature's hooks and its own dead body weight, she thought she had cleaved its head right off and the hatchet was sticking out of her face—luckily for her, it had stopped just shy of severing the elongated spine within the creature's neck completely.

Its talons were deep in her back, and she felt them dig even deeper as she tried to free herself. The frustration that now rose within her was that of having to lose one thing to gain another, like pulling a Band-Aid off but much more painful. She put her feet against the creature's abdomen and plunged them into it like pistons—the result was a nasty chunk of skin being torn from her body.

"Fuck!" she yelled and cried as she rolled around the ground, massive waves of pain pulsating and rippling through her spine. Once the pain receded to the bare bones of a dull but constant agony, she regained her upright position. As she stood over the now-dead creature, the sun finally graced the world with its light, though it was still largely hidden by the steel-gray clouds that were now dumping buckets of rain.

The blood on the front of her body was washing away, but the sieve on her back continued to bleed. She painfully attempted to dislodge the hatchet from the creature's spine and found that it was stuck for good, until the torturous thing rotted away. She also found that something else had not been so successful in killing the creature once before—massive lumps of healed flesh covered mashed and broken bones scattered along its chest and abdomen. Plus, it looked like the only thing connecting the creature's half-bashed-in face were the ligaments under the skin, nothing else.

In pain and frustration at not being able to retrieve the hatchet, she grabbed the bag, slung it over her good shoulder, and began to walk along the edge of the forest, staying a good thirty yards from the tall grass. Her blood loss had now become a very large point of concern, and she still couldn't drink enough water in the humid heat of the forest. The blood had seeped through her boiler suit all the way to her feet. "I'm in a tight friggin' spot," she said through gritted teeth.

It was about noon, and she was going to continue on in a northerly direction until she stumbled across an *X* notched in the tree before her. She looked down into the forest and saw a massive crater about two hundred yards to her left. Walking up to it, she saw that something very large and heavy had crashed here. She scanned the area and found another *X* notched in a tree straight across from the crater. She skirted the sides of the crater until she reached the *X*; with her head to the ground, she found a trail of underbrush that led up to yet another *X*. It was as if someone had left markers for anyone around to follow.

She pressed on, and by the time she came upon the sight of the clearing in the distance, she saw a man . . . he was sitting on a stump, carving what looked to be a spear. She started walking faster now, her head spinning and dizzy from the loss of blood. Making it to the edge of the clearing, she managed to shout, "HELP!" before she collapsed and passed out.

Jack dropped his spear. *Am I going crackers, or what?* he thought to himself, ready to consider the possibility that he was delusional. However, she was real, and she was really messed up.

CHAPTER

7

Jack was cooking up yet another breakfast of biscuits and gravy. The meal had grown old about a week ago, but it was just to survive. The woman with no name lay in his trench shelter with a roll of toilet paper wrapped around her shoulder, his old, torn-up, blood-soiled T-shirt blanketing the toilet paper to provide compression. The blood on the shirt had dried quite a while ago, and if she lived, he doubted she would mind.

He'd also had to make a torch to scavenge the rest of the hygiene supplies out of the pod, which wasn't as big of a stockpile as he had once thought. Half of the packages the mice and rats had already been into. Some of the packages were rank, rotting corpses, because they had gotten wet and been weighed down to the bottom of the pod that was now covered by eight inches of water. The electricity from the lightning had then fried them. Jack was also very surprised that most of the packages had started on fire as well, though they'd somehow managed to go out without setting the whole interior of the pod alight.

Nonetheless, what was left was what was left, which wasn't much: a dozen toilet paper rolls, the box cutter, half a roll of dental floss, two more bottles of antibacterial soap that were now almost completely used up in the cleansing of the woman's wounds. Lastly, a package of six toothbrushes and one single tube of toothpaste. Jack had also acquired a broken shard of mirror that had rested on the floor of the bathroom; this he wanted for the sake of having it, and even the little mirror that the six-inch triangular shard provided was sufficient.

He had undressed and redressed the woman twice now. She was a rather beautifully built woman—not that he was looking, but not that he didn't take a glance either. The first time he'd undressed her was to clean and stitch up her back. This took the remaining supply of dental floss. Realizing the scarcity of his supplies, he admitted that his idea of starting to kill everything till everything killed him was out of the picture. The second time he undressed the woman was the second morning, to check her bandages. What worried him was that she had been unconscious for two-and-a-half days now. He hoped she had not lost too much blood, for the loss of anyone, even if he didn't know them, was too much for him to bear the thought of.

He had also seen his first wolf since he'd arrived here, and it had startled him. When he peeked his head out of the trench the other morning, which he'd done every morning since the "demoose" encounter, he'd seen it. It was at the edge of the forest, on a trail, which led to the beach. The wolf had tracked her blood trail all the way back to his camp, which was a giant no-no. Thus, when she finally left, he'd begun crafting even more spears. He'd made multiple trips to the forest, kicking any spot or speck of blood he saw into the dirt or underbrush the best he could. The wolf that he'd seen was small, probably the runt of the pack, as it was too stupid to track the blood trail that led all the way to the trench. The only other possibility was that it had seen Jack at just the right moment that morning, and was now spreading the good news to all its other wolf friends, which undoubtedly meant they would be back. It was time to prepare for war in Jack's eyes, as he had already been planning a different kind of self-destructive war only three days ago.

However, with the arrival of another human being, he now thought this unwise. Jack now had someone to share the burden of surviving with—he was no longer alone on this godforsaken planet. He couldn't force himself to comprehend the possibility of her death—he would truly go crackers. How cruel a twist of fate that would be.

Breakfast was done. Jack checked on his new roommate to see if she was awake yet, but she wasn't, so he ate alone again. He pounded a bottle of water and then got back to crafting spears. In the last two days he had crafted eight in total. However, these were no normal spears—he had actually taken the time to select the straightest branches, working them over until they had become balanced at their centers. The spears were six feet long, and their tips were whittled to a sharp and very long point. If he had learned anything from his attack, he knew this woman had also suffered from an encounter with the same creature. Jack realized he needed the animals to bleed, a lot. He believed that, when a spear was thrown, the animals could break the tip off and separate themselves from the spear—but the tip of the spear would remain embedded, and the animals were not smart enough to "play surgeon." This would create a three-inch-deep, quarter-inch-wide hole that would constantly bleed.

Each spear weighed about ten pounds, which suited Jack just fine. However, he knew that throwing spears and fighting spears were two very different things. A thrown spear was to surprise the animal with a direct, forceful kinetic blow, just like a bullet from a rifle. Then the animal would run and bleed out, fulfilling the spear's purpose. A fighting spear was used to pierce not just once but multiple times, with much more force behind it. It also had to be able to withstand a blocking blow, such as a wolf trying to snap it in half. Long story short, a shorter and firmer point, a thicker shaft, and a harder wood. *Oak, perhaps?*

These were the kinds of thoughts that filled Jack's head now—he was no longer going to get maimed, if he could help it. He also had to accept that his weapons needed to be one handed, eliminating the idea of creating a long defending spear to engage these creatures. Long spears would be good to use in a trap or to line the clearing, placed at sporadic and strategic points. Jack had a lot of time to consider his new hobby of weapon and trap craft. He had not written down any solid plans, as he didn't know what his next mission might be when the unconscious woman woke up. This led him to admit that he had become stagnant, locked in a sort of anticipation of the woman waking up so he could finally talk to someone. He knew he would have to take it slowly—too much would convey the amount of time he had truly spent alone, and she might then interpret him as "crazy." Jack had already admitted to himself when she arrived that he was a hair shy of losing his mind.

Jack continued through the day as he had the previous day and was able to craft another four spears, bringing his total to a dozen. He felt the task would become more of a hindrance if he continued with it tomorrow. His plan was to make a pitfall trap to harvest bigger game; however, a trap of that magnitude would take a week or two to complete. Tomorrow's plan was to get the rough sketch down and then start gathering the necessary materials.

He entered the almost pitch-black trench shelter, where the woman was still lying unconscious. He stripped down to his boxers; he would have taken them completely off, but he thought he should keep a bit of modesty about him. Wringing the soaking clothes out in the corner across from his bedding, he then laid them out to dry for the night. Even though he had taken all the precautions that he could, he had started to suffer from a very mild case of trench foot. His skin had started peeling away from his toes. *Maybe I should just stay inside tomorrow and let my body dry out,* he thought to himself. There was no true urgency forcing him to go outside tomorrow if he chose to rest.

. . .

He was awoken by her blood-curdling screams reverberating off the walls of the small enclosure. Instinctively, Jack grabbed the bricklayer's hammer that he kept next to him and raised it. His eyes had adapted to seeing a little farther in the pitch black of night, but not by much. He waited for any sound made by a predator that had snuck into the trench; however, there was none.

"Where . . . am I?" the woman asked very hoarsely, in a dazed and confused frenzy from waking up to the sound of her own screams.

"You . . . you are safe. You fell just within the clearing, and I picked you up and stitched your wounds the best I could. You are in my trench shelter," Jack replied calmly so as to not to further disturb the woman.

"Why is it so dark in here?" she asked, still trying to get a bearing on exactly where she was.

"Because I have no working flashlight or lantern, and I was worried that if I built a fire in here it would ruin all my hard work and send it up in flames. I am sorry if it's not to your liking, but a lot of things had to come together for the small victories I have achieved. I will not risk even the remote possibility of losing this home," Jack said slowly and truthfully. He could see the whites of her eyes staring at where his voice was coming from, but those eyes had not adapted in the same fashion that his had. This started to concern him. *If she had the same run of bad luck for as long as I have, why hasn't she become used to the darkness yet? It was almost the first thing that changed in me,* he thought to himself, then dismissed the question as she interrupted his train of thought.

"Can I get some water? I am very thirsty," she asked, almost uncertain if he even existed at this point. She had begun to fade back into the gray of unconsciousness.

A moment of fumbling around, and Jack found the bottle of water that he kept next to his bed in the corner. "Here—take small sips or you'll puke it out. It happened to me the first time I came back to," he said as he gently pushed the water bottle into her shoulder so she could feel where it was.

She drank in small sips as he had suggested, and by the sloshing at the end, he could tell she had almost emptied the entire bottle. "Thanks," she said in a whisper, before she inevitably passed out again.

"No problem," Jack whispered back. He knew he was not heard—her eyes had closed, and the whites were gone. *Thank God,* he praised in his head—she was still alive and healing. For a while he had started to doubt if she would pull through, but she had. He breathed one sigh of relief and then lay down again for the night.

▪ ▪ ▪

When Jack woke up at daybreak, his roommate was gone. He got dressed and then peeked his head through the opening of the trench shelter. The woman was standing by the fire, cooking something in the stew pot. Jack climbed out of the opening, then approached his stump and took a seat.

"Good morning. How's your back?" he asked genuinely as he was warming up.

"It still hurts a lot, but I feel okay. What happened here?" the woman asked. She knew the clearing had been created by a pod; she had also figured out that was how the forest fire had been started.

"Well, that's a long story. My name is Jack. I was going to introduce myself last night, but after you drank the water . . . well, you passed out before I had the chance." Jack extended his right hand in greeting. However, he could see by the way she was standing that her right arm bothered her tremendously.

"My name is Nicole. Pleased to meet you. Are you here all by yourself?" Nicole asked, those dark, beautiful eyes probing Jack. In all honesty, her gaze made him feel just a touch uncomfortable.

They exchanged a quick handshake before Jack conveyed the story of how he had ended up being attacked by the same creature she was. He explained how the pod had been thrown by the twister, and how the storms here had tiny doses of radiation in them when the green skies came. He also explained that the mild rash he'd incurred would probably keep growing in intensity if the continued light exposure increased. He couldn't explain how he was not incurring radiation through the rainwater, or how only a certain type of storm seemed to really carry the radiation.

While he explained what had happened, she looked into him and saw that he was no longer the man he had woken up as. He was no longer a geographer—something was about him, something primal. He looked as chewed up as a dog's bone, especially his stub—and yes, Jack noticed when she would take a quick glance at it—mangled yet healed. He had become part of the primal landscape he had woken up in and seemed to be rather at peace with it. She analyzed him and found that he was not soft like the other two that she had traveled with; upon that, she decided to bend the truth just a bit when it was her turn to explain how she had happened upon his little oasis.

She said that when she had awoken in her pod, there were two others. They had not changed in the way Jack had—they were soft, and she was the one who had kept them together. She said that as time had passed on, they'd started to plot against her; she was something of an oddity, too much of a hard case for them. They had attacked her at the gorge, she said, which was true—but she added that it had been unprovoked. She said she was going to kill them but had decided against it. Instead the other two had gone back to the soft side, and she had continued toward the raging fire that burned in the distance. She continued to explain that after her encounter with the "allegato," a word she rather liked the sound of, she had bled quite a bit—that was when she had happened upon the *X*-marked trees that led her to the clearing.

Jack took in what she had said. The part that was hard to believe was that there was a soft side to this island. Now having a clearer bearing of where he was, he replied in a thoughtful fashion, which held the truth of his own opinion: "Nicole, I believe you and your previous group had a falling out, because even I can see you have that look about you. It's the look only a killer has. Now, that is neither here nor there, as I have had to go through my own troubles and losses, which have changed me deeply. However, I must disagree that there is a soft side to this island—I would say you guys had a rather nice streak of luck. To counterbalance your luck, I had to go through the hard shit.

"I think the other two will find out just how hard it is. Maybe not this week or this month, but I feel that everything here is different, just waiting for a sign of weakness. It is my best judgment that as a new group, we have three options—that is, if you want to be in company with me. We can pack up and head over there, as a pod is a much safer and nicer thing to live in. Or we toughen up, buttercup, and come to the inevitable realization—*my* realization—that the pods were only supposed to be our temporary homes in the first place. I have settled my own new home, and I have come to accept that I have to live on primal instincts, just as everything around me does to survive. It is not the world that needs to change for me—it is me who needs to change for the world, just to survive.

"There is a third option: I will aid you in going back to the site that you came from, and you can live among those who, in my eyes, will reach the same point I have. I have become too much of an animal for others' company. I am also a fair man and have never pushed people into rushed decisions. You can stay as long as you want to think it over, but when that shoulder heals up, if you have still not decided, it will be up to you to either pitch in or move out."

Nicole took all this in and digested it. What he had said had a lot more logic in it than she had initially thought Jack was capable of. The thing they shared most was that they were now both hard cases for one reason or another. If everyone was going to become hard, wouldn't it be better for everyone just to have these things explained in a calm and reasonable fashion? Wouldn't it then mean they would inevitably regroup with the other survivors? "Why wouldn't we pack up and go back over there, where there is safety in numbers? I think they would come to understand what happened if you were there to explain this hard logic to them. What if we could organize and rebuild with less strain on our resources?"

Jack could see her logic, but he didn't think that she even bought the stuff she was selling to herself. The very delicate problem they faced was that they were all somehow supposed to make it together in one big happy group. However, he saw something in Nicole that argued the complete opposite: she had made mortal enemies with the only people she knew at the time. How long before their personality conflicts gave way to people being snuffed out? Things in Jack's eyes were no longer cut and dry as they had been—there was a delicate conflict that stunk as it hung in the air. However, the fact was inevitable: safety in numbers. "You know how to get back?" he asked clearly and decidedly.

"Yes," Nicole replied, though in all honesty, she wanted to

forget them.

"This is my new plan. We will go over there and talk. We will see if they are receptive to you in particular. If not, I have no problem coming back, just as I have no problem with leaving. I am an animal now, and as an animal, I know from time to time I must migrate. It seems this is one of those times. We will eat breakfast; I will pack, and pack quickly. Then, with me bearing the load and you taking the lead, directing our path, we will make the trek over there." Jack said this honestly, as he was for meeting more people; if it didn't pan out, he always had this clearing to come back to. He also figured that his trench shelter would last on its own terms for quite a long time.

Nicole only looked at him; she had just woken from a semi-coma, and now she was being told to walk. This guy was definitely hardcore. She gave him that much credit. "Okay," she said. "Breakfast is ready."

...

They were out of the forest and walking along the beach by noon. Jack's pace was swift, which Nicole, not admitting it, was having a hard time keeping point. He had filled her rather clever makeshift bag with all his tools and ten liters of water. He was keeping a swift pace, as he knew their timetable was short with the amount of water they had.

Now that they were walking, some clarity had hit Jack like a firm slap to the face. He wasn't at all curious anymore as to what had happened between the group; whatever it was, he knew it had been bad. However, he was surprised that the group had disbanded just like that—this was "weak sauce," he thought to himself. They had had a rather light experience of the island indeed. The reality was Jack could probably kill all three of them with his bare right hand, as this world had changed him. He was stronger now, a lot stronger. He'd also decided that it was the best option for the four of them to work out whatever bullshit hung in the rank air between the disbanded trio. He would shed light on the fact that surviving was no longer a bullshit democracy in which people reacted in such an infantile manner.

Now, the fact that Nicole was willing to kill her two companions, who for all she knew were the only other people left on Earth, did disturb him, in a way. Nicole was definitely a hard case, as he was now. The personality conflicts no longer mattered; if they could not get along, they would all surely die a very immediate death. The hard question that Jack no longer liked to ask himself was, *What's the point of surviving, then, if we should come to the point where we can't even set our massive differences aside just to live? It's that fucking simple now. Either we set aside the old-world bullshit, or we die, and we should make up our minds about it quickly and not just stand with our dicks in our hands too long.* The ball was rolling now, and Jack had already come to all the conclusions he needed to. There were no more leaders to come by and hold their hands—either do and live or don't and die. *Let's get to fucking work, boys and girls—there's a lot of catching up to be done.*

By sundown they had made it twenty-five miles, as Jack had set the pace at a rigorous five-mile-per-hour walk, which was borderline jogging for Nicole. Jack had learned to keep a walk of purpose about him; everything that was to be done in these times needed direct impact. *No waiting and talking about feelings, no sewing circles—just get to work.* He like the sound of his thoughts, as it gave him a renewed sense of purpose.

They sat across from each other, each drinking a bottle of water, with no fire under the open, still-raining skies. It seemed as if Jack could no longer remember a day where it hadn't been raining. "Can we take it a little slower tomorrow? My shoulder is on fire," Nicole pleaded—the white flame of pain was almost enough to make her pass out.

"No. I dug a trench when my abdomen hung together with only a thin membrane holding my guts from spilling out. I dug after I cut my own hand off. I worked until I felt numb with pain—work makes you forget about it. I know you hurt, and badly. However, I went through my own hurts and pains alone, and I had to stitch myself back together. There are no more 'slow' days, Nicole. Work is work, and it has to be done." Jack said this as sympathetically as he could, but his bottom-line expression showed he didn't really care. It was one of those newly engrained things: "If you are still operational, you will still operate," he said, then laid his head against the orange sand that now surrounded him. His bricklayer's hammer was in his right hand as he fell fast asleep, as a man can only when he has come to a great amount of peace with things he cannot change. His hand never released its firm and constant grip from the handle of the hammer.

Nicole was now somewhat frightened by Jack. She knew he wouldn't hurt her, but he was truly an animal with no room left for mercy. It seemed as if the wounds he had received somehow hurt all the worse for being received alone. Jack would hold that grudge against everyone who hadn't been there to help him for the rest of his life.

She lay on her left side to protect her right shoulder. She was hurting a lot now, wondering how she was ever going to get across the steep slopes and hills tomorrow—not to mention the gorge she would have to jump over again. Restless, she pleaded with the rain to stop, but it never did.

■ ■ ■

They were moving again by daybreak. Each had drunk a full bottle of water, which now left them with only six liters. Their pace did not waver even as the sands they had to trudge through made the work all the more difficult. The orange sands whipped against them almost with the intensity of a sandblaster, but it didn't seem to bother Jack. It was like he was on a mission and all the nerves in his body were shot; he only bore a small grimace as the painful sand crashed into his body. Nicole was on the verge of crying out in pain, but she held it in.

They made good time and were out of the wretched desert and standing over the massive gorge at a couple hours past noon. Jack only looked at the gorge once, took his pacing steps, then bolted, leapt, and flew like a cannonball. He landed in a rolling fashion on the other side, without even breaking a sweat. Nicole stared down at him for a very long time; she was considering the stitching in her shoulder and the pain that would spark through her if she landed on it.

"Come on—we can get to the bottom of this mountain range just a little past dark if you hurry up," Jack called. "You're overthinking it—yes, it will probably rip a couple of stitches out. I'll patch you back up, Nicole." He said this with a certainty that frightened her once again. It was as if he had already made the decision that he was responsible for her care, that she had no choice in the matter—which she probably did not.

She ran, sprang, and flew. She did in fact save her shoulder—however, in a miscalculation, she practically did a belly flop onto the hard surface of the plateau. The air left her lungs, the force of the fall knocking it out of her. Jack ran to her and somehow delicately picked her up by the collar of her boiler suit, then stood her upright. "Anything broken?" he asked, this time with genuine concern in his tone of voice.

"No . . . no, I don't think so," she replied. Then she noticed that Jack had made the jump without taking his pack off, which meant he had sprung with at least sixty pounds of extra gear on his back like nothing was there.

"You ready? Or do you need a minute?" he asked as she regained her breath. Yet again, he seemed genuine.

"No . . . let's go," Nicole said monotonously, still trying to piece this guy together. Sometimes he cared, but other times he didn't. *How is his mind working?* Even if she could no longer read him or see into him, she knew for certain he was one hardcore dude.

An hour after the last hues of gray light had left them completely blind, they made camp, simply lying down where they stood. They finished off another bottle of water apiece, then went to sleep for the night. Jack was the only one who really slept. Nicole was tormented by the unending rain, and she found Jack's ability to just lie down and sleep in soaked clothes while the rain continued to freely fall upon his body annoying. Nicole felt this was very unnatural and bizarre, leaving her even more puzzled as to how Jack had become the way he was.

▪ ▪ ▪

They were moving again, and Nicole's arm was filled with white-hot waves of pain. It felt as if someone were prodding a knife into every thread of muscle and the stitching holding it together. She was glad for the first time that it was still raining, as she began to sob at the frustration of the pain. Nicole knew if she could just take a rest, it would stop, but there seemed to be no arguing with Jack. She pressed forward.

Now they were on a previously traveled trail in the midst of the tall yellow grass. The wind had even picked up on this side of the island, which was somewhat unsettling to Nicole, but Jack didn't seem to mind. It was almost as if everything that made Jack human at one point in time had been taken out of him. The other thing that had begun to bother Nicole was the feeling that she was alone, even though someone was just a couple of paces behind her. There was no small talk with Jack, yet another unsettling fact for her. She had once thought she was a hard case, but now she wanted nothing more than to be among the company she had left—and yes, she was even thinking she should apologize.

▪ ▪ ▪

The silence that hung in the air was thick as an impenetrable steel wall as the four survivors stared at each other from their positions in the now-occupied kitchen of Olivia's pod. Then Jack cut the silence down with a simple request for comfort. "Hello. My name is Jack, and if you don't mind me fetching some water, and cooking up a pot of coffee and a large dinner, I would be glad to get on with it."

The present company just stared at him in amazement and wonder. This was like a bad dream for Olivia and Matt, who, for the past six days since they'd left Nicole, had stood around talking vaguely about what they should do. Now, it seemed someone had come to tell them—the man standing among them was a dominant alpha male, dwarfing Nicole and reducing her to a not-so-welcome guest.

"S . . . sure," Oliva stuttered, pointing toward the hallway to the dry storage room.

Without hesitation, Jack walked over to the storage room, saying with a genuine smile, "Thank you kindly." He got two pots of steak-tip and potato stew cooking, as well as a coffeepot perking and burping as its contents boiled. The thick and very nice aroma from the cooking meal filled the air. Once dinner was ready, Jack dished out the servings. No one dared to refuse or break the silence; they were scared but couldn't place why. Maybe it was because Nicole seemed to have been drug back by her shoulder, the bloodstain now water-washed to the back side of her skin. It was dry for the most part, but the fact remained that something had caused her to bleed, a lot, and very recently.

Once their only three bowls were filled, Jack drank his stew from a mug, but he didn't seem to mind. They were starkly quiet, and Jack just couldn't figure out why; yet again, he had to break the silence that seemed to be so ominous to the other three in his present company. "Well, why don't we start with introductions? As I stated earlier, my name is Jack. I am pleased to meet some new faces. I used to be a lead geographer for United Geographic before they closed their doors to everyone trying leave Earth in a hurry. However, I am, as I can see, in present company, no longer Jack from United Geographic. I am forever changed, and I am who I am now.

"I do not know what happened between the three of you before, nor do I really care. The fact remains that there is safety in numbers, and if we can't all get along, then what is the point of surviving? I would find it would be best to let go of your old-world mentalities and tendencies, to unite for the sake of living. Otherwise, we might as well just pick four different directions to walk in until we all perish and die. What I am simply saying is that we no longer have time to bicker and to fight amongst ourselves.

"This new world contains enough fuck-ugly things—pardon my French, ladies—that want to kill us and do not care about our petty schoolyard squabbles. It is quite a run of luck the three of you have had, but as Nicole and I can both testify, that luck can dry up in a mighty quick fashion. When it does, if you are alone, you turn into me. That is why I am the way I am. I got to suffer and hurt by myself. I got to kill things that even the three of you put together wouldn't come out from underneath—nor should I have been able to, but I did."

Jack put his empty mug on the counter next to the electric stove, unzipped his boiler suit, and lifted his white undershirt—a very improper thing to do during a meal, but he no longer had the need for that kind of manners. The three scars that ran the entire length of his abdomen were deep, gnarly, and jagged. At the sight of them, Olivia lost her soup all over the kitchen floor, and Matt's and Nicole's faces turned pure white. The scars were unreal to the three of them—even Nicole's wounds didn't go this deep. It looked as if something had been just a hair shy from gutting him completely. Olivia rushed to the bathroom, and Matt grimly stated, "Way to ruin a meal."

Jack shot Matt a glance hot as fire. "Oh, I'm sorry your poor little eyes had to see that, just really fucking sorry, bro. Take a good look—given some time, you'll find the same thing all over your body too, if you're not careful. You people need to snap the fuck out of it! This is no longer the world in which manners are required, nor politeness, nor courtesy! This is a world of blunt impact, pain, and suffering, crying yourself to sleep while shitting yourself! This is a hard, unforgiving world, so it is time you all hardened the fuck up!" Jack's face was red and angry, contorted with such viciousness that it made Matt's hypothetical tail tuck between his legs. Olivia's sobs could now be heard from the inside the walls of the bathroom.

"I am sorry I have to be so blunt. I get that I'm just a fade away from becoming mad, but while I am still sane, I need you to understand that this is nasty business. We need to collectively and rationally come to an agreement. Now that I have said my piece, it's your turn. The three of you will individually get the chance to talk just as I have. We need to talk. I know that without socialization a person starts getting a little flakey. Give me time, and I will come to a better understanding of the terms of socialization again. But it is of the utmost importance that you realize you need to become hard—you need to change for this world. The world is done changing for us, mankind. The world is ugly now, and we need to band together and show it we can be ugly too—we can dig deep, we can not only survive but prosper.

"The simplest way to think of it is this: I am your new foreman, and I am telling you to get to work. Nicole has sort of caught on to the fact that there are no more breaks, no more begging and pleading to stop—you do or you die. It's a nasty thing I have shown you, but even nastier things lay in wait for you out there in the tall grass, in the air, on the ground—who the fuck knows how many nasty things now roam these wilds. Again, this is my view; now that I have said it, it's someone else's turn. Coffee, anyone?"

Jack said all this in a compassionate but urgent manner, hoping it reaffirmed what his scars reflected, but in a nicer, more understanding way. His dark-brown eyes showed the pain of what made him the way he was. What better way was there to warn them and try to save them? They now understood what he was trying to get at, and a silence fell upon them, Jack the only one drinking the coffee.

No one talked for what seemed like an hour. Olivia had returned with a bottle of water and stood in the corner of the kitchen by the airlock door. "Well," Matt finally said, "my name is Matt. I was also a geographer at one time, but not the acclaimed type—the kind who's hidden in a distant cubicle . . . long forgotten, as one of the present company has pointed out. I have no grasp on what to do, what direction to head in, although I have a large portion of the island mapped out. I simply seem to be at a loss, for you, Jack, are living proof of the nastiness we somehow have avoided. So, what are your thoughts on the direction we should take?" Matt asked this with honesty, as he didn't understand the concepts at hand. He looked at Jack, who was now scratching the stubble of his bushy light-brown beard.

"Well, there are only simple things. The first is establishing ourselves outside of the safety of these pods. It will happen eventually—the sooner the better, in my opinion. Then come food, water, shelter, fire, first aid, navigation, and signaling. Once we're at a point where we have accomplished those basic necessities, we can move on to bigger and better projects. Hopefully, sometime in the not-so-distant future, we will actually be living again, not just surviving, but hoping for this alone is a very dangerous thing in my book," Jack said, now calm, almost at ease. He then added, "Can I see your map?"

The map was laid out on the now-clear kitchen table. Olivia busied herself, as she wanted no part in the conversation, avoiding the thought of becoming even remotely similar to Jack. She cleaned the dishware while the others examined the map.

Deep in thought, Jack asked, "What's the scale?"

"Half an inch is ten miles," Matt replied, looking up at Jack, who was still just standing over the kitchen table and scanning the map.

After a moment, Jack looked up from the map and said, "I would suggest we walk the fifty miles to that large river that turns into a delta. Then we stick close to the edge of the forest and build our civilization there."

At the word *civilization*, Nicole let out a small chuckle and sarcastically, almost bitterly, said, "Was there anything civilized about you and your pilgrim home?"

At this thought, Jack rolled with laughter as if it were the funniest joke he had heard in a long time. Nicole shortly joined in, as both knew and understood the thing that they were laughing about. The other two grinned in a confused way, as people do when they miss an inside joke.

The planning continued; eventually, as Jack had predicted, everyone got around to saying their own piece about who they were, what they were about, and their thoughts on the situation. After long deliberations, the group decided they would enjoy the comforts of the pod for one more day; then they would pack up and leave on the first of July. July 2 would mark ninety days since they had awoken, which was a much longer amount of time to Jack than it had seemed to be for the rest.

They began growing more and more comfortable with the fact that they were becoming acquainted, and Jack seemed to relax as much as was possible for him now. They all took their final showers, had their last big meal, and enjoyed their remaining old-world comforts. For the new world was coming upon them, whether they liked it or not.

CHAPTER

The group had spent the entire morning of July 1 packing up individual and group gear. Jack had had to explain to the three the previous night that each person was in charge of carrying a portion of the gear the group would need, such as toiletries, food preserves, water, and tools. The difference was that group gear or activities were something everyone could use and/or benefit from. Personal gear and activities were things only the individual could benefit from. The point Jack was trying to make was that for a while, everything was going to mostly be done for the group's sake; personal effects and projects would be placed on the back burner until they were established as a group. Jack's example of a personal item was a toothbrush. However, he pointed out, a roll of toilet paper can be used by the entire group. They grasped the bottom line of the points he was making very quickly. Basically, for a while they were going to be a commune in which the motto was, "One must be for all and all must be for one another."

Jack spent his morning making towing sacks out of the blankets he had found snuggly tucked into the bedroom of the pod. He took the comforter and the sheet, realizing that only two in the group had nifty boiler-suit packs. He and Matt would do the heavy work of dragging the bulk of the gear.

Matt had spent his morning packing ten journals, ten pens, and ten pencils. He was also trying to form a daily duty roster, and had made the executive decision that any large decisions should come to a vote; if a vote was not unanimous, then the decision would have to be thrown out and a new one brought in. He had also created a supply list as the other three packed, and spent some time jotting down what they would be bringing. The list was pretty short. Jack had brought all his own hand tools, and they also took all of Olivia's tools as well. They now had double of everything and a new propane torch. For food, they were bringing thirty breakfast biscuit and gravy meals, thirty turkey dumpling stew meals, thirty beef stroganoff and mashed potato meals, and thirty steak-tip and potato stew meals. All totaled, it came to thirty days of rations. For toiletries, they were bringing four toothbrushes and four tubes of toothpaste, ten bottles of antibacterial hand soap, three rolls of dental floss, twelve rolls of toilet paper, four bars of soap, and forty liters of water. Each person was tasked with carrying an evenly distributed eighty pounds of weight.

Olivia had spent some of her morning, upon Nicole's request, replacing three of her stitches that had fallen out and washing out her wounds for the last time. Olivia found it odd that Nicole had asked her of all people to do this—she had no medical background, and it was in fact Jack who had learned how to stitch in his more painful but equally efficient way. After Olivia had completed her handiwork on Nicole's back, Nicole looked her in the eyes. With a sad longing in her gaze, she said, "Olivia, I'm sorry for doing what I did. I'm sorry for letting my anger show through, and I'm sorry for being such an asshole. That is the best apology you are getting from me."

Staring into Nicole's eyes, somehow changed yet still dark, it seemed to Olivia they had seen something that had scared Nicole enough for her to become a little more humbled by her past. "Thank you. Apology accepted, and I am also sorry if my stitchwork fails on you. Why didn't you ask Jack to do it?"

Nicole took a long pause, then said honestly and bluntly, "He scares me. And when the time comes that we are all alone in the woods and lonely . . . I don't want to have any misunderstandings, that's all."

Olivia's eyes widened a bit, showing panicked curiosity. "Why would he hurt us?" she asked, barely above a whisper.

"No . . . no, he wouldn't. However, I just want to play it safe around him, you know? He's hardcore but not mean about it. It's just who he is now," Nicole replied honestly, her tone reflecting a certainty that put Olivia's mind at ease.

"How long until we are leaving? Do you know?" Olivia asked as Nicole put her T-shirt back on and zipped up her boiler suit.

"Soon," Nicole replied, and then the two of them parted company to finish packing.

. . .

The group found themselves on the move just before noon. Jack had been ready to leave a couple of hours before the rest of the group. The fact was that the other three were enjoying the last comforts of the pod as long as they could. They also did not want to walk back into the rain that was now seemingly a never-ending trend. However, to Jack's liking, it was not like the rain on the other side of the island. The rain over here didn't seem nasty and bitter; it seemed to be a light drizzle, as if gently saying "hello."

Jack led the group with his right hand dragging his tow sack behind him. He had considered shaving off his beard but decided against it, since soon enough it would grow back if he did. The two women walked a couple of paces behind Jack, carrying their boiler-suit packs. Matt was taking up the rear, as he had the joy of dragging a tow sack that was half his body weight. Matt was not weak, but he was not strong like Jack yet. Jack's muscles were very large and stood out like hard steel ropes. Jack's pace was also a brisk one, considering he was dragging the same amount as Matt. However, the group huffed and puffed along, leaving a good-sized trail of trampled grass behind them. The walking was slower now—Jack had realized he could not push the others as hard as he wanted to. Even he noticed how big he had gotten, and it seemed as if he were not done growing those muscles either. The tow sack was heavy, but his muscles suffered only a small amount of strain as he broke the trail. In time, he knew everyone in this group would be big like him too, if it all panned out right.

"Can we stop for a minute?" Matt chimed in from the back of the group, his face beet red.

Jack stopped and grabbed four bottles of water from his tow sack, handing one out to each one in the group. "Yeah, we can stop," he said as he handed out the water. They all polished off an entire bottle, then began to walk again. Jack thought they were only going to make it to the halfway point at best. His thoughts were on planning a structure that, once built, they could all sleep in. He didn't think a trench was necessary anymore, as the storms seemed to be calmer on this side, and he doubted from the information that Matt had given him that a twister was a recurring phenomenon on this side.

Even though this area seemed to be mild, however, Jack kept his head on a swivel—flashbacks to the tall grass kept him alert enough. He also found it queer that they could see for miles in every direction, yet he saw not even a single bird flying in the sky. It was as if the entire animal population was on the other side of the island and had abandoned the prospects of living on this side of the mountain range. The thought dawned on him: *I have migrated, and wouldn't it hold true with the other life? What if this whole island revolves around seasonal migration? Summer was thick on the other side; maybe on this side, winter would be thick with life?* That was a curious thought to Jack.

As he mulled it over, he heard small chitchat being made among the others behind him. "What are we going to do? Bunk together like roommates with no personal privacy?" Olivia asked the group, which Jack was now part of as his own thoughts subsided.

"Well, it will conserve a lot of work and resources," Nicole replied. "Hey Jack? How long did it take you to build that trench shelter?" She was neither for nor against bunking with the other three; as long as they had a safe place to sleep, what did it matter?

Jack stopped for a moment, and the group followed suit. He had to really reflect on that, for days blended into weeks and weeks into months; he was always busy. "Well, I'd say just shy of two full months, but no offense to present company, I was working almost eighteen to twenty hours a day. I only rested when I felt like I was due to pass out," Jack replied, looking at each of them only briefly before continuing to walk.

"That means with four of us now, we could say it would take the better part of a month to build a shelter apiece," said Matt, his tone speculative but calculating. "If it's July now, it would be well into November, and who knows when winter starts, if there is a winter on this island. I think if we spent two months building a shelter that we could all sleep in, we would have all the more time to prepare for winter."

"We will have to talk to mister 'no fire' about that one—Jack doesn't like the idea of having a fire inside," Nicole replied lightheartedly, earning a few chuckles.

Matt asked, "You don't like the idea of an indoor fire, Jack?"

"No. No I do not, and you will all see why. After you spend two hard months working hand in hand to make this shelter, you will see how hard you truly have to work for a place to live. You won't like the idea either. If push comes to shove and everyone feels they need a fire, I will bow out of it," Jack replied now a million miles away in thought as he remembered the pain and toil he'd suffered just to get set up. *They will surely see; yes, they will.*

"I don't know about everyone else," Olivia said thoughtfully, "but I don't see the harm in building a chimney and a fireplace, even if we never use it. It would strictly be for the sake of having it, just in case we needed it for warmth." Even to Jack, the idea fit well. All agreed aloud that a chimney and fireplace of some fashion would be built.

They continued for a long stretch in silence again, until they stopped for the night just before dusk. Water was given out again, and they all sat in a round circle in the midst of the tall, wet grass. They were shielded a little from the wind, as the grass was a hand taller than their heads when sitting.

"I think we should build a long house," Jack said thoughtfully after taking a long sip of water.

"What do you mean?" Matt asked curiously, as his thoughts were on a Native American–style building.

"I think we should make it like a log cabin," Jack explained. "It would be around twenty feet long by ten feet wide. The roof would stand at a height of no more than twelve feet from the ground, and it would have two rooms. The first room would be the entrance; this would be the cold room, as it would primarily be used for storage. The second room would be a warm room that would house a chimney; it would be the room we sleep in."

"How do you plan on getting a roof in place?" Olivia asked. "We have no machinery." She was clueless as to any aspect of carpentry.

"I was thinking of roping one log up at a time. Matt and I could manage it. They would be very long, but as narrow as possible for the timbers. Eventually we would end up with a pyramid of them up there, which we could lash together; then we could build our A-frame-style roof off them." Jack knew it would work for a temporary roof, but he had no idea of how to build a true roof either. What they needed was a carpenter to guide them, but they didn't have one.

"Well, it sounds like a good idea, but then again, what do any of us really know about building houses?" Nicole chimed in with a light, sarcastic tone. They all laughed, even Jack.

"I can see how we would build a single-room house, but how would we incorporate interior walls?" Matt asked, as he could see where Jack was going with his idea.

"Right," Jack finally replied. "It would have to be a single room, because I have no idea either. Okay—how about a small cabin with the same concept for a roof? It would be easier to hoist the timbers to lash them together and create an A-frame—though I hate to admit it, but every spring we would have to rebuild the friggin' thing."

Jack sensed his new idea was going over well—and for right now, all their buildings and structures should be small anyway, since in a way, they were just experiments to see what would and wouldn't work. Thus, it came to a vote and passed. Jack would be in charge of sketching the project and leading the group in participation.

▪ ▪ ▪

Jack awoke before the rest of the group, just as the first gray hues fell upon the land. He had slept better than all three of them combined, since the little drizzle of rain didn't bother him compared to the buckets that were dumped over on the other side of the mountain range. Over on this side, the rain was hardly noticeable to him. He let the others toss and turn for about an hour before he woke everyone up. After everyone had finished their first bottle of water for the day, the group continued onward. Olivia and Matt were now lagging behind, their bodies truly worn out and ragged from the previous day of overencumbered travels. However, the group did continue making progress, and Jack was keeping the slowest pace he could lead at without losing his temper.

The group had traveled silently all day, the whispering wind that traveled across the plain's grass the only rambling conversation. They had made it to the river just before the final light of dusk, by which time they had all succumbed to exhaustion and wished only to sleep. Matt and Olivia were the first to crash out. Nicole followed shortly after; Jack surveyed the surroundings until all the light had left the land around them. He found that they were in a nice spot, a calm spot. It offered the essentials: a constant source of water from a very large-bodied river, building materials from the forest. The forest seemed to just pop up out of nowhere, making Jack a little uneasy. Jack knew that most wildlife would bed down under the protection of the forest.

When he finally lay down, his mind was running its endless hamster wheel of thought. He was not too sure how to build the group's new shelter. He had a general idea, but it was too vague for his liking. He would spend a considerable amount of time sketching up the rough blueprints tomorrow. He would have them collecting the firewood, and a lot of it.

▪ ▪ ▪

When the first morning rays came, Jack took a walk down to the river while the others were still sleeping. The river was running at a fast pace, and crossing it would be almost impossible. Near it was a small marsh that was thick with reeds and stone.

He bent over the shore of the river's edge, cupped his hands, and splashed the cold water on his face. "Wow! Shit, that's cold," Jack shouted, almost jumping back to his feet. *Well, it's a good thing that bacteria and parasites usually spawn in warm, still water,* he thought to himself. He then walked down the shore about a hundred yards, to the edge of the marsh. Dipping his hands under the still water, he dug out porous clay from the marsh's bed floor.

"My good and merciful God. Clay!" he bellowed. The solution to his problems lay right in his hands. This meant they could build stone walls, and possibly in the future they could make bricks out of the clay. "What an oasis this turned out to be," Jack said to himself. Without wasting any time, he got back to where the group had bedded down, rummaged through Matt's tow sack, and pulled out a soggy-but-not-ruined notebook and a pen. He began to sketch his design.

▪ ▪ ▪

By noon, Jack had his sketch finished, and the other three had just finished cutting down and processing their first tree. The three of them had begun dragging the wood to the area where Jack had told them to drop the pile, which was about two hundred feet west of the river's shore.

Jack's sketch was of a clay- and stone-walled building that would house a wooden roof. The walls would be two feet thick by eight feet tall. The outside length of the building would be thirty-two feet long and sixteen feet wide. The entrance room would be ten feet wide by ten feet long. The warm room would be fourteen feet long by twelve feet wide; on the far end, the wall would bow outward to create a natural chimney in the wall. The mouth of the chimney would be two feet wide, four feet tall, and two feet deep. The roof beams would be need to be hoisted up; this would require creating vine cordage. Then, when the thirty-four-foot-long by six-inch-thick timbers were lifted into place, six total, they would form a one-and-a-half-foot-tall A-frame. They could then lay brush and timber on the frame, and the roof would be complete. Thus, the first step was to have hands ready to carry rocks in their sacks and drop them in a pile closest to the designated construction area, which was two hundred feet west of the river shore and ten feet north of the firewood pile.

Jack began dragging all the sacks to the area where he was going to build the structure. He then dumped all of the gear out of them, separating them into designated piles. Shouting to the group, he told them that once they had finished hauling the firewood, they should come to him for their next assignment; they hollered back an "okay" in response.

Without wasting any more time, Jack laid his empty tow sack open on the ground next to the shore, then began pulling rocks out of the water and placing them in the sack. The rocks he selected were as flat and long as possible; a single rock did not span more than six inches long or wide. Jack used his right hand to pull the rocks out of the soft silt. The rhythm he was used to, the rhythm that made him full of purpose, the rhythm of work had returned to him.

After filling his sack only halfway, he found that it had to weigh at least two hundred pounds. He dragged it strenuously, laboriously up the two hundred feet inland where the piles of gear marked the spot, one deeply dug step after the next, the ropes in his right forearm bulging in accordance with the massive weight he was pulling. Once he got to the drop area, he began dumping the rocks out of the bag. Without a left hand, this meant taking out half of the rocks with his right hand; then, once an acceptable weight was reached, he poured the rest of the rocks out. With the bag empty, he repeated the process.

Jack had pulled three full bags by the time the rest of the group were done dragging up the firewood. He told them to simply follow suit—they were to grab their individual bags and start humping the rocks up to the small pile that Jack had already made. They looked at him curiously as they dug up rocks, except for Matt, who had caught on to the idea that clay and rock make solid, formidable walls. Olivia and Nicole, on the other hand, thought throughout the entire day that they were simply dragging all these rocks to make a massive bonfire ring. When Nicole finally asked Jack what the hell they were dragging all the rocks for, Jack simply smiled as his hypnotic rhythm continued, replying, "These are for a wall, and we need a lot of them."

The day went on in the same fashion, everyone grabbing rocks, dragging their bags to the now fairly decent pile, and then dumping out more rocks. The pile was surrounded by trampled trails of tall grass now. The only time the activity ceased was upon Jack's bellowed call, "Quitting time!"

Everyone stopped; truth be told, everyone in the group was thoroughly worn out. In a way like-minded to Jack, Nicole had only been using her left arm to drag her rock-filled sack so as to protect her healing right shoulder, which was numb compared to the hot pain from the laborious exertion that swelled throughout her left arm and left shoulder. Jack told the group to relax while he got a fire started, then filled the stew pot with water from the river. The fire now steady and the water boiling, Jack stirred in the first bag of steak-tip and potato stew.

They sat around the fire, too tired for conversation as they sipped on bottled water and waited for the first round of the meal. Once the stew was cooked, the pot was passed around the fire in a clockwise rotation, each person taking three spoonfuls of soup at a time. After its fourth rotation, the stew was gone, and their tanks were still half empty. Jack then refilled the pot with water from the river and made up another serving of stew.

Once the meal was finished and each person's water ration drunk, they sat around the fire, staring into its entrancing glow. Jack built up the fire one more time before he turned in for the night. He was the first one to crash out; Nicole and Matt fell asleep within minutes of each other. Olivia, however, found the pains in her body were keeping her awake. She was a hurting unit for sure; she had never even held a job and never had to lift more than a thick packet of paper. She was ever so tired, and the charley horses that filled her legs and arms made it almost impossible to get more than an hour of sleep at a time. However, sometime in the middle of the night, exhaustion overtook her completely and she fell into a deep slumber.

▪ ▪ ▪

The proceeding ten days followed in the same rhythmic flow as rocks were gathered, dumped, and regathered. It was grueling work for everyone, and none of them were sad when it ended. Jack felt confident in the number of stones they had gathered by July 14. The past ten days had consumed all thirty packets of steak-tip and potato stew, and two packets of the breakfast biscuits and gravy. They now took turns boiling four pots of water a day for drinking water. Jack was certain they didn't have to boil the water, as it tasted fresh and crisp right out of the river; however, all voted that as a precaution, they should continue to boil it anyway. Some arguments and bickering had ensued from the pure overtaxing labor between Matt, Nicole, and Olivia. However, Jack somehow managed to stay out of the small squabbles; he was a person who just did what he knew he needed to and kept going about his business, even if someone had dropped the ball on their turn to boil the water or tend to the fire. It seemed that when someone else had failed to do their job, Jack just knew he was the guy who had to do it for them; without being asked or told, he just did it. The other three were somewhat astounded by this and curious as to how he could just continue to do it.

They were sitting by the evening fire now; all had lighter attitudes about them, as they knew the task of rock collecting was done. They had made a pile that was ten feet around by four feet tall and probably weighed a few metric tons. As they sipped on water from their plastic reusable and refillable bottles, silence befell the group; other than the snapping and popping of the crackling fire, it was silent.

"So, what's next, captain?" Nicole asked, breaking the silence at last. Those dark eyes settled upon Jack with secret intentions. The intent was attraction—over the past few days, she had become more and more drawn to him. He no longer seemed hardcore; he seemed at peace, as if all you had to do was throw the man a lot of work that would eat up any other man, and he somehow just fell into his own rhythm. This recent tranquility that had come over Jack did not go unnoticed by the rest of the group as well, some of them finding it a little bizarre. It was as if his medium of meditation was hard, taxing work. That had also drawn Nicole, in her own mind, closer to the end result of attraction; she had fallen for the man who sat handsomely across the fire from her.

"Well, if you didn't like picking rocks, you probably won't like this next job," Jack said in a soft, joking voice. "What we have to do next is build, and in a timely fashion. I will let you guys decide what rotation you want to put in place for the three tasks, which are all equally important. The first: someone has to dig the clay out of the marsh. The second: two people have to be constantly transporting that clay. The third and most crucial, because time will not be our friend—clay dries out. I don't care if you get a pile of clay six feet tall in front of you that people have just wasted their time dragging to you—if the clay dries out, it will be a waste of time. You will have to be able to keep up. The clay needs to be used while it is still wet when setting the stones. The job is setting the stones uniformly and consistently at two-foot intervals. I will personally mark out the pattern in the dirt for the structure's base, while you guys take a day off—you earned it, we all have."

Jack looked at the faces around him; they had become familiar and friendly. He had become friends with these people and was glad to be in their company, for at the end of the day they gave everything they had and kept a solid pace to match his own. They were good people.

"It all has to get done, one way or another," Matt said softly. "I think for my day off I'll cut another tree down and gather some more firewood. If anyone would care to join, you know where I will be." He knew a day off was just a day to take a mental break and change gears for a little while. More like a slow day, one where you pick your own pace and do your own thing. "I also bid you guys goodnight, for I'm one tired dog."

The group returned their goodnights; it seemed everyone had the same thing in mind, except for Nicole. About ten minutes after the group had gone to bed, she crept her way over to where Jack was lying and made her move. She hunkered down next to him and delicately whispered in his ear, "You awake?"

Jack had been in the gray area just before drifting off to sleep—however, he was definitely awake now. "Yeah, what's up? Something wrong?" he asked in a whisper as he pulled himself back to attention.

"I want you," Nicole whispered lustfully, deliciously. She looked into his now-wide eyes with her own, dark liquid reflecting pools of seduction.

"What? Now? What if they wake up?" Jack responded as she started to unzip his boiler suit with a delicateness that was soothingly irresistible.

"We're all adults here; I don't think they'll stare. Do you?" Nicole whispered softly into his ear. His immediate thought was, *Would I even care if they did?*

The two of them made love by firelight, giving and receiving, stopping occasionally when someone turned or stirred in their sleep. They had to hold back giggles when they thought for sure someone was going to catch them. As the night went on in a blissful release, no one did.

CHAPTER

9

The morning of July 15 found the group in a good mood, especially upon the announcement that Jack and Nicole were going steady. The other morale booster was the simple fact that it was a day off, leaving Matt and Olivia to cut down a small poplar tree for firewood. Jack and Nicole spent the day working on getting the outline for the walls done. Jack marked off the four corners of the rectangular area that needed to be cleared of grass, planting four sticks in the ground to serve as markers. In front of Jack, Nicole cleared the grass with her hatchet; Jack followed behind, marking the outline of the walls with a putty knife in the bare earth she left behind.

By noon, Matt and Olivia had felled the poplar tree and were working steadily to cut it into manageable chunks, taking turns dragging the firewood to the wood pile. Nicole and Jack had finished the rectangular outline of the outside walls and were both now clearing the grass left inside of the clearing. They continued this until the late evening, when Jack found he had barely enough time to finish the entire outlines of the interior walls.

Nicole had asked if Jack needed a hand with anything else quite a while ago; Jack had told her that she had done a fine job, but he could get the rest of the work done himself. Thus, she was now helping Matt and Olivia drag the rest of the felled firewood back to camp. They were done about an hour before Jack had finished his task. As they ate dinner, they reminisced about old times and generally shot the breeze. Everyone turned in early, as they all knew the taxing labor that tomorrow would hold.

▪ ▪ ▪

Jack was the first one up—to his surprise, it had actually stopped raining last night. The early morning sky was still steel gray and held the potential for more rain, but the cessation of precipitation was not only due but a desperately needed relief. Jack had not brought it to the attention of anyone else, but his trench foot had worsened in the past couple of days, and now long and angry-looking flakes of dead and damp white skin had started to peel off of his feet and ankles. His feet did hurt, but it was nothing compared to being halfway gutted.

He washed his face in the stream, then started to get the tools that would be needed for the day's work ready and in position. He stuck the round-point shovel into the ground about five paces away from the thick grass of the marsh and hung two of the sacks on the shaft of the shovel. He had decided that he would do the first of the wall-building by getting the first six inches of the base set. This would make the work all the easier for the next person to take the job, as the outline would already be set with a visible wall; all they would have to do was continue to build upon it.

Upon his return to where the others were still sleeping, he filled the stew pot with water and boiled it over the flames of the restoked fire. The air was warm, and a cool morning breeze was blowing in from the south. He was trying to speculate when the shelter would be complete; however, as he had never built a stone-and-clay wall before in his life, he could only guess that it would probably be finished by this month's end.

Nicole had woken up second; after she had finished her morning routine, she sat shoulder to shoulder next to Jack by the fire. "How did you sleep?" she asked politely. Her once straight and very well-kept hair was now in tangles and knots; nonetheless, it was still a beautiful feature, and her dark eyes glowed with reflections of the firelight.

"Well. You?" he asked, pretending to stretch, then placing his arm around her shoulders.

"Good. Smooth move, captain obvious," she said noticing his overt excuse to hold an embrace.

"I know, right . . . still got it," he said with a laugh. She chuckled lightly with him.

"When do you think our house will be done?" she asked curiously, holding his gaze as he eyed her curves. They were still noticeable through the mundane gray boiler suit, which had a few small holes here and there.

"You know . . . I was trying to figure out the same thing. I think if all goes well, it should be finished by late August," he said thoughtfully.

"Hey!" she yelled, a sudden rush of excitement rising in her complexion.

"What? What is it?" Jack asked quickly, his eyes instantly beginning to scan their surroundings.

"It stopped raining! It really stopped raining," she said cheerfully—she had only just noticed.

...

The group was in full swing a couple hours after daybreak. Matt was digging copious amounts of lumpy gray clay out of the marsh as Nicole dragged the rocks and Olivia dragged the clay. They had decided about ten minutes prior to the start of the work that, instead of Jack having to run to the rock pile a million times, it would be simpler for one person to drag the rocks over to him. Jack was laying the clay down in clumps, then slapping rocks into the correct width of the wall outline. He smoothed the edges of the wall out the best he could with his hand as he proceeded to scoot backward, throwing copious amounts of clay and rock into position.

Jack found their wall would not be as uniform as he had pictured it. Once he had laid the first ten feet of wall down, he noticed how inconsistent the rocks were. Some parts of the wall were two feet thick, and some were damn near three feet thick. He truly did try his best to keep the wall uniform, but the nature of the elongated rocks did not allow for much consistency. Working in unison, one digging, two dragging, and one forming the wall itself, the group had completed the first exterior half of the wall, which was thirty-two feet along the east. There were two sections that were elongated on purpose. The first section was at the very start of the wall's south end, which was four feet wide and would eventually hold the front door. The second section was twelve feet farther north and was elongated to hold the "warm" room's door.

By midafternoon, the sky had cleared and shown the sun's smiling face, with large, fluffy white clouds strewn throughout the blue. The sun was a welcome relief to all in the company, as it had been so long since they had actually been dry. As the sun baked the moisture out of their clothes and bones, it also started to bake the clay in which the wall had started to take shape that morning.

Late evening found the group exhausted, and Jack's right hand felt as though he had gained a severe case of carpal tunnel. His back ached with dull pins and needles from being bent over all day, and when he finally stood up, two audible pops came from his knees, which even Matt could hear from better than two hundred feet away. However, when Jack looked at the progress he had made, it actually surprised him, since he had only seen ten feet at a time. He had the entire north wall, with an accompanying bow for the fireplace and chimney set. This meant he had been able to lay half of the building's first layer of wall, which ranged from five to seven inches in height, a much better margin than two to three inches. Much better. "Quittin' time!" he yelled.

Matt responded, "Yeah, we know. We heard the day's end shots from your knees, old man!" They all got a pretty good laugh out of that as they walked—staggered, in Jack's case—back to the fire. Nicole restoked the fire; it was Olivia's turn to cook. Matt and Jack stood by the fire and watched the women work. "I heard you think it's going to take until late August to finish," Matt said, striking up conversation.

"Man . . . word travels fast around here, huh? Well, if we can maintain growing the entire wall by six inches every two days, the wall alone will take roughly thirty-two very long days. Thus, we're not looking at August anymore . . . we're looking at the beginning of October," Jack replied as he watched Nicole bend lusciously over to gather more wood for the fire.

"How do you figure that?" Matt asked, kind of shocked by Jack's response.

"Well, thirty-two days from today is . . . August eighteenth. I predict a proper roof will take us no less than a month to build, which would be September sixteenth. The punch list will probably take a week, give or take a couple of days, which is September twenty-fifth," Jack replied. At the same time, Nicole caught his longing glance; he gave her a sly smile, then turned his attention back to Matt.

"Right. But what's a punch list?" Matt asked curiously, as he had never heard this expression used before.

"As my dad used to say, it's basically a list of all the odds and ends that amount to the tedious bullshit work a lot of guys used to forget about. If a man did his job properly, there were fewer punch list items, as the man had kept on top of everything he was doing. However, if the man was sloppy and didn't take the time to solve the small problems as he worked on the big ones, well, the shit added up. In short, the punch list sometimes could be a make or break for a construction company—if the punch list was enormous, and the completion date was past due, it came out of the company's profit margins, and boy, I could talk your ear off about how slim margins could be. Damn, I miss him." Jack said all this with a small smile at the joy of the memory, until the tail end, in which his expression turned to stone. The fact was, memories now seemed to be a bittersweet kind of deal.

"I see—so you have previous knowledge of construction then?" Matt asked, not seeing Jack's expression. He was done talking.

...

The days flowed in much the same fashion and yet again seemed to blend one into the other. Jack had become a little peeved with the slow rate at which the wall was being built. Each day the four changed their work position, and Olivia was not cut out for the wall-crafting process at all. It wasn't her fault, really—it was just that she had really small hands, and took way too long to shape and smooth the wall.

This had gotten Jack into some rather hot water with Nicole. The two women had become quite acquainted at this point, so when Jack yelled at Olivia and said, "You take way too fucking long! I don't want to hear how you will try harder—the work is obviously too fucking complicated for your toddler hands to keep up with the rest of us!" Nicole had been furious. Olivia had gone off and cried those same bitter tears of frustration that Jack knew all too well. He apologized on his own, but if she was receptive, it was unclear. Regardless, Jack in his infinite wisdom got to spend two days in a row hunched awkwardly on his nub to keep balanced while bent over at his knees in order to shape and place the wall. The pain was worth it, as he seemed to be the only one in the group who could maintain completing an entire six-inch layer within two days.

Jack saw Matt doing bending and flexing poses over a small wading pool that cast his reflection back to him, although Jack would keep this a secret to his grave. *Whatever floats your boat,* he thought to himself. He for one found it hard to look at his own reflection without his boiler suit on, as the gnarly scars on his abdomen were . . . well, not very attractive. It also constantly reminded him of his turmoil over on the other side, one of those memories he was trying to keep in a dark corner of his mind. Matt had started to become increasingly efficient, his body widening with bulk and ropy muscles.

The problem as they saw it this morning was that they only had thirty bags of turkey dumpling rations left. With the slow progress they were making, a return journey to the pods was going to become a reality. The queer lack of animal presence had started to strike up a lot of conversation within the group recently—birds did not fly or sing, fish did not leap or swim, and mammals were all but absent. It was if they had decided to camp in the one place on the island that was devoid of all animal life. In Jack's mind this was also a nice relief, as a battle with those allegatos every day would be a lot worse than their current situation. It was agreed that they would cut down on their food intake and hopefully be able to complete the wall before they had to make the journey back to the pods.

"We're halfway there," Nicole said as she prodded the fire with a stick.

"Yes, and it's going to be August eleventh tomorrow," Jack replied, a bit concerned.

"We will get it done, Jack. You just have to accept that it's going to take a little longer than we initially thought. I love you, but sometimes you can get a little riled up about the simplest trifles. I mean, you're cool and calm ninety-nine percent of the time when you are working, but then as soon as you stop it's like you lose your cool. Like all the worries and concerns come out when you aren't doing something," Nicole said lovingly, resting her head on Jack's right shoulder.

"I'm sorry, I shouldn't vent on you—it isn't right. I love you too," Jack replied.

...

The days continued on as they had before—by September 4, the wall was complete, and the group had one last ration packet of turkey dumplings left. Matt informed Jack that he and Olivia were going to make the journey back while the "true workers" continued on building. Disregarding the rudeness of this comment, Jack said they should all go and stick together, but Matt made it clear that Jack and Nicole were not invited. On the morning of September 5, Jack woke up to two fewer people in the party. The pair of them had left before Jack had even got up—this was an oddity in itself, as he was always the first to rise.

Jack's beard was now very untamed and unkempt—it had grown three inches from his face. Jack was the type who got beard rash, which was why he had never grown it out this long before. The rash was unnoticeable under the thick stubble brush, but it sure did itch. Sipping water from his bottle while the morning pot of water boiled, he decided he would let Nicole sleep in—since he'd been told in underlying tones to "fuck off," he decided he was going to take the day off and spend it with her.

"Good morning," he said as she stirred to life about an hour after the water had boiled. Jack had already bottled it and cleared the pot.

"Morning," Nicole responded groggily as she wiped the sand of sleep out of her eyes.

It was a warm morning, unlike the past couple of mornings, which had held a bit of a chill. The sky was a clear light blue without a cloud in sight, and the rays of the sun shone down upon them. No breeze blew in the still morning. Upon realizing how late she'd slept, Nicole quickly said, "Oh, shit. I'm sorry if I kept you waiting."

A smile upon his lips, Jack slyly responded, "I thought everyone could sleep in today, but you know how I am—I'm always up early. I thought maybe we could take the day off."

For a moment, a streak of surprise surfaced on Nicole's face; then she said in a matching tone, "You? You want to take a day off?"

Jack's smile held, and a gleam in his eyes rose. "Yes, me. That is, if you want to."

"Sure. When did Matt and Olivia leave?" Nicole asked, moving closer to the fire and then lying back down, resting her head on her left arm to keep a delicate gaze upon Jack.

"Well, believe it or not, they were gone before I woke up. Funny, huh?" Jack replied; not only did his smile widen, but the gleam in his eye changed to a look of curious concern.

"Really? Huh? Maybe they wanted to make as close to fifty miles as they could today," Nicole responded, but even her luscious expression changed to one of wonder.

"You think they're pissed off enough to leave us here?" Jack asked, not with worry, but with a weights-and-measures scale operating in the midst of his always calculating and planning mind.

"What you're really asking is whether I think we'll have to provide for ourselves. Isn't it?" Nicole asked, her speculative eyes scanning the man she had come to love.

"Yes and no. I'm wondering if my charming personality has divided the group, as you've told me—and I am working on being a more understanding individual." Jack said this with honesty and a sly, joshing smile. However, Nicole knew he had come a long way since the group's first meeting at the pod, and he was a man trying to manage a battle on many fronts.

"Yes, you are improving, honey, and I doubt this will go any further than the two of them taking a break from us. Remember, I was also rejected from their company." Nicole said this with a forced smile, because it did bother her how the two of them had seemed to abruptly change their stance on the friendship they had formed.

"Which makes me even more curious as to why. I know I'm an ass, but you have done nothing but try and make things right when I was upset. Can't they tell the difference between work frustrations being vented improperly and personal attacks?" Jack replied sternly, though it was a rhetorical question. He had become quick to apologize in these past few weeks, but it seemed those two were taking everything ultra-personally.

"Hon, it doesn't really matter. All that matters is that I'm still here, right? I still want more of you every night. I have had to hold my urges back for the sake of those two. Speaking of which, why don't we make love and forget about all this petty stuff?" Nicole said longingly, stretching out her right hand and putting it delicately on Jack's right cheek. Jack returned the invitation by kissing her hand, then her neck, then found himself south of her navel.

▪ ▪ ▪

While Jack and Nicole were enjoying each other's company, Matt and Olivia were taking their first water break a little more than fifteen miles into their travel back to the pod. Although Matt would never openly admit the thought to himself, it was a matter of reality: he was being led by the head between his legs. He desperately wanted to be in the company of Olivia's warmth. He could sometimes hear Jack and Nicole going at it in the middle of the night; he would wake up to the unmistakable whispers of pleasure just across the fire from where he slept, without a body to cuddle up to in the cold nights. He was horny—let's face it, we have all been there at one time or another.

"I can't believe the nerve of that fucking guy and his cunt!" Olivia howled, still enraged. She had been verbally vomiting all over Matt; he was just agreeing in hopes of getting in her pants, but at this rate, he doubted if she would calm down and allow it before a year had passed. He had decided to use the head on his shoulders; the minor erection he had possessed about an hour before was now in hiding, as the verbal vomit had become quite grotesque.

"Not to play devil's advocate, but even you can't buy all the shit you're selling. Jack's good shit, and so is Nicole. You're throwing the temper tantrum because she took him before you had the chance. I know how the alpha male thing works, and quite honestly, I'm sick of it! There's a guy lying ten feet away from you every night, more than ready to be a willing participant—but holy fuck, you can't get over yourself, can you?! You feel entitled to be an alpha female, but you can't understand that the guy right in front of you already thinks you are! Fine! Just fuckin' fine! But for the love of God, take a good deep breath and shut the fuck up, so your filter can catch up to your thoughts for one tiny minute! Jesus Christ, I need a smoke!"

After shouting this, Matt made his final decision—it would be better to jerk off alone than listen to one more minute of her whining. He took point; after he had a fifty-yard lead, Olivia finally started to follow him.

. . .

The rest of the day found Jack and Nicole reminiscing about those private memories that can only be shared between loved ones. They were in such high spirits by the end of the night that they didn't even care that there was nothing to eat; other appetites and thirsts had been quenched, sometimes almost more filling than a nine-course meal topped with the most robust wine or scotch. However, the day's travel continued in the same fashion for Matt and Olivia—she kept as far behind him as possible, which suited Matt just fine, since he had said what he had to say.

That night, within the last hours of daylight, birds had started to fly overhead in flocks. Because they'd been absent for so long, all Matt could do was keep his head up and ponder at why there were so many birds now flying south. "Are the migration patterns that abrupt on this island, and if so, where are they all coming from? Also, how long before we run into land mammals and reptiles? Oh . . . right . . . predators are mammals too. We've got to get a move on and tell the others!

"Olivia, I need you to keep close—we are going to make as much headway as we can, and if the weather permits, we will walk all night!" he said. She had finally almost stumbled into him as he'd paused in his amazement at the birds.

"Well, you can, but I am a free agent! I can lie down right here if I want to!" she said in a condescending, entitled tone.

"Okay! Okay! Give me your tow sack, then," he said firmly. For the first time since waking up on this island, Matt had used his "man's voice."

"No! I will carry my own share, in my own good time," she

said stubbornly—and, to Matt's distaste, very bitchily too.

"Fine! Jesus! Talking to you is as good as talking to a flat wall." He began to walk off in the direction of the pod.

"Well, you're the stupid one, since you're the one talking to a wall," she said, cackling like a school girl. *Are we in the fifth grade now?* Matt thought to himself, flipping a middle finger at her in return.

Matt continued to walk through the night as the weather permitted. The silver moonlight cast its cold glow over the land; he was surprised at how big and full the moon was. *Is that it? Is it because the cycles of the moon were impeded by the previous rains—which would make this the first full moon the animals and birds have seen since the storms ended? I hope not, because Lord only knows what I might run into if I don't get to the pod quick enough.* He quickened his stride as fast as he could walk without running full out.

Olivia was stewing in a mix of self-pity, self-contempt, and hatred for the ones she had to keep company with. *Why can't I ever get what I want?! I'm always Debbie picked second! Debbie desperate! I hate this fucking place, and I hate these fucking people!* she thought to herself.

Eventually, however, it finally dawned on her that she didn't know for sure how long she had truly been alone. The thought began to worry her—the birds were the first indication of a massive migration, and in her stupid pity party of one, she had not noticed the position she had gotten herself into. She was as good a target as a fawn without her mother to protect her, a lone sitting duck.

Getting up from where she had been pulling up grass, she began to walk in the direction of the pods. *Do I know for sure where the pods are? Do I know where I even am?* The intruding thoughts ran through her brain. She realized that she was a follower, not a leader, and because of that she had followed blindly.

She had not one idea where she was when she began her blind march, reassuring herself that she was going in the right direction of the pods. Instead of following the trail that Matt had broken, which she hadn't seen in the moon's silver light, she continued north, not west, where she was supposed to turn a couple of miles after the woods. She was lost.

CHAPTER

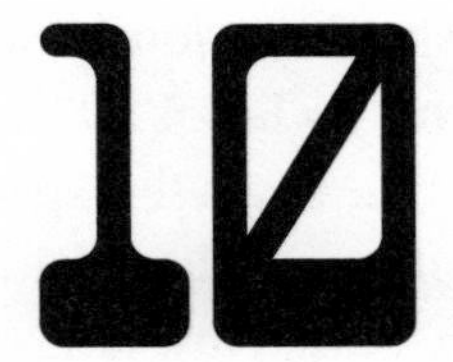

The morning of September 6 found Jack and Nicole startled out of their sleep by a squawking, singing, chirping, and cawing of over a thousand birds strong at the nearby forest's edge. Black birds, white birds, yellow birds, hawks, ravens, seagulls, geese, and other birds neither one of them could place flew in the red and orange hues of first morning light. "That's a lot of birds," Jack said, jaw dropped like a busted hinge as he stared up at the sky over the tree line.

"You got that right. I guess we'll have company today after all," Nicole said, flabbergasted at all these birds seemingly appearing out of nowhere.

As the two of them bathed in the cold waters of the river, they kept their eyes to the northern sky, birds continually flying by in the hundreds. "What do you make of this?" Nicole asked; she had never seen anything like the event unfolding in front of their eyes.

"Well, it's one of two things. The first is a massive winter migration. However, that means the things that walk on the earth will be coming soon—if all the birds are migrating as they appear to be, so will the mammals. The second is an exodus of some kind—a habitat has been destroyed, or a larger force like the forest fire I lived through has driven all the birds out of their habitat. However, that would mean animals from other biomes will be appearing, which could be a very bad thing—in nature, things are rather agitated when they have to acclimate to a new biome's conditions. In either case, I think we should seriously pound out the rest of our shelter as soon as we can." As Jack said this, he continued to stare at the now crystal-clear blue sky, a few sparse clouds hanging high in the atmosphere way off in the distance.

"Sounds like a plan, Stan. How long do you think it will take to build the roof?" Nicole asked, taking her gaze off of the birds and instead gazing at Jack's naked body, which had quite a few battle scars she had not yet seen.

"It will take three days for us to fell six trees at the proper lengths for the running beams. A week, maybe longer, for you to constantly be making vine cordage, as it takes two hands. While you're working on that, I will work on making the thatch bundles for the roof. Once we have everything ready, it will take all four of us to rope up the six beams. Then, maybe, if all hands are on deck, we could get the thatch up in about a week. In either case, I don't foresee a completion date until October." Jack said this vacantly—he was far off in the planning process, visualizing the roof on top of the eight-foot-tall clay-and-stone structure they had made.

▪ ▪ ▪

Jack and Nicole's day began in the woods. Once they found a suitable tree, they began the rhythmic chopping as a duo—Jack would strike, then Nicole would strike. *Swing, swoosh, chop. Swing, swoosh, chop.* Once the tree was cut down, the sawing began; they both had saws which made fast work of clearing the unworkable timber from the tree's branches, after which they'd place it on the stick-and-brush pile that sat next to the unfinished house. Nicole and Jack had their rhythm down to the point where in most cases they didn't have to talk about what they were doing—they just knew.

Matt found himself at his pod a little after early morning. He entered through the airlock and soon had his tow sack filled with 120 various nonperishable meal packages. By late morning he was out of the airlock door; after a quick scan revealed the birds were still flying over his position in droves, he took off, back toward the camp. However, he got this sinking feeling that he was not going to see Olivia where he had left her.

By late afternoon, he'd found his feeling was right. *She's gone. Damn it, I knew I shouldn't have left her here! Well, let's see where she went,* he thought to himself as he looked for any unnaturally straight path trampled through the tall grass. When he found one that led due north, he thought, *If I'm at the most a day behind her, I will never be able to catch up to her with this tow sack. However, if I make the run back to camp, she will have three days' lead on me in the opposite direction.* Ultimately, he decided on finding her. However, if she didn't want to be found in the first place, this would be the true slap to the face. How long could he leave the other two without food? Thus, he came to a conclusion: *I'll tow this back to camp as fast as I can. As soon as I drop it off, I will go to look for her at a breakneck jog.*

The next morning, an hour before sunrise, Matt was standing over the dwindled fire warming his hands, as the heavy fall air had started to fill the night with a chill. The tow sack lay where he was thinking of taking a quick catnap; once Jack awoke him, he would set off again.

▪ ▪ ▪

"What do you mean you left her?" Jack asked in utter disbelief. In his mind, no matter the tiff, you didn't leave a man behind. When Matt relayed that Olivia hated both him and Nicole, he howled, "Well, for fuck's sake! You go get her back!" Matt's face contorted to resemble that of a dog that just got caught pissing on the carpet.

Nicole wasn't up yet; if she had been, Jack knew she would want the entire trio to go look for Olivia, but that just wasn't an option at this point. Delaying a roof could mean snow falling into their shelter, making it as useful as an over-labored retaining wall.

"I'm sorry, Jack—I just lost my cool, okay? It won't happen again," Matt said apologetically.

Jack held his tongue from what he truly wanted to say. His final reply came calmly: "I believe you are sorry, but it is not me you have to apologize to. You are the master of your own destiny—you're a man. You get to carry the forefront of the weight which is carried on all sides by those you care for. If you do not care for Olivia, you should stay, and I will go. If we are the last four people on Earth, why should we just leave others behind? Human life right now is priceless. So, tell me, Matt, are you going? Or am I? If I'm going, then it will be you who gets to explain to my lovely Nicole why I had to leave."

With that, Matt only nodded, grabbed two bottles of water, stuffed them into his pockets, and began to walk off in the direction he had just come from only two hours previously. Once he was only a silhouette of a man's figure, he began to run.

...

Nicole woke up shortly after Matt and Jack's talk. "Where did they go? They just left the sack with the food here and took off again?"

"No, Matt is going to go look for Olivia—they got separated. She has almost a three day's lead on Matt; with my approval, he took off running back down the trail this morning to find her." Jack said this in the sort of way a man does when he leaves no room for a question or conversation, as if the matter is closed and sealed until it need be brought back to attention.

"Huh? Well, I'm hungry. Can we eat breakfast before starting?" Nicole asked, her dark eyes scanning him, surveying him, almost as if to say, *Fine, don't let me in on it, but you are not even going to touch me for a long time.*

Jack recognized this look, the look he somehow had to suffer for someone else yet again, and said, "Yes, breakfast sounds good."

After a quick breakfast, the duo began cutting and felling trees again. By day's end, they had processed two more trees. The overcrowding of birds upon all of the tree limbs in the accompanying forest began to cry a plea of, "*Can't you people see we're full up as it is? Thanks, now it's three to a limb and not two.*"

...

Matt's breaths were coming hoarse and ragged as he stopped for his first break—he had been running since he left camp, the farthest he'd ever run in his life. The sun was just past noon. He was back at the spot where they had parted company. He had already run the length of a marathon, twenty-five miles without taking a break—his horse was played out, and from here on out, he was going to be walking. Every vein stood at attention, pulsating at an alarming rate and thumping behind his ears. Every muscle felt strained and weak. His body was filled with dull pain, and his mind had become distant. After catching his breath, he collected himself, pounded an entire bottle of water down, and then began walking through the tall grass again.

The walking had grown tiresome and dreadfully long by the time the sun began to set. The distant sounds of howls, grunts, and calls that filled the air now were intense, even if they were miles away. The cloud cover was not playing in his favor, which meant the trek slowed even further. He could only see maybe ten feet in front of him by nightfall. He had cleared an additional twenty-one miles, which in his opinion was far enough. It was true that he had gained an enormous amount of stamina and muscle over the past couple of months, but the spot he was in now made him feel as if it were his first day out again. *No food for days and yet I was supposed to go on a witch hunt.* The thought elicited a chuckle, but only a small and quickly fading one.

. . .

By the time he heard a figure approaching him at a full-on sprint, he had walked another three hours and had only made six more miles. It was dark now and the clouds had completely covered the moon—he could see maybe five feet in front him. However, he could hear footfalls coming toward him, closely resembling those of a human. He got his hatchet ready and waited in a fighting stance.

It happened fast, the figure's dazed run flying straight into him. The figure had long tufts of tangled hair, two eyes, and hot breath right on top of his face. Then a voice: "Matt?" The voice belonged to Olivia—she had been running for so long that she sounded like a sputtering engine about to explode and burst into flames.

"Yeah, it's me. You all right?" he asked, rolling out from under her and pulling her up to stand.

"Run . . . animals . . . coming." Like that, she was off again, this time holding her side from runner's cramp.

Matt caught up to her, but he could barely see her silhouette against the dark carpet of night. Aggravated, he shouted, "Hey, now, you just stop! I didn't travel all the way the fuck back here to follow you and get lost! Now what has . . ."

A loud hiss from some massive creature came from behind. It was distant, but approaching rapidly. *Thump! Thump! Thump, thump!* Its running footsteps were loud in the distance, but that meant it had to be massive, whatever it was. "What the fuck is chasing you?" Matt yelled, the two of them now running at a good speed, side by side, through the cool, dark night.

"It . . . it's . . . massive . . . sleeps in . . . day . . . hunts . . . by . . . *wheeze* . . . night," Olivia responded raggedly. Matt could hear just by her breathing that she had been running for a very long time—long enough to make her dazed and tottering as she ran. To avoid making Olivia strain any harder than she had to, Matt stopped asking questions—he just kept pace as the constant hissing and massive footfalls followed them.

Daybreak came, and Olivia kept running—sort of. She was almost falling over herself, her breathing way too fast and shallow—she was going to run herself to death if she didn't stop soon. As a matter of fact, so was Matt. He was beyond exhausted and couldn't believe that they were pretty close to getting back to the area where they had parted ways. "S . . . T . . . O . . . P," Matt managed to say, but Olivia only shook her head. The footsteps and hissing were still following them, which was disconcerting in general, as she'd said the fucking thing had stopped for a breather during the day. Matt continued on as whatever it was gave chase—at this point, he was just hoping it would drop dead of sudden heart failure before the two of them did.

At last, the footfalls behind them stopped, and Olivia collapsed—she simply took a nose dive into the dirt and passed out. Matt stumbled and tripped over his own feet to avoid falling on top of her—he took a couple of good rolls and then landed spread-eagle on his back, his body resembling an *X*. He just stared at the clear-blue sky, not a cloud in sight. His breaths were labored, and he felt like this sudden stop was going to kill him.

Getting up, Matt began to take very small baby steps to keep the blood moving and the oxygen flowing. He walked a couple of circles around Olivia, who was now snoring at a fast pace, almost like someone trying to blow their nose as many times as they could in a row, then letting the snot drain onto their face. "Damn, she's in a tight spot," Matt mumbled to himself, then finally let his own body bed down before he too passed out.

When he awoke, Olivia's wide eyes were staring down at him—she had just given him a firm, hard kick to the ribs. His eyes flashed with a temporary rage, until he realized he was so tired that she had probably tried other methods to wake him before the last one did the trick. It was evening, and they probably had a couple of hours before the sun went down. "We need to get going, and quickly," Olivia said raggedly, but her body did not match what she was saying.

"Okay, but what the hell are we running from?" Matt asked curiously. His tone told her he deserved at least that if he was even going to consider one final ride on the marathon merry-go-round.

"I was walking north and I was completely lost. The edge of the large forest was in view when I stumbled upon a palm tree with no leaves in the middle of the field. I walked up to it, and then it rose out of the ground. It had a long tail that ended in a spear, and it stood the height of a large one-story house. It stared at me for a moment before it decided to lie back down. It was covered in dark-brown plate scales, and its face, legs, and small little arms were the only places not covered with scales. It hissed at me before it lay back down—and sure as shit, when it woke up that night, it began chasing me. I had to run a massive loop that took me to the same trail I left from when I started the long walk north. When I ran into you, it was still following me. I think I pissed it off." Olivia stated all this with a frustration that arose from feeling like she was not explaining it well enough. To her surprise, Matt's face conveyed that he was understanding the bottom line of it all.

"Well, if it is following you, we can't just bring it back to Jack and Nicole and say 'Surprise, guess what I brought.' We need to lose it. I think we should run back to a pod, hunker down, and then wait for it to follow our scent. Once it realizes that it can't eat us, it will bugger off." In truth, if it had followed them this far, it was not likely to give up anytime soon.

"Well, I never thought of that, plus the pod's walls are an inch of solid steel. It's like being in a tank. All right, you lead the way," Olivia replied, her tone growing more upbeat.

▪ ▪ ▪

They made it back to Matt's pod by midnight. After sealing the airlock doors, Matt put on a pot of coffee and a boil-ready meal. Once the coffee and steak tips with mashed potatoes were ready, the two of them sat down at the dinner table. They both fiendishly wolfed down their first servings, and Matt put on a second boil-ready meal.

Finally, he broke the silence between them. "I am sorry, Olivia. I really am. I should not have left you. I should have dragged you with me, if that's what it took to get you back to camp safely. I am sorry I said some nasty things to you—although they were truthful, I could have broken them to you in a more understanding and compassionate way. Believe it or not, I am still a virgin, and yes, I know exactly what it feels like to never have anyone take an interest in you—to always feel like a ghost in the room. I understand where you are coming from, but it is wrong. Jack and Nicole are good shit, and they have a deep, unaltered bond with one another. Inevitably, if in fact we are the last four people on Earth, we'll have to get together. It's either that, or the lack of connection will drive us crackers. So, I leave it up to you. I like you, and I don't expect an answer today, or next week, or even by year's end. I do hope that at some point you will open up to me. For right now, we've got a big problem standing between us and home—we need to solve that problem before we go solving others."

Olivia looked at him from where she sat in a new way, a pleasant way. She replied quietly, "I accept your apology. I am also to blame. I gave in to self-pity and threw one hell of a pity party. I'm sorry for making you run all the way out here just to get mixed up in this. I'm sorry that I talked in jealousy and verbally vomited on you. So, what do you have in mind for dealing with the monster that will be at our door by night's end?"

Matt looked into her eyes and saw that she was being genuine . . . enough. However, he had played all his cards and still ended up neither advancing nor losing—just staying neutral, like always. "Well, we wait it out. Either it will give up or it won't. We have just about a six-month supply of food stored up in here to sustain us. I do think within a couple of days, something that large will have to give up—to keep a body that big going, it needs a lot of food to do it. The one thing I wish they would have supplied the pods with is a board game . . . because to be honest, time is going to pass extremely slowly for a while."

▪ ▪ ▪

Crash! Smash! Thump! Slam! HISSSSSSSSSS! As the very late hours of night befell the pod, the giant was throwing a temper tantrum, Matt and Olivia watching from the safety of the observation window. It was massive, was probably the size of a T-rex. Its feet, however, were different—they were webbed like an amphibian's, with long, tree-frog-like digits that ended in massive talons resembling spears. It had tried to stab its nasty tail spear into the pod on multiple occasions, which only resulted in long, terrible hisses of agony.

The spear point on its fourteen-foot-long tail was about two feet long, and just under a foot wide at the base. The armor that surrounded the spear tip had cracked apart in places due to the higher-strength steel shattering the plating. It now resembled an ancient tribal spear point that had been used for way too long by a lazy hunter. The creature itself had rammed into the pod with its massive head, which did look like a palm tree made of hard-plated spikes. Its head was very elongated, following its spine to the middle of its back. When it charged and rammed into the side of the pod, it only managed to push the enclosure a few inches upon impact. The massive creature seemed to bounce off like a puppy running into a very hard wall. It had slashed, kicked, and rammed until the first morning rays came.

When it lay down only thirty paces from the pod, it slid its mouth into the dirt, making it look like a mound of hard-packed dirt that ended in a large palm tree. Its front horn stuck out far from the palm tree; if one followed it down to the ground, they could make out the shape of a massive head. The creature had given up within the first couple of hours but stayed posted, a puppy guarding the door waiting for them to come out.

▪ ▪ ▪

In camp, Jack and Nicole had finished the work on the roof beams, and now Jack had begun collecting vines and cordage. Once he filled his tow sack, he dropped it off with Nicole for her to braid rope. This process was going to be even slower than Jack had thought. By day's end, Nicole was only able to craft one twenty-foot-long, one-inch-thick length of rope. Jack had surpassed what she truly needed within a couple of hours—the pile sat next to the campfire in a mound measuring about six feet wide by three feet high.

They lay down for the night, and Jack started to worry about how far Olivia had truly wandered. If she and Matt were not back within a couple of days, his hopes for their return were going to start to dwindle. Nicole was still holding a grudge against Jack, but he knew in time it would pass, like all tiffs do.

▪ ▪ ▪

"Fuckin' A!" Matt bellowed. The scene that had unfolded before them was a gruesome one. A herd of what looked like bison with massive rabbit heads and horns were being meticulously slaughtered by the creature that had been hunting him and Olivia. The bison were being tossed through the air, impaled with that spear on the end of the creature's tail. Then it dawned on Matt—this was their chance. "Let's go—he's thoroughly distracted, and this opportunity won't last long."

They exited the pod, blood spatter painting the meadow about a hundred yards to their west. The bison were baying and crying, trying to form a rally to charge the palm-headed beast, but it seemed as if what had started as fifty strong was now down to a herd of maybe twenty. Entrails and bison split into two or even three separate pieces marked the scene of nature's battleground. After one final gaze, Matt and Olivia took off at a run back down the exact path they had arrived on, in hopes of duping the creature into thinking they were still in the pod.

The setting sun was almost fully down, bidding its farewell for the night as the two survivors ran back toward camp. The night air was cold, their breath coming out in hot clouds of moisture. Winter was coming, and fast. The cold air burned their lungs as the condensed oxygen filled them. The sounds of the distant slaughter and feast were no longer audible, and they both thought their plan had worked—if it hadn't, at least the creature would be busily gorging itself for a while, maybe even a week. There were a lot of dead bison when they'd left, but hopefully a few had gotten away so the creature would have something else to chase.

Wolves howled in the distance and some sort of guttural response bayed, a creature that neither of the company had heard before. It seemed as if all the life in the plains had just up and decided to follow close at their heels. By time of the sun's first warming glow, the two had arrived back at the fire of the camp, which was built up into a large inferno of radiant heat against the chill in their bones.

...

October 2 marked two great endings and two great beginnings. The first ending was that the roof was now completed. The group was surprised by how well the thick thatched roof could keep in the heat from the fireplace. Jack had made timber and thatched doors; Matt had made the accompanying timber frames to attach the doors to. The timber of the doors faced the outside of the house, the thatch on the inside of the door acting as insulation to keep the warmth in. There was always a fire going in the nicely finished fireplace, and the chimney let the smoke billow through. Another ending had also been reached: six months of survival.

Nicole had started to show. She was now three months pregnant, and a nice round lump of unborn baby resided within her. Jack would hear nothing of her going more than ten feet from his side if she went outside. The developing unborn baby was the first beginning. The second was that the entire southern prairie where they resided was teeming with life: demoose, bunson (Jack had aptly named the bison with their massive bunny heads), gray wolves (which kept their distance, thankfully, for now), and some creatures that haunted the night air with their hissing and grunting, somewhere off in the distance.

Winter had come, and the temperature was now quite similar to that of Minnesota in a flash freeze. It was a rare now for a day to reach above thirty below, and no snow fell—only hard dirt and instantly frozen grass remained. However, the group was in good spirits; all was going well, and they had a nice abode in which to hunker down in at night. Jack and Matt had become close—they had come to a consensus that women were to stay inside during the winter, as any bare skin would get frostbitten within thirty minutes, if it even took that long. Jack and Matt had begun planning on hunting for furs as it got colder, to the point where movement outside would become impossible. The group was safe and sound, and for the first time, they felt like they had a home.

CHAPTER 11

Malachi Smith woke up in the bungalow he had been sharing with the three other people who had come from pods just like his. They had found that the bungalow district was the safest out of all the other districts on St. Paul Island. They had met with the only two groups confirmed to have survived the floods, and each group was drastically different.

The first group, who called themselves the Saints, were the survivors of St. Paul—their island had been spared from the raging floods. They believed that they were a chosen people and that no one else was permitted to inhabit the island, making the position of Malachi and his companions a very pressing one. The group had had their fair share of not-so-pleasant meetings with the Saints, all ending in gunfire. The other problem was that no one in their own group had acquired a gun as of yet, which meant Malachi and his podmates had had to run and flee rather than fight and hold their ground.

The Saints on the island were nearly five thousand strong, and their presence could be seen most heavily on the south side of the channel that divided the north from the south. They were deeply rooted in the slum district and farming district; however, it seemed that even after three hundred years, the people on St. Paul Island had not been able to get the power back on, nor the water running. The power plant was a nuclear plant that rested on the far southern tip of the island. The water treatment plant and desalinization plant were on the far southeastern tip of the island, and both places were within the Saints' most heavily guarded jurisdiction. However, the Saints had proved to be a very primitive type of group, who still practiced the trials into manhood that involved killing what was commonly referred to as a "plague demon." In short, a "plague demon" was someone who was infected with some sort of cannibalistic disease; the uninfected hunted the infected so the disease didn't pass from one person to the next. The disease actually came from spores. If you inhaled the spores, you turned into one of those things—and as far as Malachi could gather from eavesdropping, none of the "plague demons" died until you killed them.

The second group of people were called the Risen Revolutionaries of Freedom, or the RRFs for short. They had survived the floods in a massive cruise ship, in essence a massive floating city. It had served the RRFs for a long time; however, eventually it had run aground on a reef, as they had run out of diesel fuel a long time ago. Now the RRFs were engaged in a bloody war with the Saints, which so far had proved to be a waste of time. The RRFs had tried to negotiate with the Saints to locate themselves upon the north side of St. Paul Island, telling the Saints they could keep to the south side. No compromise had been reached—from the reports that Malachi was able to overhear, the negotiations had been going on for the past four months with no progress reached by either side. As far as Malachi could guess, the RRFs were waiting for a big wave to push the cruise ship off of the reef they had become stuck on.

THE HUB

...

"We need to make a real plan, guys. We've wandered the entire north side of the island for the past six months and haven't even established a proper home yet. We need to get started on a project that will yield some actual progress," Allison said, frustrated. Her blue eyes scanned the room as she looked for some response, her long, curly blond hair ceasing its gracious flow at her shoulders.

"We need to first find a place away from prying eyes," Zoe replied, "something we could build and repair to a livable condition. Unfortunately, none of us knows the first thing about construction, other than that we used to hire people who did know to build stuff for us." Her light-brown eyes shot a fiery gaze at Allison—she was tired of talking about what they couldn't do. She wanted to talk about what they realistically could do. "If it weren't for those fucking Saints and their plastic explosives, we could still be living in our pods, snug as bedbugs. The Saints blew them all up after they stole all the food and supplies that were in them. We have no fucking tools, Allison. So what do you propose? Using fucking rocks attached to sticks?" Zoe's face was now beet red—a common feature, for now everyone was playing cutthroat blame games. Zoe's naturally straight hair hung down a couple of inches past her shoulders, swinging rapidly as she made some rather unpleasant gestures.

"Shut the fuck up, both of you, or I am going to thump both of ya'!" Michael said in a calm but warning voice, his dark-brown eyes showing no leeway for argument. His barrel-chested stature stood at attention; his shaggy, dirty blond hair, which looked progressively dirtier every day, shook in time with his head. Michael had become the enforcer in the group, which only seemed right—the man was five-foot-ten, but he carried 240 pounds of pure muscle. He was built like a brick wall—no matter how hard he got hit, he would never fall.

"What we need to do is learn. We need to learn how to create, to make things that we need. The library is the source of the knowledge that has kept the Saints running. However, I bet there are still books they haven't found yet. We need those books, and we needed them months ago," Malachi said, his British accent cutting through the stark silence that had fallen upon the bickering group. His brown eyes conveyed that this was a statement, not a suggestion—this was the plan, and they were going to do it.

"Okay . . . but how?" Allison replied, her voice high in protest. "It's almost eighty miles to get there, and the place is swarming with the Saints. We don't have guns, and it's not like we were invited. So how are we supposed to get in the place?"

"Very carefully. We will have to scout around and enter stealthy-like. If it goes as my mind's eye can picture it, they shouldn't even know we were there," Malachi replied, keeping his cool.

"I'll bite. If all the doors and windows large enough to sneak through are guarded, how are we going to get in without killing one of them?" Michael inquired; he liked the plan but wanted to brainstorm solutions while the topic still hung in the air.

"I'm thinking we enter through the sewers. They haven't been run in a long time—they're probably dry to the bone, as long as the floodgates are open. If they are closed, and the sewage has reached the manhole covers, then, like you said, we will have to kill one of them," Malachi replied.

"Sounds like a real plan to me," said Michael, looking at the two women in the group. They had gone starkly quiet, as if the bickering wind had been taken out of their sails.

▪ ▪ ▪

The plan was decided. Now came the preparation. Malachi was not the group's leader per se, but when it came to preparation, he was the one who made the plan come together. What they would each need was a backpack and a working flashlight—though yet again came the problem that the Saints were the only ones crafting the makeshift batteries needed to power them.

The Saints, as well equipped as they were, liked to stretch themselves mighty thin past the resort and casino district. They had outposts indeed—but in the shopping district, one would be hard-pressed to find an outpost that was manned by more than three people, and since the bungalow district, which had basically turned into a swamp a long time ago, had virtually nothing to offer other than shanties that were mostly submerged in a foot of stagnant water, its streets were no different. Malachi's thoughts were on taking out one of those outposts, then seeing if the Saints had the backpacks and flashlights they would need. If not, they were going to have to continue taking down outposts until they found one that had what they needed.

However, as Allison had pointed out earlier, none of them had guns, or anything beyond improvised melee weapons. They were not in the business of killing people—a stupid concept to begin with. For all anyone knew, these were the last people on earth, and yet everybody still seemed to hate each other the same as before the floods came. Still, Malachi knew he would have to get accustomed to killing people; it was inevitable. The hammer was coming down, and at this point they no longer could survive on what passed for food in the bungalow district. Not only that, it was high time that they finally made a proper home for themselves and stopped beating around the bush. After everyone was ready, they proceeded into the street and began walking to the shopping district.

By noon the group had reached the entrance of the shopping district. The district was the second largest, topped only by the resort and casino district. The shopping district was basically nothing more than a few surviving buildings, which were in much need of repair. The majority of the buildings were either on the very brink of collapsing or had already done so. The group watched them as they walked down First Street. It ran the length of the bungalow district and shopping district and all the way to the First Street Bridge, where the Saints had already blown up the only two bridges that led to south side of the island a long time ago.

Crossing an intersection, they saw that the corner of the street in front of them held a still-standing coffee shop. The shop had been looted, the useful things taken before the bridges were blown up. "Hey, someone's out there!" A voice from inside the coffee shop called out. A moment later, three Saints armed with melee weapons came rushing out from the building and toward the group, who stood only twenty or so paces away.

The first Saint, a ragged-looking punk, came upon Malachi—with a clean swing, Malachi smashed his baseball bat into the punk's left hand, crippling it. The now-furious punk swung his half paddle in retort, coming down hard on Malachi's left bicep. Malachi shouted out in pain; stunned at the blunt impact, he missed his counterstrike. His now-bashed left arm choppily blocked the punk's second swing—there was an audible snap as Malachi's forearm broke in two places. Screaming in pain, seething through his teeth, Malachi swung the baseball bat with his right hand—it came down so hard on the punk's right thigh that the bat broke, and the punk's femur shattered into a million pieces. The punk toppled backward, screaming at the hot pain in his leg, but shock only allowed for little puffs of air to come out of his lungs. Malachi drove the now-splintered bat into the punk's head like a spear, crushing his skull and killing him instantly on impact.

While Malachi was finishing off his opponent, Michael was engaging the second Saint—he was looking a lot better off than the first punk, who now lay in the street with a bat handle sticking out of his forehead. When this punk made his swing, Michael dodged it—in one swift backhanded move, he swung his lead pipe upward, crashing into the punk's bottom left jaw. A chorus line of teeth shattering in the punk's mouth followed the massive counterstrike, sending the punk into some sort of dazed, staggering dance. Blood trickled out of his mouth, then gushed as he tried to say something. Michael followed with a finishing blow down upon the top of the punk's head, splitting the skull into large pieces and leaving a massive hole where the end of the lead pipe made contact with his skull. The punk went to the pavement headfirst, dead before he hit the ground.

The leader of the little Saint outpost had passed the two men and was on top of the two women. He made a wild swing with his machete in an attempt to cut off Zoe's head, turning his back to Allison—she pounced, driving her serrated pocketknife into the leader's right shoulder. He turned so violently that he ended up cutting himself even deeper as Allison pulled out the knife. The Saint swung the machete at her right leg in a hasty attempt to put her down, but Allison jumped, driving her feet into the ground like pistons, and countered by trying to slam into him. He resisted the tackle, and Allison ate pavement as she went down.

When the leader turned around, he was met by a hard right jab thrown by Zoe into the knife wound on his shoulder. Out of reflex, he wildly swung the machete, missing Zoe's scalp by just a hair. Allison desperately tried to drive the knife into the leader's chest—he dodged and hit her on the top of the head with the hilt of his machete, which sent her staggering backward. While the leader was dealing with Allison, Zoe swung a wild right jab, which ended up connecting with his left shoulder.

The two men in the group were now coming in for the kill. Michael was the one who finished the leader off—he had the element of surprise, and right before the machete made contact with Zoe's extended right arm, the lead pipe smashed into the leader's Adam's apple. The leader flew backward through the air, landing headfirst on the pavement. He rolled and kicked while he choked on the blood that now filled his airway; within a minute, he was dead.

"Holy shit! That was close! Thanks!" Zoe shouted, receiving a small "Not a problem" from Michael in reply. The group stood and stared at the three dead bodies in the street.

"Is anyone hurt?" Allison asked, folding her knife and returning it to her pocket after she had wiped the blood from the blade onto the leg of her boiler suit.

"Yeah . . ." said Malachi through gritted teeth, his arm hurting badly. "Not too bad. I'll live, but I think I busted my left arm in a couple of places. I think it can wait until tomorrow to look at it, but it really fucking hurts. So, ladies and gent, let's get their bags and see what there is to be taken from the coffee shop. Then we'll make headway—at this point, I don't really care if we have to make fucking torches and blaze our way through the sewers, but let's get this over with." In need of a new weapon, he picked up the machete, taking the sheath belt off the dead leader and donning it around his own waist. Each Saint had a black backpack, but the group found nothing of value in any of the bags besides a pack of unfiltered cigarettes. Now Malachi, Michael, and Allison each had a backpack to haul as many books back as they could.

The coffee shop, when they searched it, consisted of four booths by the front, accompanied by four two-person tables; nothing else remained in the front. The group then searched the small back room and found what they were after. At the foot of the three bedrolls that were in the farthest corner of the gloomy back room was a lantern, which was connected to a large battery. "It'll have to do." Malachi said, as Michael picked up the lantern and the thirty-pound battery it was attached to and placed them securely in his backpack. The group gave up on the search once they had scanned the floor and found nothing but empty cans and four empty employee lockers.

They were back in the street within fifteen minutes and were now making headway toward the library in the public services district. They'd come to the conclusion that fighting from now on should be avoided, as Malachi was a hurting unit. They also came to the conclusion around late evening that they were going to have to stop and take shelter for the night in an abandoned building. The swamp that had filled the streets and buildings with stagnant water had ended in the time-share district, where distant fires could be seen by the orange hues of last light accentuating their smoke.

The group had made thirty-five miles of total progress, a very long walk. They happened by an unoccupied townhome with a palm tree that had decided to grow through the middle; its leafy branches had decided to push ever upward, through the tile-shingled roof. The group entered through the right door, which fell off its hinges immediately upon being opened, hitting the floor with a loud crash. Michael leaned the door back against its frame to try to conceal their location.

The group proceeded up the rotten, dilapidated stairway to the second floor; finding the bedroom farthest from the street, they settled down for the night, each taking a corner of the room to bed down. Even though it was October 3, it was still seventy degrees and humid outside. The last hues of daylight faded within minutes of their settling down, and the dark carpet of night surrounded the quiet tropical paradise.

...

The group was stirred out of slumber by distant but loud shouts coming from the street. Daybreak was still an hour away, but men were outside the house—how far, no one could tell. "Stay low, move slow, and keep very quiet," Malachi said in a tone a smidge quieter than a whisper.

The group donned their packs and made their way to the stairs. One at a time they crept down; once the entire group was on the main level, they slipped out the back screen door, into the blackness that still encompassed their world. They stood in the backyard, the grass around them almost waist high. They quietly slunk through the grass and hopped the fence that ran lateral to the front street, leading into the alleyway. They could see no more than two feet in front of their faces.

FLASH! The beam of light that hit the front of the townhome they had just left cast blinding hues of white down the alleyway the group was sneaking through. Loud footfalls filled the air as men, unmistakably the Saints, cleared the house the group had just vacated only moments ago. "Run . . . now," Michael said quietly.

The group began running down the alleyway, their footfalls heavy—the Saints would be on their trail any minute now. As they crossed an intersection, the blinding array of light dissipated; they hopped another fence that led to another townhome's backyard. "They went down the alley! After them!" a commanding voice shouted from the distant townhome's backyard. The Saints were on the group's trail now.

For the better part of two hours, the group hopped fences, ran through alleys, and weaved through yards. An hour into first light, the group was pretty confident that they had lost the Saints. They stood now on the edge of the resort and casino district. They had made it unscathed, but they knew the alarm would be raised. "Feel like I'm going to cough up a lung," Zoe exclaimed.

"What the fuck was that light? I mean, it cut through blocks of darkness!" Michael said, trying to catch his breath.

"I don't really know," Malachi replied thoughtfully. "All I do know is that we must have pissed them boys off something fierce to have them come that far searching for us. I mean, they would have had to have seen the bodies of their fallen comrades to justify this amount of activity and resources spent on trying to find us. So we have to keep moving, and quickly, before they starting putting together the pieces of where we are headed."

The hunt was on now. They were going to have to pull the hypothetical rabbit from the top hat, not only in order to make it into the library unseen, but to try to return the way they had just come in order to really lose their pursuers. For right now, that was neither here nor there—what they needed to do was keep moving. After the group had collected their breath and taken a very short water break, they were making headway again, jogging this time.

▪ ▪ ▪

The group traveled unimpeded until early afternoon, when they found every street that led to the services district blockaded. Saints armed with handguns and rifles stood at attention behind the massive concrete barriers, barring any chance of vehicle progression through the street. The barriers also acted as readily available cover for the Saints to take shelter behind in a firefight. The group had walked three consecutive blocks east where every cross-sectional road headed south—all were blockaded. Every blockade was accompanied by at least five armed Saints; of the five, only one of them, probably the leader of the group, had a bolt-action rifle. The other four in the leader's company only had either .38 snub-nosed revolvers or single-shot .410 shotguns, makeshift weapons almost resembling pirate flintlocks. At the third and last intersection, the group came to a stop just out of earshot from the nearest blockade.

"Well, we have two options. Either we take the chance of getting lost in the sewers, or we take the chance of snuffing out five armed men. We would have to do it unseen and quietly. If we fail at either attempt, the area will be swarming with Saints in a matter of minutes," Malachi whispered. The choice was not a hard one to make.

The group backtracked about a hundred yards and found the first manhole cover. After Malachi had a visual on the direction they needed to head in, they proceeded to uncover the manhole. Michael slipped the thin end of his lead pipe into the pry bar keyhole and, with all his might, leaned on the pipe as a lever. He got it up high enough for Malachi and Allison to slip their fingers under the lip of the cover, and with great strain, they slid it across the pavement. "Michael, you go first and set up the lantern," Malachi told him. "We'll follow you."

Nodding, Michael started to climb down the ladder that led into the sewer. It was pitch black in both directions, assuring him the sewers were unmanned. He took out the lantern, but the battery's wires were long enough that he could leave it in his backpack. He turned on the lantern, and its dim white glow cast upon the brick walls of the sewer. The sewer was rank with rot, its putrid water ankle deep. "Come on down, it's clear," Michael whispered, and even his whisper reverberated and echoed through the sewer.

The group followed suit, with Allison as the last one down. Before she made the entire journey down the ladder, she strenuously dragged and dropped the manhole cover back into place. Once she was at the bottom of the ladder and in the company of the others, they followed Malachi's lead. Malachi and Michael walked shoulder to shoulder, the two women following closely behind them. "You know where we are going?" Michael asked in a whisper.

"No, not really, but I do know the general direction," Malachi replied.

It was pitch black, like a solid wall of darkness lay just ahead of where the dim ray of the lantern cast its fading white light. They had been walking in the sewer for close to three hours, and they were sure sunset had already settled upon the world above them. As they walked, they continually came across two-way and three-way splits; the group doubted if they could even remember how many directional changes they had made. The putrid and musky water was now knee deep, and only got deeper as they walked farther in. "The water will be our way out," Michael said to the group. "We just have to keep going until the water level drops back to ankle deep."

The group did not reply to Michael's comment; they only continued walking through the sewer.

...

"CITY HALL"

"EDISON LIBRARY"

"FIRE STATION AND POLICE STATION"

They now stood at a three-way fork, each tunnel bearing the name of where you would end up over its entrance. The middle tunnel led to the Edison Library, the left tunnel to city hall, and the right tunnel to the fire and police stations. "Look at that. We could literally steal everything and get away through these tunnels," Zoe exclaimed, and she was right as rain.

They proceeded down the middle tunnel; after walking about four hundred yards, they came to a dead end. A ladder along the back wall led up to another manhole cover. "All right, we're here," said Malachi. "We need to be very quiet; if for some reason we get separated, our meeting point is the Black and White Casino." The group gave nods of understanding.

Allison was the first one up. Once she had a good stance on the ladder, she pushed up with all her might, then slowly slid the manhole cover halfway over the opening, proceeded up the ladder, and scanned the room. It was a small room, obviously in the basement, as the stonework matched that of the sewer. The room was clear of enemies, but it was also dark.

The rest of the group followed her lead; once they had all emerged into this small room, Michael proceeded to the blue-painted steel door, his lantern now casting its light against the green-and-gray brick walls. As he slowly opened the door, the hinges responded with a loud and ominous creak—they probably had not been worked since the floods began. Malachi squeezed through the door first, and then the others followed him.

They were now in a long hallway that had lots of janitorial closets, long-forgotten copy and print rooms, a supply closet, and one room filled to the brim with seasonal decorations. None of the doors led to any paths, just self-contained rooms. The four of them continued farther down the hallway; at the end, there was a concrete staircase that led up to main floor of the library. Malachi motioned for Michael to turn off the lantern; after a minute of fumbling with the switch, he managed it.

Still taking the lead, Malachi was the first one up the stairs and the first one to peer above the lip of the concrete ledge that separated the stairs from the ground floor. No one seemed to be occupying this floor. The library was massive—in the center of the main floor, there was a huge, spiraling concrete staircase that led tens of stories high. The fires that burned in trash barrels didn't start until the third floor—only then did the occupants appear.

At the third-floor landing, there were two Saints armed with fully automatic assault rifles. They were staring into the fire, paying no mind to the staircase or the main-floor lobby. Malachi slowly approached the top of the stairs, then slipped around the bookcases, some of which were standing upright and some of which had fallen down. The group followed closely behind, the books and rubbish that littered the ground making their steps silent.

Malachi now saw the directory sign that hung in the main lobby, informing visitors on which floor the material they were looking for could be located.

"First Floor/Fiction New and Old"

"Second Floor/Biography and Autobiography"

"Third Floor/Nonfiction A–E"

"Fourth Floor/Nonfiction F–J"

"Fifth Floor/Nonfiction K–O"

"Sixth Floor/Nonfiction P–T"

"Seventh Floor/Nonfiction U–Z"

"Eighth Floor/Magazines and Sundries"

"Ninth Floor/Kids' Zone"

"Tenth Floor/Teenage Zone"

"Eleventh Floor/Sky Room"

“Fuck me runnin’,” hissed a frustrated Malachi, “that’s a lot of floors. I know why they didn’t bother guarding the first floor. Shit. Well, we got to get past ’em.” The number of books this place held was astronomical, and the size of each floor alone was a mission in and of itself.

“They usually put the miscellaneous books in the U through Z section, which is probably our best bet,” said Allison, recalling all the times her research papers for college had brought her to libraries just like this one. “The magazine and sundry section is probably teeming with Saints—that’s where all the books with pictures are. We need to run up seven flights of stairs in order to get up there. How do we slip past the guards?”

“If there are guards at every flight of stairs, we are not getting through that way, I can guarantee it,” Michael replied quietly. “The fact is that if we do distract them, this place will be crawling with men at attention. We need to slip through unnoticed—a distraction is our last resort. If the elevator cables are still intact, we could climb our way up; every elevator door seems to be ajar.” He knew the odds—even if each soldier embraced the spray-and-pray tactic, the chances were alarmingly stacked against the group.

The four decided to keep to the edges of the circular clearing that the spiral staircase made. They stopped at the elevators that were straight across from the concrete stairs leading to the basement. Michael looked inside the elevator shaft and saw that only one cable remained intact. The elevators themselves had collapsed and fallen years if not decades ago. Extending an outstretched arm, he tested the cable by yanking on it. “Seems fine . . . I hope you all passed phys ed when you were kids, especially the rope climb,” he whispered before he embraced the cable.

As Michael started climbing, Malachi whispered to Allison, “Hey, you guys get what you need—here’s my backpack. My arm isn’t going to let me climb.”

Allison took his bag and gave it to Zoe to wear. "All right, and if shit hits the fan, run to the sewers," she replied in a worried tone.

"You don't have to tell me twice. Now go," Malachi responded, then slunk a good fifteen feet out of sight of the elevators, trying as best he could not to broadcast to the Saints that the group was bypassing their blockades on the stairs.

▪ ▪ ▪

It was a tremendously long climb up the elevator shaft, accompanied by a tremendously long fall if they botched the jump from the cable to the landing in some way. Michael grabbed onto the cable with a white-knuckle death grip and began swinging his legs to get momentum. On his last full, flailing swing he let go, dropped six feet to the hard concrete landing, and rolled end over end, then skidded to a stop. It was a hard landing, but not so overt as to bring attention to himself. Allison followed suit and hit the concrete in much the same way as Michael had.

Zoe was last—she botched the timing of her jump. She'd climbed a long way up the cable, believing she'd need the additional air time—she fell eight feet, her arms slapping down hard on the edge of the concrete. Murmurs arose from the Saints. Michael and Allison pulled her up from the edge and onto the concrete floor. They proceeded at double time to a nearby corner flanked by a long row of bookshelves, taking cover from the two Saints who had been guarding the staircase and were now looking at the elevator shaft.

After a couple moments of stark silence, the Saints returned to their posts. The group got to work scanning every shelf for the "miscellaneous" section that Allison had brought to their attention. Crouching and being as quiet as possible, the three moved from row to row until they found a little inch-wide by ten-inch-long plaque that read "Miscellaneous Nonfiction." The section consisted of ten long rows in the right-hand corner farthest away from the elevators, and a good distance away from the two Saints guarding the staircase.

There were two deciding factors as to how many books they could carry. The first: Michael already had forty pounds' worth of battery and lantern in his bag, which was already a good amount of weight to carry. The second was that they couldn't over-encumber themselves, since the climb back down the shaft would not be such a small feat. Michael decided to look for littler books that would provide useful information contained in small packages. The first book he grabbed was *Sailing for Rich People.* (*People who pretend they didn't just buy the boat to have a safe place to binge on cocaine in the marina, while the wife is at home,* he thought to himself). The next was *Emergency Surgery.* (*So, the patient is bleeding out because you're not a medical doctor—read this book, because I'm not an MD either.*) The following book was titled *Science and You!* (*Never graduated from high school? No problem, friend—we only use words that fifth-graders could understand anyway!*). Last but not least, *Emergency Essentials.* (*What to pack for the guy who just shot you! Bummer!*)

While Michael was perusing his books, Allison and Zoe split the large volumes they had found into two piles. The first book they found was titled *Electricity and You!* (*Why you love to stick forks in sockets . . . explained?*) The second book was *The Army.* (*And why they will survive long after they have shot you and your friends on sight!*) The third, with a slimy film on the cover, was titled *Organic Shit Potatoes in Your Basement!* The fourth book was *Fix it Yourself!* (*Leaky roof, no problem. Don't call the hall, because you can do it yourself.*) The last but by far the best was *How to Pimp Your Ride!* (*Using only the parts you could steal off your homie's beat-down shitbox wagon whip.*)

With the books divided equally by weight between Allison and Zoe, each bag weighed about thirty pounds. The books they had gathered were the thickest—as all of them came with demonstrations, color pictures, and glossaries of abbreviated layman's terms.

Allison, Zoe, and Michael met up with one another at the end of a row of bookshelves in the "Miscellaneous" section. They gave each other a nod, indicating they had gotten the books they needed, and proceeded back to the elevator shaft. One at a time, they grabbed the cable and began the slow descent back to the ground floor, where the elevator car provided a safe landing. They climbed back onto the main level of the library, where Malachi was still patiently waiting for their return. The group skirted across the main-floor lobby and descended back down the concrete stairs, creeping through the long hallway, re-entering the sewers, and sliding the manhole cover back into place.

They started walking the maze of sewer tunnels back to where they had originally entered. However, they did not end up at their point of origin as they had hoped; by early morning, they decided to emerge from the next manhole to get a visual as to where they were. They were very surprised to find they had walked nearly twenty miles of sewer.

Emerging from the manhole, Allison found they were in the rich housing district. There were no Saints close by and no visual barricades; when she decided it was clear, the rest of them emerged from the sewer. Closing the manhole with its cover, they walked to the nearest mansion, a home the size of a football field. Entering the mansion through double oak doors that were inlaid with either brass or gold plates, they found some stairs and headed to a third-floor bedroom, farthest from the front door and closest to the back door of the right wing. They were all very tired from their previous adventure; after some brief chatter about the different books they'd acquired and how close a call it had been, they all fell into a very deep and exhausted sleep.

CHAPTER 12

The morning of October 6 found the group in good spirits. They were on the move again by daybreak, and the sun shone through moderate cloud cover. It was a little below seventy degrees, but still tropical in its humidity. The massive palm trees that littered the sides of the street in groves swayed in the whispering wind. The group was staying alert to their surroundings as they walked and quietly talked amongst themselves. "Where do you think would be best to locate?" Michael asked in the midst of his thoughts. "I mean, we need a spot outside of prying eyes, and we need it to be secluded enough to provide a strategic advantage." His brown eyes showed the recesses of his mind, his very dirty blond hair flowing in the breeze.

"You can't forget the fact that wherever we decide to stay has to be remote enough to conceal the massive amount of noise we'll be making," Malachi replied, struggling to speak through his almost-stupor—ignoring the white-hot pain in his busted left arm was taking most of his mental capacity. "I mean, we now have books that for the most part show us how to get things back up and running. We need a place that is far enough away that the noise of, say, a running generator or an arc welder would dissipate before it was overheard."

"The other question I have is—do we stay on this island?" Zoe chimed in. "I mean, there is another massive body of land to our west that would provide at least the prospect of easier beginnings. This island is full of nothing but Saints, RRFs, and plague demons. Plus, we don't even know if the Saints have truly lost our trail. They could be hanging back for a while and plotting an ambush—it seems to me that they have ample time on their hands to waste." A positive expression on her face, she scanned the group with her light-brown brown eyes to see how they were taking to her idea.

"Now hear me out, guys," Allison said thoughtfully. "I was mulling this idea over in my head for a while . . . what if we built a houseboat? Look at the RRFs—if they had diesel fuel to power their engines, they would be safely floating away right now. It's like living on an island you have control over. It could be small enough for us to row it, or large enough that we would have to figure some motor situation out. We could hypothetically fabricate a steam engine to power the boat. The possibilities are endless as soon as we are mobile, but they are more than limited with no means of mobility."

The group received this idea better than the other ones before it, like the one Michael had mentioned before they had started walking. His first idea had been to see if the island had some sort of armory or military museum where they could fix up and hijack an old-school tank. However, this idea was stupid—before the floods, this island had been a hit vacation spot. No wars needed to be fought on a peaceful tropical paradise. It was even more unlikely that this island even had a coast guard before the floods. In either case, the idea of a houseboat took off like wildfire. The entire group got involved with debating the idea; an underlying tone of hope was taking root and starting to sprout. They now had a purpose.

...

As the group continued to walk unmolested by the Saints, their conversation had finally come full circle. If they were going to build a houseboat, they would need a workshop in which to build it—this simply killed the idea.

"I guess we are all just going to have to learn to live under an oppressive thumb," Michael said, his voice carrying a touch of finality. "Our ancestors did before us, and we will have to learn to tolerate it. No matter how we want to cut the question apart, it's still basically the same. We need a secret location to create a settlement away from the oppressive eyes and ears on the street. If I had to throw my two cents into the debate, I would vote for the upper-level floor of a resort or casino. We will have to clear out the plague demons from every floor we choose to inhabit. Then we will need tools and stuff to build upon our new home." With that, his mind was made up—he had said what he needed to say.

"Not to play devil's advocate," responded Malachi, "but the hotels, especially the upper levels, are either neglected and about to fall apart, or kept up by Saints—we'll have to clear not only plague demons but also the Saints. The argument we're simply having, but have reached no solution to, is the real estate we are trying to move into. Now, I want statements—let's come up with the places we definitely cannot move into."

The group stopped dead in their tracks for a moment at the truth behind his words; no one could really figure out a place where they could just move in. The problem was the unrealistic proposition that they could ever obtain or even secure an area in which to call home. That had been their true problem since day one, always playing a shuffle game with the Saints and their cronies.

"I know there cannot be more than ten miles of sea separating the tip of the bungalow district from the other island's shore," Zoe said. "However, it's winter there, and for some reason it's not here. It's like some sort of phenomenon has occurred, blocking two very separate ecosystems that are only ten, maybe twelve miles apart. We could steal two small canoes and try our luck." Upon the last sentence her argument fell apart, and she knew it. Even the other three knew by the grim look on her pleasant face that she had realized her mistake. "Luck" was no longer an option—sooner or later, it would run out. They all knew that the same phenomenon that separated the two island climates would probably hold true on two sides of the sea. One was calm and tropically beautiful, and the other was cold and untamed.

"Well, it's obvious," Allison replied. "We need to become able to defend ourselves. We need to start playing offense with these fuckers. We need to acquire guns—that way we can properly defend ourselves. Then we need to acquire the bigger guns, the kind that are mounted on turrets and shit. After that we need to start fortifying a location, and take shifts on watch and on duty. There are only four of us, so we will have to pick someplace small and easily defendable. It should have multiple floors—we can rig the first couple of floors with booby traps, and live on, say, the third and fourth floors after fortifying them. Or we take over a mechanic shop—but it has to be somewhere of great strategic advantage. Then, after we have fortified and know what the fuck we are doing, we can start the process of building whatever we want.

"I don't want to omit the fact that a certain time frame is involved here. It's not like we can stand against close to five thousand strong, or even fifty strong. We need to make quick and powerful movements of strength." When she had finished her statement, her face was flushed; it was quite a mouthful to spit out all at once.

"Damn, she has a point," Michael admitted. "The one flaw I do see in it, though, is preparation. If we're going to do a so-called blitzkrieg, we need to find out if they have any boats that are operational at the private marina. It would be a bitch to get in there, but that is where we would gain the guns to make our stand. The problem there is, if we show a presence at or interest in the marina, our enemy may catch on to the fact that we are trying to outwit them and leave. If they had some kind of operational supply ship that we could just happen to commandeer, then there wouldn't be the need to do all this sneaking around. We just attack full blown, no holds barred—as long as we all go into it knowing that we are either boom or bust, no bounce, no play." Faced with all this, the notion of just getting the fuck off the island seemed to be a rather good one.

"It's time to either shit or get off the pot," Malachi responded. "We walked twenty miles in the wrong direction if we are considering going through with this plan. If not, and we want to just keep buying more days alive on this island, then we are twenty miles in the right direction." After that, he waited impatiently for a final conclusion to come around—his arm needed to be set badly.

"All right, but just one more counterpoint which will only take a moment," said Zoe. "If we do get down to the marina, say there aren't boats, not a single floating raft—then what? We'll just be holding our cocks in our hands. If we plan this all out right, we can gain more control over the situation—why not?

"All I'm saying is, what if we build a boat ourselves? I mean, there are a ton of still-usable parts and pieces on this island; we could rework a boat trailer and a boat hull into proper condition and go from there. Because not to piss on anyone's parade, but I think if any boats had moving parts—like an operational engine—we would have heard them a long time ago. I don't doubt the Saints have a very few nifty tricks, such as batteries and generators to charge those batteries, but I don't think they have any mobility set up yet. If they had, they would not be so dead set on staying on an island that has remained stagnant all these years after the apocalypse. I think we are going to have to build this bitch from the ground up. Who knows—maybe people will start defecting to our little hideout in the bungalow district once they find out we have power and a plan."

This time Zoe had said what she meant to say, and there was a logic to it. They all knew nobody really went into the bungalow district—there was nothing left of the place other than rubbish and swamp-encrusted bungalows, most of which had fallen in on themselves. Only a few had survived.

"Okay, if I may clarify—our plan, then, is to gain weapons, then materials, then fortify our little encampment, and then start building a boat?" Michael asked.

"Yes," said Allison, "but don't forget that while we're doing all this, we need to keep an eye on our food and water supplies. Once we have an accomplished little settlement, I think people who are tired of living in the dark will come out to the light. Not soon—maybe not even in our lifetime—but I think, if nothing else, we will spark a revolution, like a second renaissance."

That ended the discussion. She looked at everyone in the group, and they were all sure of their plan. They continued on toward the bungalow district.

...

It was the night of October 9 that they finally made it back to the bungalow district. There were twenty Saints gathered around one of the putrid and disgusting pools on the backside of a distant resort. The group had been spotted by the Saints, impeding their progress—they had to take the long way back. This included jumping fences, long periods of sprinting, a couple dives back into the sewer, and then back out again. It had been a long week for the group, and they basically collapsed in unison upon their retreat to the bungalow they had been hiding out in. They were all malnourished and suffering to various degrees from dehydration; their main goal now was food and water. They had enough to fill their stomachs tomorrow, but not enough for the next day or the day after.

Late the next morning, the group found themselves commiserating over their assigned tasks. Allison had finally set and splinted Malachi's arm; for the time being, he was out of the running, as his entire left arm was a mass of purple and blue bruising. It was now on the other three to bear his load—and at the moment, they were talking about how exactly they were going to go about intercepting a supply drop.

"Well, should we head off and figure the details as we walk?" Michael asked.

"That sounds like a good idea—it's a long walk," Zoe replied with a light smile.

"How are we going about this, then? I mean there is usually quite a crowd that shows up to receive the supply drop. Plus, it's delivered to the welcome and info center, which doesn't offer a strategic position," Michael said as the group started to head down the swampy street.

"Yes, that is true, but if we hit the supply drop before it ever makes it to the welcome center, we won't have to deal with a crowd," Allison replied with a faint grin.

"That's a good idea, except for the fact that it's five to three at that point—and those five are usually armed with fully automatic rifles," Michael told her frankly. He wasn't seeing where Allison was going with her idea.

"The supplies start in a rowboat, which takes them all day to ferry the crates of food across the channel. Thus, while the armed Saints are busy jockeying the crates from the channel to the horse-drawn trailer, we take them down one at a time while their hands are full," Allison replied, her face now bearing a full smile. Now Michael saw where she was going with it.

"Plus, if we can get the horses and the trailer back to camp, we will then have mobility: a makeshift horse-drawn carriage," Zoe chimed in before Allison could finish with that exact point.

"Exactly," Allison replied.

. . .

The group had made good time that day, as the Saints were occupied with their own travels to the welcome center. The three of them were now settling down for the night in an abandoned penthouse apartment complex. They had only dared to go up to the third floor, as the complex had seemed to settle at a forty-five-degree angle—the ground it rested upon had gone soft. They were just a mile away from the resort and casino district; they were fairly certain that they could make it to the dock by the twelfth, as the supply drop was usually loaded every two weeks two days prior to its arrival.

The night air hung warm, but the winds had picked up outside the complex. A cool draft could be felt seeping in through the windows and cracks in the masonry supporting the leaning tower of the penthouse.

"Allison, are you awake?" Michael whispered into the dark corner of the bedroom she was residing in.

"Yes. What's up?" Allison replied groggily; she had almost fallen asleep.

"Say this plan goes right, and we get the horse-drawn trailer . . . won't everybody be looking for it once it disappears?" Michael asked. It was a rhetorical question—he knew the answer was most certainly yes, but he was hoping Allison had another ace in the hole.

"Yes, they will, but remember, we will have two full days after tomorrow to sneak around them, and probably another day for them to give up on waiting for the supplies that will never arrive. Either way you want to look at it, we have two days' lead. Goodnight, Michael."

Allison said this with finality to try to get Michael to calm down for the night, but even she knew Michael was the kind of guy who only slept when a task had been completed. Sure, he might lie down and keep quiet so the others could get some sleep, but his mind was always on and firing when there was work to be done. Only when a job was done did he sleep.

...

With the morning came heavy rain, the first real storm they had seen in months. Lightning touched down upon the vast and now-turbulent sea; the winds blew the rain in painful sheets. This, however, was a very good turn of weather for Michael and the two women—he knew it would give them more stealth and concealment, as most people stared at the ground when it rained to shield their face from the whipping water. The group was mobile again within the first hour of daybreak, and they kept a steady pace as they made their way to the channel.

The hours passed as they walked and the storm continued. The gutters and sewers were now overflowing, the rank, putrid water they had once contained now running rampant among the streets. The stench was a horrid one, and the water was now ankle high. Determined to press on through the cutting winds, the group skirted the western side of the resort and casino district; by noon, they were in the services district.

They were now crouched as they crept around the buildings

and streets, where armed men still guarded the barricades. The men stationed here obviously had their supplies delivered to them, whereas the other barricades and outposts of the resort and casino district had been abandoned. From a safe distance, the group viewed the crowd that had assembled in and around the welcome center. It was a good thing indeed that they were not going to try and take the supplies from there—it looked like a giant hornet's nest in a suspended period of rest while it rained. If they were to approach, the swarm would surely come down upon them.

They crept, crawled, rolled, and snuck their way to the channel landing, which required a lot of cautionary movements. It also required the patience to observe the patterns of the guards' routine and the timing of their breaks, where they would stop and banter with each other. The night was rushing in, and the small rowboat delivering supplies was still busily ferrying them across the channel. The group waited in the shadows until it looked like most of the supplies had been loaded on the trailer and the horses had been attached via a pull bar.

The channel walkway was concrete, about ten feet wide. Running along the walkway was a six-foot-tall flood wall and six inches of water that had already flowed over it. Twenty feet or so away from where the rowboat landed and dumped its load was a stairway. Six guards were jockeying the goods to the trailer from the channelway. The trailer was ten feet to the left of the stairs, and it seemed two guards were always at the top loading the trailer while another two went back down to the channelway, where they grabbed more crates to load onto the trailer. Fourteen feet to the left of the large trailer, there was a pump house; on its far wall, kitty-corner to the trailer, Michael, Allison, and Zoe stood observing the guards' routine from cover. Their foes' assault rifles had ignorantly been left resting against the left side of the trailer, closest to the group. The last two guards out of the six were fairly preoccupied with attaching the pull-bar assembly to the horses. They were no more than ten feet directly in front of the group, placing them within striking distance.

Michael counted to three with his fingers; once the third digit came up, he took off like a flash. Allison followed him, while Zoe made a mad dash for the automatic rifles. The guard closest to the advancing duo ducked and dodged Michael's swing with the lead pipe, as he had seen him coming out of the corner of his eye. However, he did not see Allison coming up from behind him—she drove the knife down into the guard's left shoulder, but to her dismay, she missed the artery in his arm that she had been aiming for. The man cried out in pain as the knife slid from his flesh and ragged, black leather overcoat. Zoe was now steps away from the automatic rifles that lay against the trailer.

The guard who had just been stabbed drew his .38 police special too hastily, fired from the hip, and missed, the flame from the shot suppressed by the heavy rain. The other guards were now scanning for the action and returning to the trailer.

The second guard, who'd been attaching the pull bar to the horses, now realized how close the danger was—he pulled his gun and fired blindly into the trio of fighters. It was hard to make out who was who. The bullet whizzed by, and there was a ricochet somewhere off in the distance. Michael swung again at the thug who'd been stabbed only a moment ago, but he dodged the swing. Then Allison came with a failed uppercut of her blade—when the man dodged Michael's pipe, he also lurched in a fashion that made the blade simply cut into his leather overcoat.

A shot rang out, and blood splattered Michael and Allison. Zoe, now armed with a fully automatic rifle, sent a bullet downrange—it hit the guard Allison had stabbed midchest, the power behind the shot causing him to fall to the ground.

The guard standing at the front of the horses let out another shot from his revolver. The bullet punched a hole into Michael's shoulder and lodged itself deep in the muscle; as his back had been turned, it made his body do a contorted dance, whirling around to see the man who had just shot him. A shot rang out from a guard who was now coming around the tail end of the trailer, the bullet passing Zoe's head by about a foot. Another shot came from an enemy who had followed behind the first guard to round the trailer; his bullet went way low and ricocheted at Zoe's feet. The two guards walking their crates up to the trailer from the channelway dropped what they were carrying and took cover behind the wall nearest to the stairs that led up to the trailer.

Allison was first to react, driving her knife down like a dagger into the eye of the man she had stabbed earlier. He went into death throes, flopping around like a fish. Michael ran and tried to tackle the man who had just shot him, but he failed, staggering a little too far to the left and allowing the guard to dodge. Zoe took a potshot at the two men who flanked her at the end of the trailer; as she dove behind the trailer's temporary cover, she shot, but it went so far off in the wrong direction that one could tell she hadn't even tried to aim.

The two guards flanking Zoe took shots in return—both missed, as they were trying to hit a moving target that had now dived for cover. Another shot rang out, but this one was followed by a mist of crimson. As Michael was getting to his feet, the guard who'd shot him previously did so again. This time, the bullet rang as true as judgment—it punched a hole through the back of Michael's head and out his left cheekbone. Michael dropped to the ground like a sack of dirt.

Allison took off like a bolt and was upon the man who'd just shot Michael down before he had time to react. Her blade violently thrust up and into the bottom of his mouth, just shy of cutting into the man's brain—the man could only stare as Allison ripped the blade from his mouth. She grabbed the stunned man, his wide eyes just staring complacently at her. Holding him by the scalp with her left hand, she jigsawed the blade into the man's throat, showering herself in a bloody crimson.

Then a shot rang out, accompanied by more crimson mist. Zoe had just squeezed off a round that punched through her closest attacker's neck, sending his left hand to clutch at the wound as he fell to the ground. An unsuccessful bullet returned in exchange, fired by her other still-advancing attacker. Zoe returned fire, and the bullet hit him point-blank in the chest—it sent him airborne, flying backward like a man hit with a cannonball in a cartoon. When he landed, they continued to trade shots. The first bullet to leave the man's revolver hit Zoe in the left bicep. Zoe returned another quick round into the man's chest—his response shot missed her neck by a hair. Reflexively, she pumped three rounds into the man's chest in quick succession, then two to his face, splattering brain matter and skull fragments everywhere.

While the rapid muzzle flashes of gunfire raged on between Zoe and her attacker, another flash appeared near Allison—she had finished sawing the man's neck apart, and the blast was the man's final muscle twitch pulling his gun's trigger, sending a bullet through her left shoulder socket. It shattered and blew apart her shoulder, her entire arm going limp with white-hot pain. She had finished the man off before his neuron signals got to where they needed to go, resulting in the delayed fuse behind the shot that had severed all motion in her left arm.

Zoe, still reeling from the shock of the firefight that had just gone down, never saw the man she had shot in the neck get back up. But he did get back up—and from ten paces, he took aim and shot her in the chest. With the adrenaline still violently pumping in her body, she never felt the shot until after her rifle rose and blew the man's head clean off. When she did feel it, she was fairly certain she was out of the fight. Her whole body seemed to fight the idea of getting up, or even taking the next vital breath—but somehow, lung-shot as she was, she managed to stand up. Looking around placidly, she started rambling over and over, "I want to go home now, I want to go home now."

Allison rushed up to the pile of fully automatic rifles and threw them on top of the trailer's already stacked load. Keeping the only one with a sling for herself, she proceeded to tell Zoe to get on the trailer. Zoe climbed up on top of the three crates that sat directly at the front of the trailer, stacked to act as seats. Allison checked to see if Michael had a pulse—and by God, he did. She dragged him the twelve feet to the front of the trailer, bringing him to rest on the crate bench.

As she started to climb up herself, the two guards hiding behind the channelway's six-foot wall came rushing up the stairs.

Needless to say, a fully automatic rifle aimed at a choke point only three feet wide does nasty things to a body. Even if the bullets miss the two fleshy beings, the stairway acts as a choke hold—the ricochets, with nowhere to go, end up hitting either the people in the middle or the wall, which sends hot chunks of concrete into those standing there. Thirty full rounds went off, cutting through the silence like a concussive cannon. Concrete chunks flew and dust filled the air, along with the crimson spray of disintegrating body parts and limbs being severed by sheer force alone.

The aftermath was two cowards spread across an area ten feet wide; if they had come up while their friends were fighting, they probably would have killed everyone in the group that now rode away in the horse-drawn trailer.

...

Luckily, there was a massive stock of medical supplies in the trailer. After taking the long way out of the services district and entering the resort and casino district, Allison started patching up everyone, including herself, the best she could; in a past life, she had graduated from medical school with a degree in physiology.

She had bandaged and cleaned Michael's wound the best she could, but it was a rather large hole in the front of his face—she didn't know if even a doctor with an operation room set up could fix it. *It's not like a man can walk around with a hole the size of a tennis ball in his head.* She grimly doubted that Michael would survive for long.

However, Zoe's chest wound was luckily through and through—the impact had narrowly missed her lung, the bullet's kinetic impact merely breaking four of her ribs. Her bicep was just a flesh wound and would only require cleaning and bandaging. Allison's shoulder wound would take some serious surgery to fix properly—splinters of bone and bullet fragments pointed like spikey projections out of her skin on the top side of her shoulder socket. Still, she had also been lucky, walking away without a wound to the major artery that ran through her left arm. Allison had high hopes for herself and Zoe, but even if Michael did survive somehow, she doubted he would want to live—the entire structure of his face on the left side was gone.

The main objective now was focusing on getting back to base with the supplies. Once she had patched everyone up the best she could, Allison drove the horse-drawn trailer through the western outskirts of the resort and casino district. She led the horses all night through the dark shopping district, then through the morning and into the evening of the next day to their final destination.

When they arrived in the late evening of October 13, Malachi couldn't believe the condition they were in. "Hey guys, how . . . oh fuck. Are you guys all right?"

CHAPTER 13

The morning of October 14 found three survivors burying their departed friend. The rain had stopped sometime in the passing of the night—when, none in present company could tell you.

Michael had come alive in a fit of seizures sometime in the early morning. His convulsions and screams had lasted ten minutes before Malachi shot him point-blank in the head. It was not a malicious act; they'd all known it was coming. Someone had to put an end to his screams and the tormented reality that he was already dead; there was nothing any of them could have done to help him. The bullet he had originally been shot with, before the second one killed him, had sprawled into four separate pieces located in four separate regions of his brain.

Allison said that there was nothing she could do for him other than to pray and hope, but that hope regressed into a bitter reality: a man cannot be expected to wake up with half of his face and a quarter of his brain gone, then somehow come around and say, "How do you do?" No, the bitter truth is simple: he wakes up and goes into terrible seizures mixed with slurred screams, and one of you who can't take watching another man suffer in such a way gets the courage to put him out of his misery. That happened to be Malachi; since he killed his friend, he decided it was only right that he should bury him.

Malachi put Michael's body over his shoulder like a limp sack of potatoes. He walked him up to the top of the only field that hadn't yet turned into a swamp and buried him the correct six feet deep. He walked back to camp and invited the rest to say their words; once they had all said what they had to say, which was between themselves and the deceased, they took a long, solemn walk back to the camp in silent reflection.

It brought tears to their eyes when they had to take account of what they had gained from their friend, who'd risked it all so others could continue. They were all distant, in their own worlds, dealing with the grief upon different terms. No one spoke; no one could even bring themselves to chance a glance at the others.

Allison was in charge of medical supplies; she tallied them up and made a list of what they had. Malachi did the same for the weapons and ammunition. When Zoe, who was dealing with her grief in her own way, was told to tally the food, she screamed with rage and bitterness that she hoped they would all just fuck off and die. With no bitter words of retaliation, Malachi did her job as well, tallying the food they had and making yet another list.

When it came time for everyone to read their supply lists, it was more of a time for everyone to move on. They knew they only had the day to grieve over the loss of their friend. What made it all the worse was he wasn't here just to hear them say, "You did good . . . really good. We owe you, and we have a debt to repay." But that was the bitter end, wasn't it? That he wasn't here—he wasn't around to get that good old "Atta boy!" and a pat on the back. He was dead, and that was that.

They stared at each other for a long time. Then Malachi said what he had to say, in a tone that suggested it would be wise not to ask him a single question at this time. "We have enough weapons and ammunition for me to feel we can truly defend ourselves. We have enough fresh food, pickled food, and jarred water to last us about two months at three square meals a day. Allison's list suggests we have a decent stash of proper medical supplies that she can use to treat any wounds we may incur relatively well for a while. The bandages are what she thinks we will run out of first, as two in the group have bleeding wounds." He choked up here—on the list, *three* had been scratched out to TWO in bold letters. Another reminder that Michael was no longer with them.

"I will be taking the rest of today, and a little piece of tomorrow morning, to grieve. Then I will be scavenging for tools, parts, and pieces we can use to make a fortification here. If anyone wants to join me, they are more than welcome to. If anyone wants to stay here, I will not judge them. The sooner we get fortified and ready to brace for the impending shitstorm I feel is already on the way, the better odds we have of living. Me personally . . . I will no longer run. If I die . . . I die. But I will die fighting!"

CHAPTER 14

The next morning, a few hours before noon, found Malachi standing at the end of First Street. The street led from the general bungalow area to a reserved, private bungalow area that Malachi assumed had at one point served only the richest tourists. It was located in a cove; as the years had passed and no maintenance work was done, most of the secluded cove had been submerged. First Street ended in five-foot-deep floodwater—it would prove to be a rather good boat launch, as it had a gradual slope into the swampy cove.

Two hundred yards to the east, the road continued until it was obstructed by an eight-foot chain link fence, whose gate acted as a barrier between the common bungalows and the secluded and private bungalows. It was a ten-mile walk through a foot of swamp water to get to where Malachi now stood at the naturally occurring boat launch. The area was very well concealed; the dense tropical flora that surrounded the fenced-in private bungalows was so thick that one would have to jump the fence and make their way through the hundred-foot plant cover to see what was on the other side. Across the fence, there was a dense two-block stretch where the public bungalows had collapsed a long time ago. This would prove to be an area the oncoming enemy would instinctively flow into, before they reached the main gate that led to the private bungalows.

Malachi knew for certain that this was where they should fortify and build their boat. Their time was limited, so the boat they were going to have to build would more or less be a raft. Malachi doubted if they even had more than a couple of days before a very angry swarm of Saints was storming down upon them. His general idea was to focus all their attention on the making of the boat—this would prove to be their only salvation. While two people worked on the boat, the other person would be on lookout detail, as the private section only had four massive bungalows that did not offer very strategic positions. They would have to make a defensive hold-out or blind of some kind that would serve as their fighting structure. Once that structure failed or the enemy became too thick, the boat would be the hypothetical Alamo of their potential last stand. With the pressure they were operating under, things would have to be done quickly. The first step was to get all the supplies from their old camp and bring them down here. The horses would grow restless and disobedient within the next couple of days, since no one in the group even knew how to take care of them. It was sad to admit, it but the fact was, they would have to run the horses until they either died or gave in to exhaustion.

When Malachi returned to camp, the two women had just finished lunch, which was a good thing—it meant they were ready for work. "All right, guys, here's the deal—either you're in or you're out. But I got to know right now—we have a very short amount of time to do a lot of work. So, Allison, are you in or out?"

With downtrodden eyes, Allison replied, "I'm in."

Malachi looked at Zoe, who was distantly trapped in a thousand-yard stare. "Are you in or out, Zoe?"

Zoe snapped back to attention and slowly said, "Why not."

"All right, that's very good to hear. Now, we need to get the stuff loaded back on the cart. Then we are going to head down to a cover that will provide us with the best odds of getting the fuck out of here," Malachi responded. Before he finished what he was saying, he'd begun throwing boxes on the trailer. The other two followed suit, but slowly, like they were being dragged out of a trance. "Come on, shake a leg," Malachi shouted in hopes of getting them to hurry up, but they only stared at him for a moment and continued on in their same set pace.

The trailer was loaded just past high noon. Malachi sat in the middle, with Zoe on his left and Allison on his right. He manned the reins and led the horses back the way he had just come. As the hours started to roll by, Malachi started to realize how truly short their time frame was, and how quickly horses got tired of dragging a one-ton trailer through a foot of swamp water.

Early evening was already upon the group by the time they had reached the secluded bungalows. Malachi led the horses to the large bungalow on the south side of First Street. There was only one other bungalow on this block, besides the one whose porch they were now unloading the trailer's supplies onto—the porch itself rested only half a foot above the knee-deep swamp water. There were two other large bungalows across the street on the north side, staring vacantly at the group's activities.

The trailer was unloaded and the porch full of supplies by the last hour of daylight. Malachi unloaded the books from the group's backpacks, then set up the lantern in the midst of the supplies on the porch. Allison and Zoe were placidly looking upon the sad, worn-down horses, which were filthy and frazzled.

"Hey you guys, can you come over here for a quick second?" Malachi asked as he racked the action of a fully automatic rifle. The two women walked shoulder to shoulder; in the dim light that the lantern cast, Malachi could see they had been crying over the horses' conditions.

"It isn't fair, you know. We should let them go," Zoe said in a quivering whisper.

"You're right, it isn't fair," Malachi replied with understanding. "But neither is our situation—and I hate to say it, but the horses are just collateral damage at this present juncture. I need them, and so do you. If a time comes in which they are still kicking and we have no need of them, I will let them go. Sound fair?" The group had lost almost all morale after Michael died, but the sulking that followed was too much. Malachi was hopeful that the two would snap back to reality, and quickly, as grieving time was over. It was time to either live or die, and mourning an old friend who had died so others could live was simply a waste of a life if the others did not at least try to live.

"Fair," Allison mumbled back.

"Now, what we need to do is start moving the furniture, and everything that isn't bolted down, to the furthest intersection in the east. We will block off the east, north, and south roads with stuff we can use for cover. We will then have a position that we can defend. We'll need to get this done by first light; then we will start building a boat. We need to hustle up the pace and work fast, as I think we will be lucky if we have until tomorrow night. Now, if you're in, follow me." As Malachi said this, he took a piece of tie wire that was wrapped around a nearby banister and secured the lantern to his right belt loop, then put the battery back in one of the backpacks and donned it. With a way to work through the night, they got down to business.

They started with the bungalow whose porch they had filled with supplies. The main room was the first to be vacated of its furniture. Three large leather couches, a large oak coffee table, brass table lamps, you name it—all were thrown in the first pile on the entrance road along the east side of the intersection. They continued to clear the house, taking mattresses, wardrobe closets, chests, trunks, dressers, etc. Then they would jockey them to the pile and drop them in no particular order, no purpose other than forming a makeshift barricade. Once the entire bungalow was emptied of its useable dunnage, the group moved on to the next house on the south block. They started in the main room, working their way in turn through the study, then the kitchen, then the bedrooms, continuously stacking. Desks, chairs, tables, fridges, coolers—all the household items that were not truly bolted to the floor went into the making of the barricade.

When all four bungalows had been cleared, the group was still embraced in the full darkness of the night. The three-walled barricade looked like a soggy yard sale gone wrong. The barricade itself was five feet thick at its thinnest area, and three feet tall. Each side of the wall, which left open only the west street that faced the cove, had a twenty-foot span of barricade. Malachi then told the others to take a minute to catch their breath and drink some water. While the two women went on a "coffee break," Malachi toted three fully automatic assault rifles and accompanying magazines, with twenty rounds per magazine. At this first station, they each would have a rifle with an accompanying four magazines.

Once Malachi had finished arming the fortified position, he took a quick break with the women, who were standing on the porch with the supplies surrounding them. As he took sips of water, he let them in on his thoughts. "All right, good job, guys. That was some nice hustle. Very nice. Look, the sun is just starting to rise." *Sip.* "Now, here's what is going to happen when they do come—whoever is on watch at that barricade we just made will shout out." *Sip.* "Then the two who are working will rush up to the barricade and engage the enemy. Now, the very important thing to remember is that one person must remain loaded and firing while the other two are reloading. The order doesn't specifically have to go like that, but just keep in mind, someone always needs to be covering with suppressive fire." *Sip.* "Now, what we need to do is cut down two very large palm trees. Zoe, since you increased the most in participation on this last stretch, I think you should take the first watch. Me and Allison will start cutting, and once those two trees are down"—*sip*—"we will need the horses to drag them so they're floating in our makeshift boat launch. After that, we will tether the two large palm trees together. As time passes, we will hopefully end up with something that floats." *Sip.* "Sound good? Good. Let's get to work."

As soon as he had finished his jar of water, his gasps for air in the one-sided conversation finished, he was off like a bolt toward the tree line, carrying one of the eight tomahawks from their weapons cache.

...

The day continued unmolested by outside interference. However, with early evening came the distant howls of large motors. Malachi was now taking watch, while Allison and Zoe were cutting out a ten-foot-long, five-foot-wide section of bungalow wall. The two women had already cut the tops of the leafy palm trees off and had just started on cutting out the section of the wall that formed the west side of the main room of the same bungalow that housed all the supplies on the porch. They would have liked to cut it sixteen feet, but that would have meant taking a load-bearing post with it, which was not a good idea—the whole bungalow would cave in. They worked methodically with the tomahawks that they both knew were meant to cut flesh, not thatch. They were implements of war, not very good crafting tools. It took the rest of the day to cut out the wall, then drag it onto the nearby trailer.

The horses were now getting rather stubborn and did not

want to willingly cooperate in the act of dragging the trailer into the swampy launch. The plan was to lift the buoyant wall off the trailer via the water. They led the horses out to the water and one at a time began tethering the wall chunk to the two palm trees. It was taking a lot of effort to get the balance just right. After tying the wall chunk to the two palm trees, they used up the entire hundred-foot roll of inch-thick polyester rope. They came to the rather unfortunate conclusion that they would have to begin making cordage, leading Allison to take watch as Malachi and Zoe foraged the dense flora for vines. As the group's progress continued, the raft's walking surface grew to ten feet wide by ten feet long.

Whatever machines were slowly making their way through the bungalow district also continued in their progress. The sound of bellowing engines began to become more intense—Malachi knew it would not be long until they had company. He assumed they had less than four good hours, and night had already fallen upon the group, adding to the unsettling feeling. Whatever the machines were, they were big.

■ ■ ■

"They're here!" The shout came from Zoe. Malachi and Allison dropped the last of the cordage they were using to secure what would be the last section of the walkable space on the raft. The raft was a total length of thirty feet, the palm trees at the front extending fifteen feet past the fifteen-foot-long by ten-foot-wide main surface. There were only two paddles, and those had been found in a mounted wall display over a mantel in one of the bungalows. The paddles were not large; they were of solid oak and only had a reach of four feet, which would mean a lot more effort from the group to row.

Now Malachi and Allison were running toward the shouting

Zoe. They were approaching the barricade when they saw lots of lights just beyond the gate that separated the secluded bungalows from the public bungalows. When they had made it to the barricade and each had taken up a rifle, they could not believe what was waiting for them.

On First Street, twenty feet from the other side of the gate, stood three wood-framed, steam-powered vehicles. Each vehicle bore a steel turret that sat at the fore of its flat standing surface. An M60 was mounted to each turret; to the rear of each one, concealed behind a large plate of steel, was a gunner, the three racking their actions almost in unison. Behind the turrets were large steam-engine assemblies which looked fit to power a large locomotive. The wood runners, struts, and planks looked liable to burst at any second under the immense weight of the engines; these were operated by four men in the rear of each vehicle, with an extra to steer the rear-wheel drive.

Behind the massive vehicles, there stood fifty equally agitated and pissed-off men. Each held the same primary weapon, a single-action bolt-operated .22-caliber rifle; they carried a wide range of secondary weaponry. They held ten rows of five behind the vehicles, but there was one man who stood in the forefront of all the artillery that was about to come down on the three of them. Malachi had never seen this many coming. He'd thought maybe ten at a time at first, until a final response that looked considerably like this. He had not expected the final response to come first.

The man who stood in front of the artillery brigade put a fist to the sky—the engines to the steam-powered vehicles died, so deafening before that the silence that now enveloped the soon-to-be battlefield was stunning.

"My name is Chief Charles! These are my people! You will be punished for the murders of Alec, Jarome, Shadica, Pontelus, Weva, and Rafadaman! *Fire!*"

The concussive blasts that followed caused each of the three to drop to the ground, not even daring to peek their heads up as the three M60s tore into their barricade. *BO-BO-BO-BO-BO-BO-BO-BO-BO*—the concussive blasts trampled over each other, no gun letting the others complete the range of their echoes. It lasted an entire minute, which felt like an eternity to the receiving end—halfway through that minute, bullets started to pierce through the barricade. The only thing that saved the group was that they had all gone prone; the turrets' mobility would not allow the guns to descend to the level where their targets were. Thus, in that minute, fifteen hundred unsuccessful rounds had been fired.

The chief had a wide smile on his face, in a false assurance that no man could have lived through that barrage. However, that smile disappeared very quickly when three heads popped up, returning a full mag apiece at the steam vehicles—as the steel was very thick, a massive number of ricochets filled the air. To the chief's dismay, his troops scattered into the tree line on the other side of the gate. Even the chief himself followed suit as the bullets began whizzing past.

"All right! Full war! Attack at will!" the chief ordered. The now-dispersed groups were regrouping into smaller outfits before they attempted to hop the fence. It also appeared that the men on the M60s had blown their entire load on the big show of force—the steam vehicles had been completely vacated.

"Okay," Malachi asked, "Everyone all right? Good. Remember, one loads, the others fire—now keep your flanks covered. Let's show these motherless bastards who the fuck we are!" he bayed—and in response, the Battle of Bungalow Bay began.

...

The first dull hues of daybreak cast their illuminating presence upon the battleground. A few potshots had been exchanged as the Saints formed ten squadrons of five soldiers apiece. They were now approaching the fence of their own accord. As they did so, the group took notice of their approaching positions. In the western distance of the cove behind the group, small but powerful gasoline engines could be heard coming upon the bay. The engines eventually died as the skiffs they powered emerged along the cove's shore.

At first, the group thought that they were being flanked—the squads exiting the eight two-man skiffs were different. Four squads at four men apiece, they had cleaner clothes, and they did not brandish homemade firearms, either, they brandished old army revolvers, and one had an old army rifle.

"I think they're RRFs," Allison called out upon seeing the approaching squads. To the group's relief, she was correct—the new arrivals bore black tactical vests that displayed a white spray-painted patch in the center, reading "RRF."

The group refocused their attention on the front line of the approaching Saints. Eight of the ten squads took cover in the dense flora—there were now four squads on either side of First Street. The other two squads began to run through the flora; when they emerged from the protection of the forest, each squad began to take aim at the group behind the barricade.

The first squad, standing ten paces to the north of First Street and twenty paces from the edge of the forest, began firing. The bullets smashed and crashed into the barricade while Allison and Zoe returned fire. Allison's shot struck true, downing one of the five in the squad, while Zoe dove for cover behind a nearby tree. Return fire was engaged upon the group, and Malachi let out a burst from his automatic rifle, punching three holes through another man in the squad.

The two flanking squads were now twenty feet into the

clearing of the swamp. While they ran, so did the RRF squads, now only fifteen feet from the shore of the cove.

The Saints' second squad fired upon the group behind the barricade, their muzzle flashes lighting up the surrounding flora. A bullet from the barrage found its way to Allison's neck—the .22-caliber ball only took a small piece of flesh in passing. Allison courageously returned fire at the second squadron, her bullet downing the man who had just shot her.

The concussive *pitter-patter-twang* of bullets impacting upon the various surfaces of the barricade was intense. Malachi and Zoe returned fire, each releasing two bursts to pepper and rip apart another faceless man from the Saints' second squad.

The two flanking squads, one now approaching from the far north of First Street, the other approaching from the far south, were now forty feet into the clearing of the swamp. As the four RRF squads approached at a full-out sprint, only forty feet from the cove, the dense flora lit up like a morbid Christmas tree—multiple stray bullets from the accompanying artillery orchestra found their way past the RRFs, whizzing by or landing a couple of inches away from the midsection of each man.

The third Saints squadron was now firing upon the barricade, catching Malachi off guard. Three bullets had made their way through a small gap in the barricade's cover, and all made forceful contact with Malachi's body. The first blew off the top half of his right ear. The second punched clean through his shoulder blade and exited through his chest—as he twisted around in agony, a third bullet lodged itself in his chest. Malachi fell backward and landed softly against the surface of the swamp water—he descended through a foot of water, only stopping when his body made contact with the pavement below. While Zoe picked him up out of the water and got him back to his feet, Allison returned a burst of bullets, peppering four men in the third squadron and killing the fifth.

In return, squads four, six, and seven all rained down suppressive fire upon the barricade, forcing the group to take cover and reload while they had the opportunity. Zoe snapped Malachi out of his daze as she let out a bloodcurdling scream: "Are you hurt?! Can you move, can you fight?!"

Malachi only nodded, dropping the magazine out of his rifle and replacing it with a fresh one. He was still in a dazed stupor due to shock, but he knew this was their last stand—he was most certainly going to die, and soon. With a deep breath, he rejoined the fighting.

Two more flanking squadrons were now approaching the barricade, only 160 feet away. The RRFs continued to run up the cover, still well over a hundred yards away from the group in their barricade. The RRF sergeant from the fourth squadron, the only one with a rifle, stopped running and took aim. He downed two men in the Saints' northern flanking squad. Squad four of the RRFs proceeded to rush up to the front line while the sergeant continued to pick off the Saints in the distance, one by one.

In unison, Allison, Zoe, and Malachi made a stand, each pumping a full magazine of suppressive fire into squads six, seven, and eight. Allison downed two men in squad six, but to her dismay received two .22-caliber slugs in return. The first blew out the shoulder muscle right above the collarbone of her right shoulder; the second grazed the entire length of the right side of her head. The graze started just below her temple and ended at the back of her skull. She fell backward into the swamp.

Zoe peppered two men from squad seven—as she emptied her magazine, she was struck by a ricochet that fragmented into two pieces. The first fragment landed in the spot where the neck connects to the back muscles of the shoulder blades; the second fragment landed three inches below the first, in her shoulder blade itself. Malachi's spray went all over the place, wildly, and to his frustration, not a single bullet landed within three feet of any of the men lining the forest. His wounds had made it impossible to even somewhat accurately operate a firearm.

Too busy dropping behind cover and collecting Allison from the swamp, the group never saw who threw it, or where it came from. The tear gas grenade blew up the center mass of the barricade, forcing the three to hastily start a dazed retreat toward the Alamo of the raft. The smoke offered them concealment as they hacked and coughed their lungs out—they made it forty feet down First Street.

The RRFs were now approaching the front line as the group retreated. The two flanking squads of Saints were coming upon the barricade, and the eight squads in the dense forest took a moment to help their downed comrades and reload.

Once the Saints saw that the group they were after had taken flight, they began to embrace a full-on charge after them. The RRFs were now approaching the four bungalows the group was stumbling away from, the front line of retreat blindly stumbling into the approaching RRFs. The sergeant, seeing the pile of supplies lying on the front porch of the bungalow farthest west, called on the first squadron to pick up them up.

The Saints, only missing a fifth of their initial group, looked like an ominous and oppressive tidal wave coming toward the RRFs. Squadrons two and four of the RRFs were made quick work of as a volley of a hundred rounds rained down upon their very unfortunate position—they had made a rash judgment call, leaving them out in the open as they tried to get to the cover of the eastern bungalows. The massive body of Saints had made it before them, and a quick exchange of fire killed the eight men in the two RRF squadrons before they could take more than two Saints down with them.

Realizing that half of his force was gone and the Saints were overwhelming his troops, the sergeant quickly called out the order to retreat. He ran up to the trio of mangled survivors and led them to the first two skiffs. The RRFs in the third squadron called out that they were going to cover the first squadron for as long as it took them to secure the supplies.

Bullets rained down upon the two western bungalows the surviving RRF squadrons were using for cover. The consecutive rounds of exchanged fire were deafening, and within two minutes the third squadron was viciously torn to shreds by another volley of a hundred rounds. The first squad, in the nick of time, began running back to the skiffs as the Saints started to fire volley after volley. One man took four separate bullets before he dropped, but the other three made it with the supplies, spreading out to three separate skiffs. The sergeant had ordered Allison, Zoe, and Malachi to use their remaining magazines for covering fire as the three survivors of the first squad embarked.

Within thirty seconds of their departure, the firing ceased. The Saints lined the cove's shoreline, hooting and hollering in victory, while the tattered RRFs and the three pod survivors had barely made the desperate escape.

▪ ▪ ▪

The aftermath of the battle was simple: the Saints had won, and the RRFs had lost. It had been by happenstance that the RRFs were in the area. They had decided to try to covertly sneak into the north side of the island—an attempt to secure an inhabitable location, as things on the cruise ship had gone sideways lately. The Saints had lost eight men, and seven were wounded. The RRFs had lost twelve men, and three were wounded. Malachi and Allison were hanging on by threads, and Zoe was just barely better off than the other two.

It took the skiffs fourteen hours to reach the port side of the cruise ship, where they had to be hoisted back on board. The people who inhabited the cruise ship had crafted the skiffs from modified lifeboats; they ran on biofuel made from whale and seal fat, which three of the four skiffs had used up by the time they were hoisted back amongst the main deck. Malachi and Allison had lost consciousness about an hour into the skiff ride, and Zoe had followed suit three hours into the trip; thus, the sergeant had been forced to lose another skiff, making his three men take on three passengers. It had been an uncomfortable ride, with the supplies making the cramped spaces even more limited.

If it were up to the ship's leader, Ramone, he would have had the three thrown over the starboard side. However, the sergeant pointed out the tactical advantage of the group—they had been on the island. Even if they were of no other use, they could be used for information. It was agreed to patch them up with only the medical supplies they had gained from the trip; after they were patched up, they were to be thrown in the jail.

In truth, the medical doctor aboard the cruise ship gave them the best care she could, using their preexisting medical supplies as well—what Ramone didn't know wouldn't hurt him. Then the ship's police force took the three prisoners to the jail, locking them up in their own cells to be questioned individually to see if their stories were consistent. The trio of survivors lay in their cages, tranquilized, medicated, and alone.

CHAPTER 15

The last hours of November 3 found Malachi, Allison, and Zoe in fairly good health. Their wounds had begun to heal, and their white-hot pain had turned into a vivid and throbbing one, taking only half of one's concentration to ignore. For the past couple of days, Ramone had been persuaded to be more appealing to the trio, instead of subjecting them to isolated interrogation. They were shuffled up nineteen flights of stairs, where they had an escort of six armed police in patchwork clothing. One would not have been able to differentiate them from common thugs were it not for the spray-painted white chest patches that read "Police."

Once on the sixteenth floor above the main deck, the trio was deposited in the captain's mess hall. This was the fourth room back from the bridge that overlooked the bow. The captain's mess hall was furnished with the last intact and somewhat visually appealing furniture, even though the old cracked material was more cloth patches than leather. The trio was told to sit at the rectangular table, which had three steel chairs on one side and three on the other. They sat in the chairs closest to the door, their backs to the stairwell. The overhead lamps had long been replaced with makeshift bio-oil lanterns that cast very dim and seedy lighting.

The police who had brought them to the captain's mess hall were now lining the wall that held the door to the stairwell. A moment after everyone had settled into position, three men came through the far door, which was directly across the mess hall from the stairwell door. The first man, who sat in the middle chair, was tall and muscular. He had brown eyes, accompanied by dark-brown slicked-back hair and a very full brown mustache. His Colombian accent shined through as he said a very warm "hello." The second man was the sergeant who had been part of the failed island invasion. He was stocky and very agile, his every stop showing a subconscious calculation of stealthy movement. He dispensed with the pleasantries of introduction. "How you answer the next question will determine if we even get that far. Do you understand?" the Colombian man continued, not a waver in his complexion.

"Yes," Malachi said, matching the quick-fire response from before.

"Good. How did you end up inhabiting the island where the Saints reside?" the Colombian man asked.

"We were left behind by the Lexington Company," Malachi replied. "Instead of sending us to Mars like they promised us—although we shouldn't have been naïve enough to believe them, as all of us combined could never have reached the monetary minimum—we were put into hibernation. Our pods never left the Earth's surface. Instead, they remained here for three hundred years. We woke up in the midst of your and the Saints' quarrels, knowing nothing of our surrounding land or the history of what has happened in past three hundred years. We had to live in secrecy and shadows, and even then the Saints found our pods and blew them up. We were then forced to take shelter in the bungalow district, since there was nothing of value to the Saints there.

"Recently, we began toying with the idea of fortifying an area in which we could build a boat to get off the island, hoping to make it across the channel to the other island. However, we overstepped our bounds, and our action caused a greater reaction. We stole those supplies—I do hope your men did not leave them behind, because among them were books containing information on how to build, farm, and live. Now, when they tracked us back to the bungalow district, which was not hard, their reaction was fifty-plus Saints, accompanied by three steam-powered turret tanks. At this point, we should have been killed, but their machine guns could not pivot far enough down—as we lay prone, the bullets whizzed past us by inches.

"When we were overcome by our enemy, your men showed up. We were retreating, just hoping to make it to the raft we had built and paddle out of range. Thanks to the man sitting to your right, we lived—and now here we are."

Malachi kept his eyes firmly locked on the Colombian's, which were filled with doubt. However, the story did make chronological sense—and it was possible. The Lexington Company had a widely known background in regards to anything that sounded like a far-fetched story of misery. This was probably a true one—word of mouth through the generations had taught how fucked-up the Lexington Company truly was.

"I am Ramone," said the Colombian man politely. "The man to my right is Sarge, whom you have already had the pleasure of meeting; the man to my left is Vincent." It seemed as if a unanimous switch had been flipped; the three speculative interrogators were no longer summing up the group's motivation but were actually pleased to meet the trio of survivors. Still, Vincent's demeanor remained slightly untrusting.

"I am Malachi. The woman to my right is Allison, and the woman to the right of her is Zoe." His reply was polite, but at the same time he hesitated; the transaction that had just occurred almost seemed like a quiet swell before the storm.

"Now, I think we could become friends, the six of us," Ramone replied. "We have use for all the able hands we can get. We lost fifteen men total—the three who were wounded and made it to the ship after your retreat died, just two days after their arrival, mostly from infection. Sarge and the three of you are the only survivors of the battle. I had sent out another sixteen men who met the same demise a day before you and Sarge returned to the ship. This puts me in a very hard position—I have lost every trained gunman under Sarge's command. This is not the fault of Sarge—he is a great leader and combat trainer. It is a fault of mine. I underestimated the situation." His voice was casual, almost as if they were old chums shooting the breeze in a downtown pub.

"I have led this civilization for the past six years. The first five and a half of them went swimmingly. However, these past six months, the ship has been marooned on this reef, and the hull has given way like paper due to a lack of efficient upkeep and repairs—proper maintenance stopped about a hundred and fifty years after the flood. We have done the best we can; the original cruise line staff had children, and taught their children how to take their position when they passed. Every generation has succeeded the other in the same way.

"However, our numbers have started declining, starting about fifty years ago, when my father ran this ship. A sickness caught on board, like a plague, if you will—it took the lives of half the ship's residents. It seemed the population never really grew after that, but instead remained stagnant. In the past two months, I have lost three people a day to malnutrition and the sickness that follows from it. We have collectively thrown one hundred and eighty funerals in the last two months. We have made desperate attempts to come on land, but the Saints keep slaughtering my people. This small island is no longer a reality. My people will have to journey to that larger island we know nothing about. This is where you guys come in, if you want to save just shy of two hundred souls." Ramone said this less as a statement than as an appeal, a desperate appeal. His charm made Malachi feel as if he had a duty to these people now.

"What do you need to happen and what is your plan are the real questions," Allison replied politely but firmly, knowing they were all still in recovery. "That would have to be told before we could make an informed decision, knowing all the facts."

"I'm glad you asked. Now, out of one hundred and seventy-three souls I have on board, only fifty are in good enough shape to work. Only ten of those men are master ship technicians; they have been working feverishly to obtain a working design for a ship which fifty men could build in one month's time. However, if the malnutrition continues among my people, ninety more will die in the upcoming month; that would be more than half the population. They have been working on this plan for over a month, and they keep coming full circle to the conclusion that it cannot be done.

"This led me to follow through with Vincent's proposal: he suggested that we send in a team of spies that would have to move very quickly. They would steal the SS *Vanessa* from the Saints. The Saints have completed building their ship; their population grows, and so does their demand for food. The steam ship *Vanessa* is a fishing boat. If we commandeered the ship, we could fit almost everyone on board, once the fishing equipment is removed. We would throw a Hail Mary and hopefully land upon the greener pastures of the larger island.

"Now, that is where the three of you come in. You know the land better than any of us, and you know how to get to the private marina where this boat is stored. It is stored in a channel lockup . . . a ship garage, if you will. You will be allowed this entire week to get ready if you decide to take the job. If you decide to not take on the job, Sarge will be forced to pick the three most competent people we have, but they will know nothing of the Saints' island. So, my real question to you is, will you do it?" Ramone finished with a plea in his tone, as if begging the three survivors to do the task at hand.

"Yes," Malachi replied, without even consulting Allison or Zoe. "But we will need proper supplies. Also, how far do you think we could get that last skiff to go?"

"That skiff's engine is almost burnt out. I would say you'd be lucky to make it the entire mile and a half to the southern shore," Sarge replied, as he was in charge of the maintenance of the ship.

"Well, we know absolutely nothing about the southern part of the island. I think we could manage it if we could get some proper gear," Malachi insisted, which got a raised eyebrow from Zoe.

"We have the three auto rifles and three magazines apiece that you brought with you. We have no food to spare, but we do have three working flashlights, three bowie knives, and a box of fifty homemade matches. Would that be sufficient?" Sarge replied inquisitively.

"Yes, I suppose it will have to do. Give us two days to strategize, and then we will be off." Malachi's response received cockeyed glances from both of the women in his group.

"Excellent. Now, I do not want to waste any more of your time. You are free to roam the main deck as you please, but do not stray from there—the rest of the ship is for my people only," Ramone stated firmly. The trio nodded in response.

...

The group found themselves in the foremost bow of the main deck, vacantly gazing at the stars unfolding around them. They were deep in thought and conversation as to what was best for their group, not the RRFs.

"I feel it's a win-win situation—they need a ship to get off this boat and over to that island, and we need a ship to do the same. We are all going to the same place—and yes, time will tell if we decide to stay with the RRFs or leave them and press forward on our own," Malachi said, staring vacantly over the bow at the gentle breakers down below them.

"I don't feel like we have any choice in the matter, Malachi," Allison replied, gazing at his calm demeanor. "I feel like we are constantly being oppressed and forced into painted corners. We are always the ones who are bending over and taking it. Why don't they send a few people with us? I mean, isn't that fair? What the fuck do we know about operating a steam engine and piloting a ship? I mean, who knows how big this ship is—would the three of us even be able to pilot it?"

"You're right, Allison," Malachi responded sincerely, "but what choice do we have? We will not be fed, we will not receive lodging, and better yet, all the people are destined to die, as their leader is obviously beyond his depth. I'm sure he was a good leader when this rusty and dilapidated cruise ship actually drifted with the currents—by the looks of the stern, they cast massive nets to catch a massive number of fish. However, now they know they can't even drop a fishing line. They are starving, dying, and destitute." He knew she also knew these points, but for some reason she was only seeing the situation from a narcissistic viewpoint.

"I don't think we should wait two days," Zoe replied thoughtfully. "I mean, we know what we have to do. We have to run, hide, sneak, and crawl our way back to the marina. We have nothing to discuss on the topic of strategy, since we don't know what the south side of the island has in store for us. All I know is that if we don't act and quickly, we will all die, including everyone on this ship. The other thing that still puzzles me is how these people have avoided becoming cannibalistic. I mean, no food, but human meat is all around them; when you are facing death, it would be impossible not to consider the option." She was not trying to say that the people were cannibals, but it did bring up a good point—three people a day died either from alleged malnutrition, or from the sickness that followed, their hosts had said. Sickness could be from too much human meat, and "malnutrition" could be from getting randomly selected to be snuffed in the middle of the night to mitigate the death rate.

"I have to agree with Zoe on this one—I don't think we should starve that long for no reason. I mean, as soon as we hit land, we could steal and sneak the food from the Saints' outposts and camps along the way. We stay here, and maybe we will be let in on this alleged cannibalism." Allison let out a little chuckle—she only thought Zoe was being funny—but Zoe was dead serious. Still, just the sight of Allison's chuckling brought a weird and welcome roar of laughter from the group; it had been way too long since they had really laughed.

"All right, then—it's decided," said Malachi. "We will set out tomorrow morning—after we sleep on the deck, I suppose, as we were told to venture no farther than the main deck. I'm curious as to why, but in the short scheme of things, I don't really much care." He said this with finality, after the group had calmed down from the laughing and giggling that they had just embraced moments before. However, this finality was overruled by Zoe and Allison, who engaged in reminiscing about life before the group's collective and terrible decisions to agree to the shady contract and bondage of servitude offered by the Lexington Company.

▪ ▪ ▪

Allison was the first to wake up the next morning. The sun was about two hours into its journey across the sky; the cool night air had chilled her bones and made the gradual warmth of mobility returning to her shoulders a long, painful process. She woke up Malachi and Zoe once the pins and needles accompanied by the throbbing pain in her shoulders, neck, and head had settled into her body's dull daily rhythm.

The group was handed their three backpacks, each of which was accompanied by the promised gear: three automatic rifles with three magazines, a flashlight, a bowie knife, and one box of matches, split between the members of the group. Sarge had selected four fit men to operate the booms and hoists of the main deck, lowering the skiff with the three of them inside down to the surface of the calm sea. Malachi detached the rigging and proceeded in pulling on the motor cord—it took a complete half hour of priming and pulling to bring it to life, sputtering and complaining.

They were off, headed north toward the southern shore of St. Paul Island. The motor kept a relatively good attitude about its cylinders being burnt out by the use of biofuel. As the journey progressed, Malachi became more and more surprised by how the motor didn't burst into flames. Dark-blue smoke pulsed out from the exhaust pipe, and the heat could be felt a good couple of feet away from the motor.

The journey was a short one; before noon, they beached upon the white sandy beach of the southern shore. However, the motor by this time was fried, the smell of melting plastic a good indication of its overheating. Malachi urged Zoe and Allison to get out of the skiff quickly, as the motor seemed hot enough to start on fire. As they ventured up the sandy shoreline, the engine never started ablaze; only little puffs of smoke radiated from its melting, now very warped and sad-looking plastic casing.

THE HUB

The sandy landscape continued for miles as the group proceeded toward the massive wind turbines that stood hundreds of feet tall. As their journey continued, the truly monstrous scale of the turbines became more pronounced. The sandy white shoreline was traded now for tan dirt and scattered rocks that eventually merged with a vast prairie of tall grass, before it descended upon a very thick and dense tropical forest.

The group walked eight miles, progressing at a very slow pace; after several hours of this, they came to another unanimous decision that they had overestimated the actual healing their bodies had accomplished in the past couple of weeks. They had to stop frequently, as one person or another would ask for rest as their healing wounds began to rekindle, the white-hot pain of injury returning due to prolonged movement.

After they had passed Port Amy on their ventures to the edge of the tropical forest, they decided to bed down for the night. Port Amy was concealed in a cove. Until they reached a junction of higher elevation, it would be impossible to see in its entirety. The port looked like a ghost town that had been abandoned since the floods had come. Its cranes at one point had jockeyed countless tons of freight that now stood dilapidated and mangled, like rusty remnants of a once-great statue. The actual concrete surface of the port had mostly crumbled and washed into the cove's deep waters. It looked archaic, and it truly was. It was an old remnant of the way things used to be, a great contrast to how they were today.

After viewing the steel graveyard of the port, where rust had long replaced what was once a burgundy red, the group decided to bed down for the night. The orange hues of sunset made the steel frame an extraordinary sight to behold. The group gazed upon it until the dying of the light, the beautiful but bitter remnant fading into the black carpet of the night. They did not light a fire, as their day on the south shore had been a hot one, and they did not want to give up their position. Worn out from the day's strenuous activities, they fell into an exhausted sleep.

...

The group slept through the night undisturbed. Upon daybreak, a ray of light from the morning's first golden hues landed upon Malachi's closed eyes, disturbing him from his sleep. To his dismay, his chest was hot with a pain that made his body so stiff with agony, he could hardly roll over to shield his eyes from the sun's bright glow. It took an enormous amount of effort—he had to literally use every muscle in his body to get up, to save him from further agony burning through his chest. Once up, his right ear began its dull ringing; this had become a constant side effect from part of his ear being blown off. The ringing was quiet enough not to drive a man crazy, but audible enough to impede proper hearing. It was as if a mosquito had become trapped in his ear, one he could not get out for the life of him.

As he woke up Allison and Zoe, he found that they had an equal amount of trouble getting moving as well. As a gentleman, he lent a helping hand to get each one to her feet. Once the group was up and fully awake with dull and throbbing pain—as well as suffering from dehydration—they began to make headway into the overgrown and very dense tropical flora. Massive palm trees made up most of the canopy, other trees of nondescript nature occupying the spaces the palm trees did not. Eight-foot-tall ferns covered the lowland ground, and massive tangles of vines hung from the tall tree branches, making straightforward progress nearly impossible.

The three of them trekked through the dense flora as lizards, tree frogs, salamanders, and snakes began to wake up to the warmth of the day. Colorful birds sang their songs as the morning hours progressed, the life that could be seen all around them unfolding further.

"How many of those windmills do you think there were yesterday?" Allison inquired as the group continued to make its very slow and tedious progress through the thick vegetation. "I mean, as massive as those things were, I would assume they alone could power this entire island."

"I thought the exact same thing," Malachi responded quickly, to distract himself from the burning hot fire that was raging in his chest. "I counted twelve in the first row we crossed through to get to the other side of the wind farm. I did not, however, count how many rows there were, as we were walking through that wind farm for a very long time. I would say it would be safe to assume at least a hundred."

"I read one time before hibernation that one of those things could power an entire household for a day. It would also be safe to assume that a hundred houses could be powered from the farm," Zoe said, joining in the conversation. She found herself thinking the Saints were a very curious and backward people. In another world, they could serve as fodder for future discussions at parties for endless hours.

"Then why don't they use the stupid things?" Allison replied, the topic sparking her interest as well. "I mean, three hundred years, and no true utilities are ever put back into service? It begs the question—what in the hell have the Saints have been up to for all this time?"

"I couldn't say, I really couldn't," Zoe replied. "It's like the Saints are the most backward, primal, reclusive civilization that could have the luck to take over this island. If the Saints could be wiped off the face of the earth and the RRF sent back on their happy little drifting journey, I dare say we could have made something of this place. If all the people from the pod program—we don't know how many there were, but let's say fifty or so, for the sake of argument—were to all have been placed on this island and woken up in the same fashion, I think we would have had the power and water running again. Maybe not with a hundred percent efficiency, but efficient enough to live comfortably. That's what I personally don't get. The Saints have an alleged workforce of five thousand strong, yet they don't even have the lights on or the water running. I mean who thought shitting in a hole outside would be better and more agreeable than shitting on a toilet with running water and sewage lines?"

The positivity that followed just from having a normal conversation was startling to the group, but in a good way. They embraced this change, long overdue as it was.

Malachi was the next to speak. "The question that has been troubling me is this: the Saints seem to have regressed back to a seemingly primal state. Now, hear me out—they have learned how to make rifled barrels, cartridge ammunition, and steam engines. What if one were to argue that they were, yes, very primal and very slow to embrace new ideas—but the ideas they *have* embraced, they are excelling at? They have all the books in the library except for the few we have stolen. With that kind of knowledge at our disposal, I would agree that we would have excelled at a much faster rate. However, what if the people we are dealing with had a leader in the beginning who only possessed an eighth-grade level of education? They would have a basic understanding of things, but they were very far from having complex knowledge. Over the past three hundred years, the Saints have had to struggle through a high school diploma's worth of knowledge without a high school level of education, much less higher levels of education or professional skill sets.

"With no teachers and no concept of anything structural, they had to spend years conferring among multiple . . . shall we say *communes*, all of them studying one thing. Say one commune of a hundred people studied basic arithmetic and then gradually advanced to complex trigonometry. Then another commune of a hundred people studied basic English and then advanced to complex literature and the understanding of complex sentence structure. Once these individual communes had figured out the complex nature of each subject, never once intermixing with the complex knowledge of one another, you'd see a very drastic gap in knowledge.

"For example, the steam engine. The people with math skills and the people with chemistry skills, due to no one really being able to convey what they mean rightly to each group, played a very long and dry game of telephone. It took hundreds of years for a middleman, maybe even the present-day leader, to understand all the necessary concepts and bring them to a head. This is where the *aha* moment comes in. It took them forever to understand each other—that's why they focus on excelling in one particular facet. Adding more complicated systems would cause another . . . say . . . hundred years of nonprogression, as another middleman or leader would have to arise to explain and interpret all the complex structures involved in, say, electricity next time.

"This is what I personally have been mulling over in my mind the past couple of months." His (long) statement finished, he was now rather red in the face and winded, causing multiple very displeasing muscle spasms in his chest. But for some primal basic social reasoning, it felt worth it.

Allison and Zoe just stared at Malachi, astounded by his profound and in-depth thoughts on the subject of the Saints. They in fact were all surprised at their existence as true people—this type of self-expression had never entered the group's dynamic until now. Before any one of them continued on in the conversation, they had to take a moment to digest how primal they themselves had become with the absence of talking and engaging in rational debates and pleasant conversations.

"You know, Malachi, I think you might be on to something even deeper than that," said Zoe. "I think you just broke whatever spell has been cast on us, blocking the simplest pleasantries of our old lives for some reason—you have sparked those back to life again. I think, sir, you just opened a larger door than you thought," she concluded, trying to convey her honest feelings in just the right kind of way.

The group, the spark of hope for their future lit, continued walking in the same fashion as they had before, debating and conversing about the similarities and contrasts between the Saints and the RRFs. It was as if a blind man stumbling around in a dark room, the plug of a lamp in his hand, had finally found the outlet with which to brighten the room, or a janitor fumbling around with his massive key ring had finally found the key to the utility room to replace the busted fuse, returning the normal activity of life to full swing in whatever building he maintained. However, like Malachi, that janitor would go on with the normal business of keeping the other parts of that same building flowing smoothly in other ways. Nevertheless, they had each experienced what counselors would call a "breakthrough."

CHAPTER

16

Noon of November 6 found the group emerging from the dense tropical flora of the forest. They had not slept well, as Malachi had developed a fever and had begun having coughing fits late in the night. The coughing had now grown worse—Malachi's chest was on fire, and his windpipe felt as narrow as a straw.

The group was now stopping for a rest while they took in the terrain that lay before them. It was mostly tall, swampy grass, small farming houses, and fields that could be seen randomly scattered throughout the clearing. The clearing itself was long enough that it blended into the distant horizon. There were plumes of smoke that rose mightily into the crystal-blue noonday with a few wispy frost-white clouds. The contrasting plumes of steel-gray smoke drifted ever upward of their own accord. The wind was gentle and the sun warm.

The group had regressed into a downtrodden atmosphere, as Malachi had to save every breath he could for walking alone. His coughing fits were to a point now where the group would have to come to a complete stop to allow him time to recover every time they struck. The group also desperately needed to find water, as everyone was suffering from moderate dehydration.

"We need to stop at one of those farms—one of them is bound to have water," Allison said as she tried to wet her lips with a dry tongue.

"I am in favor of that idea . . . *whew* . . . myself," Malachi responded hoarsely, followed by a few haggard coughs.

The group began to plod through the ankle-deep mud. Eventually, it might just prove to be great, very nutrient-rich soil; however, at the moment it proved to be a great nuisance to the group. They continually grew a foot in height, as the mud would stick to their boots; after every hundred yards, they would have to painstakingly flick off the mud that seemed to grow on their feet.

The grass and reeds were waist high by afternoon, and it took the group an entire hour to make a single mile of progress. As they plodded on, they kept a constant eye out for either a road or a nearby farmhouse. The farmhouses seemed to stay at a continuously far distance from them due to the lack of headway they were making.

The last hours of daylight fell upon the group in a bad way. Malachi had started to slow to a pace that would give a tortoise a fair race. They had made only four total miles and, at the moment, were determined to walk as long as it took to make it to the muddy road that had become visible only an hour or so ago.

The group continued until Malachi collapsed like a sack of potatoes upon the surface of the dirt road. It was midnight, the stars and moon illuminating the clearing in dim silver hues, which only made Malachi look done in. He was wheezing and puffing unconsciously as the utter exhaustion took him down into the black depths of unconsciousness. His clothes had evaporated their sweat hours ago, meaning he had stopped perspiring due to severe dehydration even longer ago, maybe close to late afternoon.

Allison and Zoe took only a moment to scrape the mud off

their boots before each retired in much the same way as Malachi had. Although they were not even near the tight spot he was in, they were just worn out, maybe even more so. There had been moments that Allison and Zoe had had to pick Malachi up by the shoulders and drag him a couple hundred yards before he regained his somewhat-intact ability to trudge on. Even without saying anything on the topic, Allison and Zoe both knew if Malachi did not get rest and water soon, he would surely die.

▪ ▪ ▪

Allison and Zoe were standing shoulder to shoulder as they shared the same bitter tears. At some point last night Malachi had suffocated on his phlegm, and since he had nothing in his stomach, he did not vomit. Instead, all they could see was the thick, stringy mucus that encompassed his entire face, cementing between his desperately wide-open mouth and nose. The flies now feasted upon his corpse. Allison dry heaved in an attempt to control her sickness. They had nothing to bury him with, so they simply tried to fold his arms across his chest. However, rigor mortis had set in, disallowing even that act of kindness.

They stood and stared for what seemed like an eternity in the dull morning hues of light. A farmhouse could be seen to the west, about a quarter of a mile down the dirt road. They watched until the growing light made the entire scene so grotesque that they had no choice but to leave their friend behind, lying like a stray animal that had been run down. Their pace diminished, and they took the longest walk of their lives. The quarter mile seemed to stretch somehow into noon, puzzling the two of them extraordinarily.

Once upon the farmhouse, they could see a farmer harvesting coca leaves to the north side; large plumes of smoke rose from the processing hut that turned the leaves into cocaine. The part that struck each as odd was the fact that, even after all these years, cocaine was still at the forefront of some people's thoughts; this was beyond them. In the processing hut a fair distance away, hundreds of white bricks weighing at least two hundred pounds apiece were stacked into a three-cornered wall to shield the two men in the processing hut from the wind.

Allison led the way into the farmhouse, whose only occupant was a very old and very small tan-complexioned woman. She was sitting in a wooden rocking chair and had a massive quilt thrown around her. It was at least eighty degrees outside, and here this old woman was wrapped up like it was the dead of winter.

The two women made their way into the kitchen, which had two ten-liter jugs filled to the brim with water. Zoe smelled the water and decided it was potable. Quietly and as quickly as they could, she and Allison drank a liter apiece from the same jug; afterward, the two of them decided it best to take it with them.

They were in and out of the dilapidated little farmhouse with no glass windows in less than ten minutes. They proceeded to walk westward down the dirt road, planning to continue until they either found an intersection that had a road that went north or that hit the west coast of the island and headed north along the shore.

By last light, despite expending very little effort, neither one of them said a word; they only motioned when they needed to exchange the weight of the jug between them. They simply had nothing to say, as the same man who'd seemed to bring forth the flow of social conversation was the very same man who'd ended it. They felt as if they were distant observers of the tragedy as they curled up inside themselves mentally. They were detached, wandering like people do when they are thousands of miles away, somewhere else completely. They had not a care nor a concern in the world. *An ambush? Fine, bring the bullets—in fact, I'll give you my own gun and ammo to use.* This was just one of the many disconnected thoughts that Allison had. *Walk? For what? Why the fuck do we keep doing things that only end in the same way: loss?* Zoe thought just a moment later. The two of them were battling a war against their own subconscious enemies on all sides.

As the final orange fare-thee-well from the sun departed, the two women sat down, took equally shared swigs from the now half-full jug, and then lay down in the middle of the road. Both of them gazed at the stars with no general interest; it was just something to look at.

▪ ▪ ▪

It was late the evening of November 13 when they saw it a mile in the distance, maybe even a little farther, at the very southern edge of the slums district. Massive gray concrete buildings that looked to be at least twenty stories in height jutted out of the street, resembling a concrete jungle. The streets were narrow, and one would be hard pressed to say they were anything other than a mass collection of alleyways. Row upon endless row of tall concrete slum apartments could be seen for miles from the little foothill that Allison and Zoe stood on.

They had traveled unmolested; the farmers were pleasant when the women ran upon them growing various crops, even extending a pleasant "hello." It seemed as if the Saints' presence was in the urban districts alone; like Malachi had pointed out, they did what they exceled at, living where they knew how to. This point grew increasingly true as the day found its way into night. It seemed that every balcony was ablaze with fire that could be seen for miles. This was the hypothetical hornet's nest, one that would force the two women out of their haze. They had wandered and said nothing to one another since Malachi's passing. Zoe was the one to break the silence.

"I have a plan," she croaked, the absence of talking making it seem unnatural to force her larynx to perform the ancient task.

Allison nodded in response; she too knew it would take a while to warm up her voice to the idea of speaking again.

"What if we steal some villagers' clothes, drop the backpacks and trade them for burlap, and then either find or make a stretcher to carry one of those massive bricks of coke? I mean, who would think us anything other than the peasants bringing the hypothetical party to the door?" Zoe said, her voice seeming an unnaturally forced thing.

"Sounds good," Allison whispered as she sat down on the road. Zoe, knowing what her body language meant, followed suit. The two of them bedded down on the open road again, while the stars mixed beautifully with the little specks of blazing balcony fires in the distance.

▪ ▪ ▪

The next morning, both Allison and Zoe were up before sunrise—they had a lot of work to get done. They would have to backtrack about five miles south on the dirt road to get to the coca farm. Hopefully they wouldn't have to gun anyone down, though they tended to doubt it. They polished off the rest of the water from the jug, and when the first dull, golden hues of light descended upon the land, they were off.

They were making good time, as a day not walking through a boggy swamp was a good day indeed. Their attitudes had somewhat changed from last night; they were leaving the bullshit at the door when there was work to be done. They continued on, not saying a word to one another. Their posture was alert and ready, not like the one they had embraced for the past week, heads down and backs slouched.

While they were walking, the sun's smiling face began to grow wider, as did the golden hues of the morning, allowing the duo to see the small farmhouse they had passed the other day. Surprisingly enough, the farmers were already in the coca field, and the fires for processing the coca into cocaine were being rekindled from the previous day's coals.

The two women racked their automatic rifles, then proceeded to turn onto the dirt road that led to the farmhouse. As they approached, they heard voices coming from inside. They were not the pleasant kind of voices that greeted friends or even strangers with common courtesy—no, these were harsh, cold voices. The Saints. Allison and Zoe took nearby cover behind a small patch of palm trees halfway between the dirt road and the small farmhouse, then took aim at the front door of the farmhouse and waited for the Saints to come out.

"Aim for the head. If we don't blow too many holes in their clothing, it will provide excellent disguises," Allison whispered so quietly that even Zoe, who was standing two feet away from her, could hardly make out what she said.

The duo stood patiently waiting for what seemed close to a half an hour as the Saints shouted at the occupants; the latter's scared, submissive replies were garbled up, making it hard to truly understand what they were saying. However, through the general tones, Allison and Zoe could make out the gist of it.

When the three men finally came out, they shared wide grins and laughs, looking as though they were three chums coming out of a bar at closing. Their laughs and grins came to a swift end as two of the three men's heads exploded into a mist of gore and crimson. The third man, truly stunned by what had just occurred and the two very close reports of rifle fire, did not react in time. He stood frozen like a deer in the headlights when the six bullets that came from two equal bursts of automatic fire violently peppered his chest and abdomen, his limbs flailing rigorously. He was dead before he hit the ground.

The two old women and three young men who had previously been in the farmhouse came rushing out the front door, making a break for the cover of the field. As they passed the man working the coals of the processing fire back to life, he followed his fellow farmers—it was more than likely his family running past him.

Thus Allison and Zoe were left alone while they donned the now-faceless dead men's outfits. Once dressed, they proceeded into the house and found another water jug and a couple jars of pickled tuna and carrots. They stuffed the jars into their backpacks, which they would now keep, since their disguises had changed.

Once the two of them exited the farmhouse, they headed directly to the cocaine-processing hut. After looking around the general vicinity of the thatch-roofed and cocaine-brick-walled hut, they found a rickshaw that was the perfect size to accommodate a two-hundred-something-pound brick of cocaine. Allison pulled the small rickshaw to the smallest brick wall; with the help of Zoe, she struggled with the topmost brick, then jerkily jockeyed it into the rickshaw. The mud was thick around the processing hut, and Allison, who decided to take the first shift of pulling the rickshaw, had a very hard time getting it through the muddy and boggy field and back onto the road. It took nearly an hour for her to drag the cart a mere fifty yards, as the two bicycle-style tires dug deeply into the mud. Once upon the dirt road, Zoe handed off the water jug to Allison as she took the next shift of pulling the rickshaw. She found it a much more pleasant resource than Allison had as it glided smoothly across the dirt road.

The progress back toward the slums was slower. With every mile came a shift change, where they exchanged the pulling of the cart for the carrying of the water. At the rate they were walking, they were only able to hold a two-mile-an-hour pace; the load in the rickshaw was heavy, no matter how easily the vehicle glided on the road.

An hour past noon found them fully embraced by the warmth of the sun, returned to the spot where they had camped the previous night. They wolfishly ate both cans of pickled tuna and carrots, as the irregularities in their meals had made them both malnourished. Once the small meal had been consumed, they were back at it. Zoe was the first to pull the rickshaw this time around.

The looming concrete jungle they were approaching became proportionately taller as they continued toward the slum district. By the time they embarked upon the first alleyway, the now-massive, ominous concrete apartments were revealing their exposed rebar and rusted, speckled, spotted beams. Each held cracked and eroded concrete walls, playing into the stark contrast of the ominous grayness that accompanied the district. Two armed Saints were standing guard at the first intersection, about a hundred yards north of where Allison and Zoe were now embarking upon the maze of concrete alleyways. They seemed to get progressively narrower as one continued into the heart of the district.

"Do you believe this shit?" the very tall, lanky Saint said to the small, very scrawny Saint. "Chief Charlie must be throwing another month-long party with his concubines again. Wait," he added, catching sight of the two women—"*those* are concubines. Look, he sent two of them this time to get the stuff. I've never seen him do that."

"Strange days these are indeed, brother," the smaller Saint replied.

Allison and Zoe overheard the two guards' conversation, knowing it had just given them their perfect cover story.

"What's your business? You know it's dangerous to be out this late without an escort." The taller of the two men addressed Allison and Zoe with a forced authority.

"My business is to get this brick to Chief Charlie," Allison replied. "Dangerous as it may be for you, the same does not apply to us—you know the punishment for messing with one of his concubines is quite a nasty one." Her smooth, rational tone and stone-faced complexion drove the point home further—she was in control of the situation, not the lanky man.

"Yes, we both understand that fact," the short and very tenacious little man said nastily. "However, maybe the two of you would happen to have a nasty little accident, neither of you able to say who did it. Since the high and mighty chief seems to be the only one allowed to consume cocaine without a ration limit, would you be so obliging as to give us some of what's in that brick? Or we take the whole fucking thing from you. Which will it be?" Allison and Zoe did not doubt the short man would kill both of them to feed his terrible little habit.

"Here's how this is going to play out," Allison said—then without notice or hesitation, she quickly whipped her slung rifle to attention and pumped a ten-round burst into the little man.

Zoe replied by grabbing her rifle from atop the brick of cocaine, dropping the rickshaw and sighting the rifle on the man before he could draw half his pistol out of its holster. "Don't you fucking dare!" she shouted.

He froze, the shots that had roared from the muzzle of Allison's rifle still reverberating through the maze of alleyways in a powerful thunder of echoes. "All right . . . you got me! Don—"

The man's voice stopped as another quick thunder rolled through the alleyway. Allison let another three rounds out of her rifle—the first two hit center mass and the third passed with little effort through his throat, where a fountain of crimson spewed from. The lanky man dropped and tumbled, gripping his throat until the final death throes were upon him.

"That's for Malachi, you little bitch!" Allison's new voice

shone through, and in all honesty scared the living daylights out of Zoe. Allison's personality had spun a one-eighty, and this violently dangerous and fierce woman had arisen from the battle within her subconscious. She was no longer the Allison of yesterday—the new Allison wanted to kill, wanted to get even with bloody payback. Her eyes were a fire of malicious victory, and Zoe herself shrank within herself. This new Allison frightened her.

"Let's go—we've still got a few hours before dark. I'll take a shift with the rickshaw," Allison said, handing over the jug of water she had dropped. A little more than half the precious water contained within it had spilled upon the concrete. Zoe took the jug without saying a word; instead of placing her rifle back on the cart, she carried it with her free left hand. Allison picked up the pull bar of the rickshaw and took point, leading Zoe, who was still trying to digest how easily and freely Allison had just wasted two people. Sure, they were bad people, but the old Allison would have successfully talked her way out of it, not just blown them away.

...

Progress was slower now, as they had to navigate the shrinking and zig-zagging alleyways that were pleasantly illuminated by all the firelight of the balconies. Allison had made it very clear to Zoe that they were not going to stop until they hit the channel or died trying to get there. They kept a steady pace, and as they traveled they found that while the guards had posted positions in almost every alleyway during the day hours, there was nobody on night shift. The alleys were vacant, clear of almost all Saint presence besides the watchers on the firelit balconies, who seemed to be not the least bit concerned with the presence of two women, splattered in blood, dragging a rickshaw full of cocaine down an alleyway in the middle of the night. The slum district was as crazy as it could get. Zoe could never have imagined a time when someone could drag a monumental amount of cocaine down a street and not have somebody ask a few questions.

They continued through the night, the fires growing less and less abundant the farther and farther north Allison and Zoe went. A bridge could be seen in the distance of the straight-shot alleyway they were now walking down. The alley had grown wider—with maybe a hair on all sides, two cars could pass through side by side. The two women were approaching the bridge now with a little more pep in their step; Allison was pretty sure that it was the remaining structure of the First Street Bridge, which simply meant they were very close to the channel.

By daybreak, the two women stood at the edge of the channel; after a lot of vigorous effort and strain, they got the cart down to the channel walkway. "The story now, is that we have been told by Chief Charlie himself to deliver this brick of cocaine across the channel for the brave warriors that fought in the bungalow battle," Allison said, and Zoe nodded in understanding.

When the channel was embraced by the warmth of the sun at high noon, the two women stood at the edge of the walkway, where an unoccupied rowboat sat. To keep their cover, the two women hefted the brick into the middle compartment of the rowboat, then disembarked from the walkway into the small vessel. Sitting side by side, they began rowing, veering ever so gently west as they slipped into the private marina's channel that headed due north, leading to the marina itself.

"What do you think a boat lockup would look like?" Allison asked, as she frankly had no clue.

"Well, if it's supposed to be a boat garage, I would assume it would have a large door, right?" Zoe responded.

The rowing dragged on for hours—the north marina channel spanned a complete ten miles, frustrating the two women immensely. They were lucky to gain a mile and a half an hour after fighting with the southbound current; they had to take very quick water breaks to avoid backtracking too much, as the current could very well push them out of the marina's channel. They pressed on until the silver moonlight of an hour past sunset was upon them.

Finally, they reached the marina itself. It was a massive marina that could possibly take days to go through. Upon further inspection, they found the marina had few boats that were actually floating, and even fewer buildings. What structures there were looked like floating compounds of rusty steel and moldy, rotten wood.

They systematically rowed to every individual floating compound, which proved to be boat lockups after all. Most of them were left open, their double doors tied back to allow for a simple glance in, which meant the women could easily determine whether the buildings contained what they were looking for. The search dragged on until they crossed the path of an odd duck. This structure was massive, not like the others—it looked like a small castle and had a fresh coat of paint over its rusty, dented steel façade. Also, the massive wooden doors were locked shut, and they seemed to go as deep as the channel floor itself. The women pulled the rowboat up to the boat lockup's adjourning dock, tied it off, and then disembarked.

As they walked along the dock, creaks and cracks from the rotten wooden planks were present with every footstep. They walked the boat lockup's entire north side, the longest side of the rectangular-looking castle. At the far northwestern corner, they found a small wood door reinforced with iron that was also locked. They also heard voices coming from within the lockup; they sounded like men stirring from a deep sleep.

"Here's the story," Allison whispered. "We are here to bring a celebratory brick to the workers and/or guards of this lockup, from Chief Charlie." Zoe again only nodded; she had been running off pure fumes for the past eight hours, as they had been up for almost two consecutive days.

Allison rapped the back of her hand against the door firmly. After three attempts, the door was finally unlocked, and a dark figure opened it a small crack. "Who are you?" the figure asked.

"We are Chief Charlie's concubines. He sent us to bring you a motivational party gift," Allison replied.

"Well, what is it? Why did he send you so late?" the shadowy figure inquired.

"He sent us this morning—the channel proved a great force to battle as we rowed the supply boat up. The gift is rather large, and it will probably take four men to get it out of the rowboat," Allison replied.

"So, you're telling me you want me to wake up three other workers in the middle of the night, impeding our four hours off, to grab this party favor for a boat that isn't finished yet," the shadowy figure replied sarcastically and outraged at the joke.

"Yes. The gift is to encourage you to sleep less and work more—that's all I know," Allison replied subtly. Now she was worried about the boat's condition. *If the boat wasn't finished like Ramone had thought, then how are we supposed to get out of here and off of this island? In a fucking rowboat?* She could see it in Zoe's eyes as well—they were both extremely concerned.

"All right! Give me a minute." The shadowy figure disappeared. His voice could be heard from inside, barking orders to wake up, to get the lights on, to get the power generators back up, and to meet him at the side door.

▪ ▪ ▪

Three workers, six guards, and two strangers now stood in an overly illuminated boat lockup, all staring at a massive brick of white cocaine. All but Allison and Zoe were in awe.

The boat lockup was a hundred-foot-long, thirty-foot-wide enclosure that was barely tall enough to allow the two massive steam stacks to rest under the fluorescent lights. The steamship that sat docked in the center of the lockup was seventy-two feet long by eighteen feet wide. It had a massive boiler and a massive engine without any of the fishing gear attached or built; one wondered where they would have enough space to put the fishing equipment, as the motor assembly and boiler took up almost every foot of the boat's hull space. It was crafted out of wood, and looked to be complete except for the addition of the fishing equipment.

"Chief Charlie has asked me to assess one thing," Allison said, the nine others staring at the brick with excitement, yet thinking it was a joke at the same time.

"What's that?" the foreman asked. He was dressed in brown overalls and no shirt, revealing his hairy body in a rather unattractive way.

"Before you dip into that, he wants visual proof that it runs," Allison said with a seriousness about her. All stares strayed away from the brick to examine her.

"All we have to do to snort this here entire brick is to turn it on?" the foreman asked seriously. A feverish sweat came over his entire body, making him sheeny with anticipation of the euphoric high that was just waiting for him.

"Yes. Show me and my fellow concubine the steps, in a simple enough order for us to be able to start it up; we can then convey to Chief Charlie that it truly does work in a way we can understand," Allison replied, Zoe now following her lead. The plan couldn't have been simpler if it had slapped Zoe sideways. They were going to learn how to run it, and then once it was up and going, they were going to commandeer it. Brilliant!

"Okay, fellas, you heard the lady. It ain't no lie this time, he finally came through. So let's give them an abbreviated and simple tour so we can get high in a short moment. Follow me," the foreman said, his two colleagues snapping to attention and following closely behind him.

They boarded the port side of the steamship, and the foreman began a very quick but effective presentation. They started with the bow, which had a captain's cockpit that stood right in front of the massive boiler. The captain's cockpit was relatively small, little more than a steel framework holding a small tin roof over the cockpit. The captain would have to continuously operate the wheel and the two levers that worked the boiler and engine. The first lever, to the right-hand side of the small wooden steering wheel, was the one that controlled the pressure of the steam in the boiler; more steam equaled more wood and water. A second person would have to continuously feed the boiler's stove with wood and operate the turn wheel controlling the intake of the seawater via a pump. The foreman then explained how the farthest lever controlled the steam intake to the engine, and the throttle more or less controlled the power and speed. While the captain controlled both parts of the separated system, there would have to be a third man to control the oil usage and watch the oil pressure gauge with a keen eye, as oil kept the pistons running smoothly. Too much could clog the system. It would take three men to run it; however, Allison was fairly certain she and Zoe could get it to go.

"Now, priming takes about thirty minutes, and to do that we would have to open the doors so the smoke from the burning wood can get out. Once the priming is done—as in, the boiler has steam, and someone cranks the pistons to life to get the momentum going—you are all set. But I suppose you need to see it, huh?" the foreman asked. Allison only nodded her head rhetorically.

The three men unlocked the main and largest door. After having the help of the six guards to pull the doors open with the chain assemblies attached, the men wrapped the chains around their designated posts on the accompanying docks around the boat lockup. Then they re-entered the lockup, started the fire in the boiler stove, waited the thirty minutes, and spun the crank, feeding the engine enough steam for it to idle.

"Good. Very good," said Allison. "However, we have to make sure it can do this for an hour. So, I'll make you a deal between the two of us. You and the boys have a party, and we will watch it idle for an hour; then, once this is accomplished, all you have to do is shut it down for us. How's that sound?" she inquired cheerfully.

"You sure? I mean, do you want to party?" the foreman asked politely.

Everyone can read between the vague lines of cocaine. Partying can turn into all sorts of rather bizarre and fanciful things, the likes of which you probably regret greatly the next morning—unless of course, you have a couple lines cut out. Then all is well, for a while, until the coke runs out.

"How about we get this test done and then join the party?" Allison said with a fake seductiveness, fooling the foreman into complying.

While the nine men were breaking out lines and having a very grand time, Allison and Zoe conferred between themselves. After some failed attempts, they finally got the hang of the boat and were making very slow progress out of the lockup. The men, nostrils now filled with powder and eyes red and bulging upon the need for more and more, were utterly distracted by the time they realized the boat had drifted out of the lockup and into the marina.

Allison and Zoe were now shouting directions at one another, back and forth, as Allison operated the throttle and steam in accordance with what Zoe was telling her was available via the gauges. Once they had it under real power, they were making swift headway down the marina's channel. By sunrise, they were out of the networks of channels and traveling south along the west coast of the island. They both could not believe their run of luck and only wished that Michael and Malachi were there with them to experience the victory firsthand. They were once and for all moving on to greener pastures—or so they thought.

CHAPTER 17

Allison and Zoe arrived at the port side of the cruise ship's bow in the late hours of November 16. The crew on the main deck had heard the boat's arrival, and Ramone had seen them miles off from the bridge of the cruise ship. The crew on the main deck threw down lines from the skiff booms and rigging, which Allison and Zoe used to tie the steamship off. They then slowly powered down the steamship. Once all the steam and pressure from the boiler had been released in a great single puff from the overflow stack, they began climbing up the rigging ropes, up to the main deck, which was a physically draining task in and of itself—they were so famished they almost passed out several times on their way up to the main deck.

Once they'd successfully climbed over the railing of the main deck, the two women were greeted by Ramone, Sarge, and Vincent. They were then hustled back up to the captain's mess hall. There were three jars of pickled cod, and the starving women fiendishly chowed down on all three, split equally between them.

"So, where's Malachi?" Vincent asked rather stupidly.

"He died so you and yours could get a ride on the steamship, while me and mine suffered and buried yet another friend," Allison replied. The fire came back up in her eyes, and it was lost on no one that she still had her automatic rifle slung across her back.

"I am sorry for your loss. I do not mean any disrespect, but what is the condition of the steamship?" Ramone asked with an urgency about him.

"Well, at the most thirty people could get a ride at a time. There are two storage bays. One, which is the largest, is stocked to the brim with cut wood to burn in the boiler stove. The second, which is a lot smaller, is maybe three feet tall, six feet wide, and six feet long. That one is empty and could store cargo. A speed that two crew members could safely manage would be eight miles an hour. The little speedometer says it can go sixty, but I highly doubt it. There is so much shoveling and stacking of wood in the stove just to run enough steam to get to eight miles an hour. That is the status," Allison replied as she finished the last portion of the cod.

"Thirty—that's all? Are you sure?" Ramone asked, shocked. He'd thought the steamship would be larger.

"Technically, twenty-eight—this may be your ship, but that one docked next to yours is ours. Thus, it's twenty-eight," Allison said to drive home the point of who was in control of the situation.

"Are you being serious? You think we are playing games?! I should throw you overboard!" Ramone shouted back in frustration.

"I should put a couple of plugs in you just for saying that, so I guess we're even. Now, shouldn't you be going over your naughty and nice list? That way you can pick the twenty-five other people—obviously you'll include yourself, Sarge, and Vincent. Wow, I just keep doing your job for you . . . isn't that funny.

"Now, Zoe and I will be waiting for you in our ship. It is your responsibility, not mine, to have all the people and gear you need in my ship by noon tomorrow. If you are not ready and think for one second that I won't sail that bitch into the sunset with only

Zoe, then sir, you are a daft and ignorant fool. I am still trying to figure out how you got elected in the first place, since you are a weak and a very impotent leader. Good day." Allison said all this in the casual way one does when they are deadly serious and don't care if other people believe it or not—actions speak a lot louder than any garbage heap of concluding arguments ever does.

The men stood there contemplating what had just happened, all their jaws dropped just enough to create a small parting between each one's lips. Allison led Zoe out; as she said they would, they returned down the ropes into the steamship. They found that the little storage bay served as a very nice pop-up shelter, where they slept comfortably until dawn the next morning.

▪ ▪ ▪

Sunrise found the two women awakening from a very restful night's sleep. Once truly awake, they began running over the ship, double-checking the gauges, looking for leaks in the intricate pipework, and so on. They were sure they had enough wood to make a couple of full voyages; the only deciding factor in whether they were truly going to make it back was the weather of the storm cell that kept the two islands' weather systems separate from each other.

The hull of the steamship was thick; its passengers would have to sit among one another on the higher upper decks. There was one right over the condenser that would seat twelve people shoulder to shoulder in three rows of four. The other was over the rudder of the ship and could only seat eight shoulder to shoulder. If massive waves did arise, since there were no "oh shit" handlebars, it would be very hard for the crew to remain on board. Until they knew for sure what kind of weather they were facing, the two women thought it best to try to take as many along with them as possible.

Once they had done their routine check of the steamship and

gotten her prepared, the two women sat on top of the first deck, taking in the sun's warmth—it was now visible over the bow of the massive cruise ship that sat next to the steamship, dwarfing it in its shadow.

"How long do you think it will take to get to that island?" Zoe asked, trying to spark the light of conversation that Malachi had always been so good at. Zoe really missed Malachi and wished he could be with them now.

"Between us, I have not one faint idea," Allison replied. "Maybe a couple of days, or a couple of weeks. All I know for certain is they'd better bring a couple of fishermen along, or we will all surely starve to death, or come very close to it." She pulled out a pack of unfiltered cigarettes she had found at the first farmhouse they'd gone to for food and water, after Malachi had died. "Smoke?" Allison asked, a lit cigarette already parting her lips.

"Sure, I'm hip," Zoe said with a light smile, which received the tiniest grin back in response. She took a cigarette, and after she lit it began puffing the smoke out. It was obvious to Allison at this point that Zoe had never smoked a day in her life before this one.

"Wish Malachi and Michael were here. I think they truly would have enjoyed this moment," Allison said, her glistening blue eyes looking upon the crystal-blue waters that surrounded them. A light breeze had rolled in, and it was a welcome relief.

"I do too," Zoe replied, flicking her quarter-smoked cigarette into the water.

▪ ▪ ▪

An hour before noon, a decent-sized group of people were standing at the railing of the main deck of the cruise ship. They came down the ropes in twos; when they were all aboard, there was a total of twenty-three souls. Twenty of them were RRF residents, and three were yours truly, Ramone, Sarge, and Vincent. Among the twenty residents were ten of the ship's master technicians and ten fishermen, leaving Allison and Zoe as the only two women on board and the only two crew.

Each passenger looked the worse for the wear; Allison and Zoe figured that none of them weighed more than maybe 150 pounds soaking wet. The rest of the hour was spent receiving supplies from the cruise ship. The supplies were hoisted down by rope in large five-gallon pails. Larger objects were lowered down to the steamship by ropes after being tightly bound and secured.

Most of the equipment being lowered onboard was fishing supplies, consisting of rods, reels, line, and tackle accessories. The other equipment varied slightly, but it all in some way, shape, or form pertained to the byproducts of whale and seal fat. There were multiple fifty-five-gallon drums of biofuel and bio-diesel lowered and stowed below deck. Lanterns and oil were also brought down in five-gallon pails.

While the RRFs were busy loading the steamship, Allison and Zoe took that time to get the boiler going and the engine primed. Once all the decided cargo was aboard, including building tools and fire axes, they gave the all-clear to cut the tethering lines and cast off. They were off by half past noon, making western headway.

The ship had no difficulty cutting through the gentle Caribbean-like water as they motored on toward the larger island. *Chug . . . chug . . . chug . . . chug . . . chug . . . chug.* The motor hummed as Allison steered and Zoe called out what both the engine and the boiler were doing. After a half an hour, they were set at a six-mile-an-hour pace; due to all the added weight, this seemed like a reasonable speed. The chop increased with almost every passing mile; their speed would idle down to about four miles an hour before Allison would call out to Zoe for more steam. They were burning through the wood as the ship continued to take on more chop. By early afternoon, the white-capped waves were about three feet tall, but the steamship was still cutting through them with a smooth bobbing motion, proving the waves were no challenge up to this point.

Chug . . . chug . . . chug . . . chug . . . chug . . . chug. With the pistons firing faster now and the steam being eaten as soon as it was produced, Zoe called for a partner—she received Gus. Gus was probably the healthiest out of the group; he picked up his job without complaint, simply grabbing a log from the storage bay in the hull and tossing it up to Zoe, who fed it into the boiler stove.

The waves had now become tremendous. Why Ramone thought it was a good time to banter, Allison would never know. The waves they were now facing pushed against the starboard side of the ship; the last one almost capsized the steamship, and made Allison turn into the current that was drawing and pushing them southwest. The sun was setting, and a panic started to rise in her—pretty soon, they would be in the middle of the worst of it and in complete darkness.

"So, I talked with the other two in my committee, and we agreed that we'll go back as soon as we drop off these twenty good people. That sound fair?" Ramone asked a bit loudly over the now-raging storm and the engine's deep and fast-paced chugging.

"Sure! But look . . . this ain't the fucking time, Ramone! Look what we're going into!" Allison screamed as the scene unfolded in front of the group of weary travelers. The sky had turned a bright neon-green color, and the accompanying flat-black wall clouds made it an even more perilous sight. Rain came down hard upon the steamship, stinging the skin with its cold. The temperature had risen and the air was very humid, but the rain was contrastingly cold, almost cold enough to freeze instantly upon contact. The winds were gale force, giving rise to the tumultuous sea, and the waves that beat into the bow of the steamship after a twelve-foot rise were immense, sea mist spraying the entirety of the ship with each crashing breaker. The wind had no true direction—it would whip at the ship from the north, then the east, then the west, then the south, and not in that particular order. Their vision became grainy as the light radiation from the storm and the stinging sea spray mixed with the freezing rain, stinging at their eyes in an odd sort of symphony.

They were in the worst of it now—the waves were so massive one could not verify the horizon, and this particular wave took the ship higher and higher, climbing with the roar of the engine. *CHUG! CHUG! CHUG! CHUG! CHUG! CHUG!* Then, once upon the top of the crest, a weird sort of spinning suspension lifted the steamship off the water's surface. Everyone who didn't instinctively grab on to something flew off the face of the ship's higher decks; their silhouettes were blue, then black, and then they were gone. The ship had become engulfed in a massive cyclone that kept bringing them higher and higher out of the water. The steam engine, unfed, choked and then died; no one had seen to its operation, as all who were still aboard clung on to any available surface with white-knuckled death grips.

They were continuously carried higher and higher, until that nasty sensation of falling overcame everyone left onboard. Allison took a daring look as the ship flew through the air like a saucer. The air had become very, very cold—pellets of ice whipped and bit into each person's skin. They were plummeting through the air and rapidly approaching the turbulent sea.

FLOP! CRASH! SPLASH! The steamship impacted the water with such kinetic energy that they literally cut through a rogue wave and plummeted to a hard stop on the other side of it. The ship forced its way through a hundred yards of water before surfacing. The storm still raged on, and the ship was graciously pointed into the oncoming waves; without a motor, they rode the steamship up to the crest and then it was sent plummeting backward into the sea.

Anyone who had a good grip remained—all who had lost their grip fell victim to the black abyss of the thrashing sea. Ten souls in total were left; somehow Ramone was one of them, as well as Allison and Zoe. Sarge had fallen victim to the darkness, and Vincent hung on to the burning-hot steam intake pipes, which had for the most part welded his flesh to themselves.

Once the ship rolled properly upright and through one last rogue wave, it had somehow passed through the brunt of the storm. They could not see but could feel that they were on calm waters again. The oil lamps had been lost, as had the steam engine; not only had it become flooded but with the raging toss through the rogue wave, it had lost its exhaust. The boiler had exploded due to the massive pressure change, killing three people in its going. However, no one had heard it blow up over the rapid claps of thunder and the monstrously frightening orange lightning.

It was very cold now, and every surface of the ship seemed to be frozen. The dull glow of the fire in the boiler stove was still visible. Zoe, beaten and battered, got a few logs in to feed the now very dull red glow of coals. She stoked the fire the best she could, but in the end the coals and wood were wet and the fire went out. Allison pulled her flashlight out of her pack; after a couple of good whacks to the palm of her hand, it eventually came back to life. While people were generally recovering, some still vomiting from the vicious and violent motion, Allison opened the storage bay before it completely froze shut. She found a drum marked "biofuel" and a steel gallon pail. Taking her bowie knife, she forced the lid of the biofuel off. She then dumped the entire gallon pail into it and brought it to where the boiler stack used to be. Placing it in the boiler stove, she then lit it with one of her matches; it went up in an angry, engulfing flame. She then closed the stove door. The heat and light that radiated through the now-vacant and open space where the boiler used to be engulfed every inch of the ship in golden firelight.

"Everyone, we need to gather around this fire if we want to survive. Soon your adrenaline will be gone, and you will more than likely go into shock with the sudden temperature change. Gather round, and if you need help . . . shout," Allison said as everyone except Vincent gathered around the fire.

"H . . . he . . . help!" Vincent cried out, getting the attention of Ramone, Allison, and Zoe. The scene Allison's flashlight uncovered was a gruesome one. Vincent's melted flesh bound his hands to the steam pipes. His fingers were now frozen to them as well due to the rapid temperature change—cold freezes hot things a lot faster than cold things.

"It fuckin' hurts! Come on, help me out!" Vincent bayed and howled.

"You're in a bad way, Vincent. We are going to have to cut the pipes and then thaw your hands over the fire," Allison replied, trying to keep down the sickness of seeing his warped and unnaturally mangled hands.

Ramone grabbed the fire axe from the storage bay, then systematically cut through the one-inch copper pipes. Once Vincent's hands were free, it looked as if he were carrying two three-foot-long batons, as Ramone had chosen to cut as far away from the man's hands as possible to avoid a tragic and accidental blow with the axe head.

Nine survivors were now closely huddled around the blazing hellfire of the biofuel, which was only bright enough to send its rays across the deck, not into the surrounding water. The group was no longer cold but beaten, bruised, hurt, and scared. They did not sleep as the hours of darkness passed—fear of being sucked back into the raging storm disallowed that. They said nothing as the long night passed, every four hours or so requiring another steel bucket to refill the burning stove's inferno.

...

When the first morning light came, the group suddenly and very stupidly found out why the steamship had been drifting so gently. They had run aground upon the shore of what looked like a red, sandy desert. However, it was way too cold to be a desert—the winds that were carried off the desert's surface were bitterly cold, maybe slightly warmer than thirty below zero.

Upon Allison's return for more biofuel, she found it had become like a thick, viscous stew. She knew they would have to bring all the biofuel drums up to the warmth of the fire so they wouldn't completely freeze. She gathered the other seven people—excluding Vincent, who had just unfrozen his hands from the large sections of pipe—to labor as a team, making short work of bringing up all of the drums. However, each person found that even a few minutes spent away from the fire were long enough to incur a very mild case of frostbite.

For a good couple of hours that morning, the group either sat or stood and watched the flames, soaking in the true despair of their situation. Ramone and his stupidity only made things all the worse. "Well, couldn't we fix up this boiler and get it going again? I mean, we probably have the tools!" Ramone said, rather out of his depth.

"You know something? I think you are the stupidest fucking leader there has ever been in the history of the earth!" Allison shouted. "How are we supposed to fix pipe connections that you hacked off with an axe, with no torch or solder? How are we supposed to put a boiler back together with no iron or steel? Ya' fuckin' twat!" Her rather cool, collected underlying tone suggested she was close to making an action that Ramone would regret.

"I'm sorry, but what are we going to do? We can't just stay here!" Ramone whined in his defense.

"For starters, you can shut the fuck up from now on! Then allow the rest of us some peace and quiet to do some actual thinking! Do you know how to think? Or do you need a refresher course in that too?" Allison replied in barely collected fury.

▪ ▪ ▪

It was going on noon, and not a single person had shot their hand up with an idea. The lightbulbs were not going "ding" with inspiration. Rather, people were starting to sink into a stupor brought on by extremely cold conditions. Allison and Zoe were at the cargo hold looking over what they had left with a feverish pace so they could get back to the warmth of the fire, as their boiler suits were not insulated.

"We have a whole lot of nothing! We've got three extra buckets and a couple ten-foot sections of chain," Zoe said, emerging from the cargo hold with the items.

"What are you thinking?" Allison asked, intrigued.

"Well, if three people can huddle around a fire bucket, taking extra care not to spill it, we could start walking with them—it will provide warmth," Zoe replied with a smile.

"That's a good idea, except for the fact that one bucket, as I am sure you have noticed, burns in less than four hours. So someone would have to be in charge of rolling one of those barrels, which would take an absolutely horrendous amount of time. Not only that, but a man away from the fire for more than a couple of minutes gets frostbite. My hands are proof, and so are yours—and so is the area not included in the ten feet of warmth the biofuel emits. The entire deck is encrusted with ice." Allison said all this with the smile of a friend shooting down a bad idea but who was nonetheless grateful for someone starting to think outside the box.

"What do you propose? Because if a gallon only lasts four

hours, that means we will burn six gallons every day just to stay alive. Also, if we don't move, and quickly, we are all going to be so far into starvation that we will regress into the only activity we will be able to do, which is feed the fire until the last man drops dead from starvation. This entire journey feels like a massive fubar to me. No proper planning, and now everyone is constantly relying on us to get the job done correctly. Well, how come we are always supposed to save the day? Fuck me!" Zoe replied.

Leaving the buckets and lengths of chain at the storage bay's opening, they returned to the warmth cast by the burning biofuel, which emitted rank black smoke that made everyone in the company stink. Vincent's hands were beginning to turn gangrenous at the fingertips, adding to the stink that mixed in the air.

▪ ▪ ▪

The entire day passed without a single good idea. However, upon Allison's next return to the storage bay, she found there were multiple runs of one-inch copper piping that spanned twelve feet in length. *Ding!* The lightbulb went off. Without a moment to lose, she grabbed the adjacent fire axe and cut out the four runs of twelve-foot copper piping. She then returned to the group, and as she warmed her hands, she conveyed her idea.

"We are in a boat, a mode of transportation. Now, the current should push us down the coast if we get caught in a good one. If not, we can stay to the shallows and push the boat along with copper piping. One must be ever so delicate so as not to bend the living hell out of it—thus, we gently push our way down the coast and hopefully somewhere warmer. How's that sound?" Allison asked the group.

"Sounds good," Zoe said, excited and almost cheerful. "All right—you and you, you're up first with me and Allison. Grab a length of copper and then meet up at the bow to push this bitch off the shore."

The four of them met at the bow, and with a lot of gradual strain they were able to break the ship free. Their three minutes were up, so they quickly shouted to the other four able-bodied people to get the ship to turn if they could—but the main goal was to keep it off the shoreline and from running aground again.

It took an entire hour, with two four-man crews taking three minutes on and then three minutes off, to get the boat turned in the right direction, going south with the current. Their progress was agonizingly slow—they could never get the boat more than twenty feet from shore, as the water was a little over eight feet deep. They had run aground a couple of times, but incurred nothing worse than the scraping of rocks against the bottom of the hull.

The job continued throughout the night and into the next morning; with the progress as slow as it was, barely a quarter mile an hour, they managed four total miles. They were waiting for a current to take them, but gradually they realized that a current would never come to them in this shallow water.

When noon came, the group came to a unanimous decision that Vincent's job would be to watch the shoreline; if they started to run aground, he would shout for them to get up. Now, this plan worked, but at the same time it didn't. Every thirty minutes at the most, Vincent's shouts to wake up could be heard, and each group took turns pushing the boat out; this meant the group in total never got more than thirty minutes at a time to lie down. It took until afternoon for them to actually get some sleep.

Then, Ramone actually raised a somewhat intelligent point, and the crew changed gears for a moment—they had forgotten about the water jugs that were tucked in the furthest corner of the cargo hold along with the fishing equipment. While Ramone started to thaw out water jugs, the two fishermen who were left began casting lines and tethering them to the side of the main deck. They cast ten lines out in hopes of fish. After an hour of running around and completing multiple tasks for the hopes of food and water, they returned their attention to the pushing of the boat around the coast.

...

The mundane tasks were now a continual ebb and flow of rather boring and cold routine. Each morning came with the checking of the lines; throughout the night, two or three very small fish would be caught, offering little more than a snack split evenly among the nine people. Then there was more pushing of the boat along the coast. At noon the lines were checked again and the same snack-sized meals were shared, along with very small sips of water, just big enough to keep them from dying.

Ultimately, during a small nap, they ran aground on some rocks that halted their progress. The day of November 23 found them with a recently departed Vincent. His gangrene had overcome both his hands, which gave him a bad case of blood poisoning. The crew, rather without remorse, threw him overboard, as the only grim feeling now was that they were no longer going to get to take real naps.

With some gentle but firm effort, they got the ship off the rocks it had run aground on and began their journey onward yet again, with no real loss incurred.

...

The morning of December 2, there were now only five left in the group. The two fishermen and one cruise ship technician had died due to pure exhaustion, dehydration, and starvation. The group now had to be continuously on watch, as they had no relief group left anymore; Ramone was placed on line duty. The fish that were reeled in now actually fed the group somewhat, as there were four fewer mouths to feed. The water was growing dangerously low, and as they crossed into the shores of the plains region, they were desperately awaiting the delta that would take them up the river.

Everyone, including Allison and Zoe, looked like victims of some horrible prison. They all had lost what little fat reserves they had left; if they were to lift up their shirts, their ribs would be visible. Malnutrition had made every task more difficult, and if they didn't find somewhere that had an actual abundance of food, they were going to die sooner rather than later.

▪ ▪ ▪

The morning of December 4, the group was now at three members—Ramone and an RRF cruise ship technician had passed sometime in the night. Their corpses were frozen to the sides of the hull they had sat against, the last drum of biofuel resting half empty next to their frozen bodies.

The group now consisted of Gus, Allison, and Zoe. They were making headway up the delta, which they'd caught sight of off in the distance yesterday. The current was very strong, which made making progress without bending the copper poles a very difficult task. By night's end, they were down to two copper poles, but the group had some relief—each line had caught a decent-sized fish. It was Zoe who reeled them all in, cleaned them, cooked them, and then cast the lines out again.

▪ ▪ ▪

Gus had died from dehydration three days ago, leaving only Zoe and Allison alive on December 19. The two were no longer able to make any headway due to their severe muscle loss and the pure exhaustion that came from severe dehydration, making everything a fog of confusion. The ship marooned itself thirty miles north of the delta they had entered through.

"She's really starting to show now, huh?" a voice in the distance said.

"Yeah, according to her, she's in the second trimester," a second voice replied. "She doesn't like that I keep her penned up in that little house of ours when you and I go hunting. She says she'd rather come along no matter how round she's getting."

This took a while to register with the two forsaken women in the boat, who were swimming in the depths of delirium. "Are those people, Zoe?" Allison asked.

Zoe replied, "No, you're having another fit." Then it dawned upon the two that they had both heard the distant conversation.

Allison got to her feet—now scanning the snow pack, she saw two dark silhouettes approaching the ship. "H . . . hey! Ove . . . over . . . here!" she managed to say loudly enough. The two men heard her cries for help.

"Now, what in the world do you think that is?" Jack asked Matt.

"I think it's a boat of some kind," Matt replied curiously.

"In the middle of winter, though?" Jack replied, even more curious.

CHAPTER 18

It was noon on December 23 when Allison woke up. She was swaddled like an infant in a demoose-hide blanket, lying only a couple feet away from the stone-and-clay fireplace, the fire it contained radiating a welcoming warmth. Nicole and Olivia were stitching up a demoose-hide jacket and pants they had tanned in the recently constructed smokehouse. Matt and Jack were off selecting a pine tree for Christmas, as the group had decided they would start celebrating and participating in the old-school holidays. Matt and Olivia were on better terms now—not so far as to say they were in a solid relationship, but they had shared some intimate moments together.

"Hello there. I'm Nicole, and the woman to my right is Olivia," Nicole said as Allison woke from her second full day of slumber.

"Hello . . . water, please," said Allison in a croak—the dehydration had impacted her voice. Nicole simply pointed to the very used and worn plastic bottle that sat next to Allison. The two other women continued to stitch the clothing together using utility knives and dried cordage. Practice and necessity had made them very good at making clothes for not only themselves but also for the men.

Allison sucked the water down almost entirely too quickly, stopping herself just shy of becoming sick. There were four beds in a row along the wall across from where she lay. The beds were made out of timber and dried grass, which looked pleasantly comfortable. Olivia was sitting on the end of the bed closest to the fire; Nicole was sitting on the bed adjacent to Olivia. The two continued their work as Allison took in her surroundings. The fire had an overhanging spit where a stew pot sat, and the smells of fresh meat and boiling water filled the room with their pleasant cooking aroma.

"Where's Zoe?" Allison asked inquisitively. As she slowly stood up, her malnutrition almost sent her face first into the dirt floor of the quaint little stone-and-clay cottage.

"Well," Nicole responded compassionately, "the woman you came with didn't make the long walk back. She . . . well, as Jack told me, she just collapsed and gave one deep, long exhale. As the snow is too thick and the ground is frozen, they couldn't bury her. Since we are a caring kind of group, we placed an engraved wooden cross by the river with her name and the date she passed on it."

"How much do you trust this Jack? I've been playing the worst game of telephone since October," Allison replied bluntly.

"Well, he is my forest husband," Nicole replied, a speculative and deep scanning gaze across her face.

"Huh," Allison said, bluntly yet again.

Without any clothes to her name besides her boiler suit—which had been removed, soaking wet—she proceeded naked out the front warm-room door, then through the dimly lit cold storage, where all the fishing line, reels, and accessories from the steamship had been placed. This room also stored fresh meat, dry wood for burning, wood chips for smoking, and cordage—lots of it too. Allison walked out into the snap-freeze air; when she saw the wooden cross headstone, she approached it.

The snow was deep here, and she had to follow the trail that had been broken days previous to place the wooden headstone. She looked upon it and its background: freezing tundra and a rapidly rushing river that was undoubtedly the one they had traveled on. Bitter tears rolled down her cheeks, almost freezing as soon as they left her eyes.

"Why? Why am I the one who survives when all my friends have died, and more than likely that whole fucking cruise ship? Fuck!" Allison howled toward the sky in much the same fashion a lone wolf does.

Her hands and ears were stricken with frostbite by the time she decided to return to the little cottage. The smoke billowing from the stone chimney looked surreal, like a pleasant little painting one would find hanging in someone's living room—the snow-covered trees in the background, a massive pile of brush here, a huge pile of firewood there, and another massive pile of stone. She was taken aback at the scenery of it all.

...

Everyone was back in the cottage and unwinding for the night. Jack and Matt had just returned with a nice-sized but small-enough pine tree that they placed in the cold storage room. Tomorrow they would build a stand for it.

Allison was off in a distant place until Jack came in. He was a pleasant kind of man, although his body was strewn with lots of large old scars and quite a few newer small scars. His stump even had a little glove on it, which he probably wore to appease his wife, as it looked "cute."

The group gathered on the ends of their beds. Jack and Matt were taking off multiple layers of warm clothing, layer upon layer being shed. It made Allison wonder how many there were. To her relief, they stopped at six, their boiler suits underneath showing tattered stitchwork with demoose hide and cordage. To the best of Allison's reasoning, she thought the men used them now as a type of long underwear. Nicole and Olivia were dishing the stew into bowls made from large bones with accompanying spoons made of wood.

The group of women ate in silence, and the men only nodded at Allison's presence. The two men softly spoke of their day; one could tell they were close friends now, but some subjects were dropped right away. To Allison, this indicated that it wasn't always so friendly between the two.

"How do you like the stew?" Jack interrupted the silence for a transition that was needed if the group was going to get acquainted with their potential new bunkmate Allison.

"Fine. So, you are from pods as well, then?" Allison asked the group. However, she wasn't too concerned with a response. Her mind was still on the passing of everyone in her group and the survival of everyone in this group, making the pain all the worse.

"Yeah," Jack replied, "I'm number seven. Matt is number eight, Nicole is number one, and Olivia is number four. We have had a rough go of things, but I think we did pretty good, all things considered," he said positively, with a warm, welcoming sort of smile.

"Yeah . . . all things considered. I was in a group of four as well. Three of them died. You did extraordinarily, if you ask me. And I am not naïve enough to consider parting from your company until the thaw comes, if there ever is one here," Allison said in a very hollow way, like she was an empty vessel with nothing left of herself.

"Right. Well, if you want to stick around until spring, that is fine by us. However, everyone works around here—no free lunch, as my friend Matt here would say. If you want to, you can help either outside or inside, but I will leave that to you.

"We are not an unfair group. We are genuinely good people. We know you will need some time to get acclimated. You will need time to overcome your grief and loss, time to heal both physically and emotionally. We have also suffered and felt loss, and I am telling you to take your time—don't rush it. If you are looking for stuff to do to keep your mind occupied for a while, don't hesitate to ask. If you need time alone, that's good too."

Jack's words were genuine and compassionate. He knew the tight spot Allison was in right now, and he accepted it. It seemed now that everyone came from a tight spot, if they had survived.

aaron C Lende

09/09/17

The Traffic Stop

BY AARON LEMKE

A light breeze stirred the leaves on the ground with a drifting shuffle. The air was crisp and had a slight scent of pine sap. The sky was clear, without a cloud in sight, the stars shining bright and vivid.

Alex walked quietly around the back of his squad car to his trunk. He motioned to the rearview mirror for his partner to pop the trunk. The shadow in the car moved slightly over the center console of the cruiser; then the trunk sprung open and the taillights flashed twice, like two rays of light splitting the darkness around the back of the car. Alex was temporarily blinded by the trunk lights because his eyes were so adjusted to the near pitch-blackness. He grabbed his pale-blue lunch box from the trunk and closed it as quickly as possible to avoid any vehicles on the road spotting their location.

Walking to the driver's side, Alex gently opened and closed the door as he slid into the worn upholstered leather driver's seat. With the short time he had while the dome light in the cruiser would remain on, he put the lunch box on the center console between him and his partner. Then the light faded, and all in the car was black again.

"So, what's on the menu tonight?" Tex asked, curious as to

what his midnight snack was going to be.

"I made up two ham sandwiches and the usual fixings. I also picked up two bottles of Coke from the last gas station stop," Alex replied, knowing his partner was hoping for some food with a little kick to it.

"You know I'm going to have to make up for the lack of flavor with tomorrow's chili," Tex said with a chuckle.

"Don't make it too hot now—last time I could taste the spice in my mouth for a week after," Alex retorted, loudly chuckling back.

The two men took out their sandwiches, their eyes adjusting again as they ate in silence. It was a quiet night, and after all, it was rare for anyone to be driving down Highway 60 at 2:45 a.m., except for the occasional semi.

Halfway through Alex's sandwich, he heard a faint echo shoot through the night air, vibrating the cruiser's windows ever so slightly. He put his right hand on the key in the ignition and started the cruiser, then took the sandwich and placed it in the lunch box. His left hand went to the window switch and lowered the window; his right hand then went back to the key, and he shut off the ignition again.

Alex listened. He heard nothing for a few seconds; then the roar of an engine about a thousand yards away echoed through the valley and into his ears. He took a second to analyze the noise and the pattern of roaring and revving. *Eight hundred yards now. Vroom, bum, bum, bum, vrooooom, bum, bum, bum. Six hundred. Vroooooooom, bum, bum, bum.*

Alex rolled the window back up and started the cruiser, putting the car in drive but keeping the lights off and his foot on the brake. Tex knew from previous incidents like this one that it would be wise to put his sandwich down and secure anything that might want to slide around.

Alex looked at Tex and said quietly, as if muttering to himself,

"Two hundred yards, V-6 engine with a glasspack on the muffler, about ninety to one hundred miles per."

Tex nodded but did not respond. He clutched his right hand against the bottom of his seat and reached his left hand for the belt buckle at the same time . . .

In one moment, everything happened, as if all the parts in a well-oiled machine had started working together on demand. The Pontiac Grand Prix raced past the squad car with a tremendous roar, the engine muffler working together with all other parts to propel the car at a dangerous speed, with swiftness and control. The tires on the cruiser spun with a loud and hideous shriek of rubber, throwing dirt and gravel against the rear wheel wells. The Pontiac flew by only a second before Alex flashed it with the lights and flowed a healthy dose of gasoline into the lines and engine. Tires squealing and bawling for traction, the Crown Victoria cruiser went from dirt to asphalt. In less than eight seconds, the Crown Vic was at ninety miles an hour, the Grand Prix only one hundred yards in front of its flashing headlights. The two cars came to a gradual stop; the Grand Prix pulled over and stopped, seeming to comply with the flashing lights.

"I will be damned, Alex! Every time you hear a car, you know exactly when to engage chase before you even see it! You got the driving skills, and I got the people skills. Now let me do my part, partner," Tex said, his voice an octave higher from the new adrenaline rushing through his veins.

Tex got out of the cruiser and walked up to the back of the black Pontiac. Putting his hand on his Taser, he approached the passenger-side door with extreme caution. He was looking for any hint of movement or quick action that would indicate a threat.

Tex reached the tinted passenger window and knocked on it. The window lowered, and a loud boom followed.

Without warning, another machine started up, and it was far

more effective than a car. It was a man's will.

The Pontiac roared in retort to the fallen officer, then bolted in an open-throttled blast of gasoline. Alex sprung the door of the cruiser open with his left hand and grabbed the shotgun with his right. The Pontiac gained traction in the tires and started to make performable speed and grip. Alex gripped the black carbon-fiber pump with his left and shouldered to his right. *Vroooooooom, bum, bum, bum. Motor is not steady with the drive terrain yet. Seventy-five yards . . . two-second travel time at fifty-five miles an hour.*

Boom, clink, clack. Psssst, scrape, thud. Boom, clink, clack. Smash, crumple, flip, smash.

With shotgun in hand, Alex ran to his downed partner and dropped to his knees. He grabbed his radio with his left hand and pressed the button down firmly; then, with a waver of shock and disbelief in his voice, he relayed the message that his partner was down on Highway 60 by the old Henigan Ranch.

Alex looked his partner in the eyes and grabbed his left hand with his. "You are all right, you are all right, you are going to be fine." But every time he repeated this, he believed it less and less.

Tex's breathing was shallow and fast. He grasped his partner's hand harder, showing white knuckles, and whispered, "Maybe I lost my people skills, huh? Did you get . . . him? I could never do it you know. You are a good cop and frie . . ."

Alex stared into his partner's eyes as he faded away, the life draining from his face—stared into the now-blank abyss of what were once the portals through which Tex took in life. Standing abruptly, he stumbled a few steps before his body jerked and heaved up his stomach's contents. After his bout of sickness was over, he looked to where the Grand Prix had crashed.

It was an elegant mess. The boulder that the Pontiac had nosedived into was now a jumble of flame, crushed rock, and compressed metal. The driver had been launched clean through the windshield and made a mess against the boulder just five feet above where the crumpled car now lay. The passenger was screaming and crying for mercy from God, and now for mercy from Alex. The fire would consume him, and the car was too mangled to get him out . . . or was it?

Well, just for him, it is, Alex thought to himself.

Alex walked back to where his lifeless partner now lay and sat down next to him. He watched the flames as they wrapped around the car heap, breathing in the smell of vomit, burning rubber, and burning flesh. *I got him, partner, don't you worry. I will see you on the next side.*

Alex put his right hand over Tex's eyes and closed them.

Acknowledgments

We would like to thank the amazing team at Beaver's Pond for making Aaron's book a reality and for staying true to his voice.

We would also like to thank our family, our friends, and our church community for supporting us throughout our journey of grief as well as love and hope.